HER BEAUTIFUL MONSTER

By Mandi Bean

Martin Sisters Publishing

Published by

Ivy House Books, a division of Martin Sisters Publishing, LLC

www. martinsisterspublishing. com

Copyright © 2012 Mandi Bean

ISBN: 978-1-937273-66-8
Fiction/Thriller
Printed in the United States of America
Martin Sisters Publishing, LLC

DEDICATION

To all of my family, friends and loved ones who stood by me,
especially my mother and father.

ACKNOWLEGEMENTS

A special debt of gratitude is owed to my editor,
Melissa Newman, whose talent is remarkable.

An imprint of Martin Sisters Publishing, LLC

Chapter One

The Beautiful Boy

"Only love can break your heart." ~ Neil Young

Fuck.

Shit.

Balls.

Sammy was five minutes late to class. Normally, five minutes lost did not mean tragedy or impending doom. Five minutes lost every single class, however, added up, and the professor was beginning to notice. She could feel his beady, vermin-like eyes roaming over her whenever she was in the classroom, forcing her palms to sweat and forcing her stomach to flip over. Couldn't he see the way her tee-shirt clung to the sweat gathered in the small of her back? Didn't he know she had run the whole way from the farthest parking lot on campus in cheap, worn flip flops, with her bag banging painfully against her side? Maybe if he did see all that, and maybe if he did know how hard she was trying, then he'd go harass someone else. She was doing her best, damn it. Someone had to notice.

The campus was relatively small and easy to navigate, even though Sammy had been extremely intimidated by the mere thought of traversing a college campus upon being accepted to the university. Sammy was embarrassed by her freshman naiveté whenever she thought about the previous academic year. How had she ever been afraid of getting lost? The Student Center, a large, formidable-looking building was the epicenter of the campus with its cafeteria, pizzeria, commuter lounge, administrative offices and handful of classrooms. Clustered about it were the academic buildings- to the left was Dickinson Hall, Dali Hall, and up on the hill slightly behind the Student Center was the largest, most technologically advanced building on campus; the most impressive learning environment the university had to offer, what with its seven floors of classrooms, offices, conference rooms and state of the art computer labs. Sammy thought it was a real shame she never had any real reason to venture inside. Such a luxury was only afforded to the future educators strolling about the campus, probably because the education program was what brought in the notoriety and funding. The building was called University Hall and Sammy had always been thoroughly disappointed by the lack of creativity in the title.

To the right of the Student Center were the music building (always in a perpetual state of renovation), the theater and broadcasting buildings, and the math and science buildings. Needless to say that, as an English major, Sammy rarely ventured to that side of campus. She did enjoy the modern architecture of the buildings though, and honestly appreciated how the physical structures appeared scholarly and inviting all at the same time. The co-eds playing Frisbee on the greens between buildings probably had a lot to do with Sammy's admiration of the campus as well. What it lacked in rolling hills and scenic views, it made up for in the essence of college life; would-be Dylans and Springsteens composing on acoustic guitars perched upon concrete steps in the fading light of a September evening, Greeks gathering to discuss their social calendars with letters proudly displayed on apparel and liter cups filled with something delicious held in their hands, and students lounging on various benches or right on the grass with heavy textbooks open across their laps or paperbacks in hand. She was passing such serene scenes of campus life as she sped along the main path of the campus, the wide, paved road that led up and around one side of the hill the college was perched on, and met the highway back along the other side. The uphill was what killed her, and it started as soon as she exited one of several massive and absurdly expensive parking garages at the end of campus closest to Meadow Lane- the road that led to the parkway and the turnpike and the big city. Not much of a runner, she took in large gulps of air as she ran through the white plaster statues that crowded the exit of the parking garage. The statues were of people, but the features weren't clearly defined and they were more creepy than anything else, especially artistic. And now they were cumbersome to boot; it was hard enough navigating around the real people on campus. Sammy didn't believe she should have to swerve around fake people, too. The parking garage gave way to the main theater seamlessly; both were white with red accents. Beside this most bizarre building combination ever, was the amphitheater. Students were lounged on the stone steps, reading, writing, laughing, listening to music and Sammy was jealous. Their throats weren't burning, their thighs weren't quivering. Then again, Sammy supposed they might be but really, that was personal and none of her business.

The path continued upward, as she passed the art building on the right with its myriad of interesting and delightfully bohemian students gathered outside, welding pieces of metal together or spray painting things black as a symbol of awful consumerism. The library was behind it, was always crowded and had a chic café inside where the more academic than social population gathered. Dickinson Hall, which happened to be Sammy's current destination, finally came into view. Located halfway up the giant, pain-in-the-ass hill, it was one of the oldest buildings on campus and was home to the English department. Thus, it was Sammy's home away from home. It was brick with blue accents, and only four stories tall. It was long though, with meandering halls that almost made the place a labyrinth. The main entrance was located off the main path and Sammy turned sharply towards the automatic doors and barely waited for them to slide open and allow her entrance. The smokers puffed away and barely noticed Sammy's mad dash inside – English majors were far too concerned with the plot of their own lives to worry about schedules.

Sammy's flip-flops smacked against the linoleum floor and nearly caused her to slide to her demise, and she made an immediate left to the stairs. The elevator would take too long and would deposit her too far from the classroom. She took the stairs two at a time and gracefully made the last few strides before sliding into the last classroom on the right of the nearest hallway. She almost passed it; the vanilla tones of the hallway made everything blend together. Each classroom looked the same. Often, she'd have to spot the professor or another familiar face to be sure she was in the right place.

As quietly and as humbly as possible, Sammy claimed an uncomfortable seat in the back of the classroom, which was one of the largest in Dickinson Hall (named not for the poet, but an alumnus who had made a generous contribution). The building was always sweltering because the air conditioning was never going to be fixed apparently, and there were no windows in the classroom, just more shades of mediocrity and neutrality. Sweating on top of sweat could hardly be described as one of Sammy's favorite pastimes. With a grimace on her face, she bent over to retrieve the various, required books from her bag, and soon felt burning eyes upon her. The color flew from her face and she flicked her wide, brown eyes to the professor, but his gaze did not meet hers. Pontificating from the front of the sterile-looking classroom, the professor's eyes were closed in academic rapture as the sound of his own voice brought him closer and closer to scholarly orgasm. But if the douche bag with the doctorate had his eyes closed, then that meant someone else was staring at her and making her uncomfortable. Her eyes darted to the left.

There was nothing but a fiercely average wall.

Her eyes darted to the right.

Beautiful, blazing, brown eyes assaulted hers. Heart stopping, she gawked in surprise at the young man so intensely scrutinizing her. His face was the perfect picture of silent and discreet contempt. Defined features and pinched, thin, pink lips oozed extreme levels of boredom and apathy. His clothes were made of fabric woven from pure sarcasm; the denim jacket hanging off his left shoulder and the exposed tee-shirt, strategically ripped to give the girls a little bit of a show, were both calculated enough to be careless and cool. Sammy shakily exhaled as this image of beauty rolled his dark eyes away from hers and scribbled something or other in his thin notebook. Sammy slowly resumed what she had been doing (what exactly had that been?), but her thoughts were irritatingly preoccupied with the young man beside her.

Their eyes did not meet for a second time that day.

The class session ended, and she watched him collect his books, an action that reflected her own. Tucking her hair behind her ears, Sammy made special note of his decision to muffle and obscure the intensity of his eyes with dark shades. It wasn't like it was sunny out or anything, but she supposed the glasses did add to the image and the mystique. She had to admit it was all very sexy. Forgetting to breathe, and feeling slightly perverted, Sammy stared as he left. Her mouth was wide open, and she didn't care. He was gorgeous, and he had been staring at her, too. Staring or glaring? Did it matter? Sammy debated the issue as she rushed from the room, hurrying before the professor stopped her to discuss her punctuality, or lack thereof.

The guy in shades had been of particular interest to Sammy since the very first day of class. He'd walked in with an effortless kind of grace, and chosen a seat without much thought. Sammy was elated he had chosen to sit next to her for today, but she was envious of his ability to choose to sit anywhere. Sammy had to weigh the options, carefully consider the social implications and social ramifications, and nine times out of ten, she sat by herself, far from other students, to protect herself from her own painful insecurities and near-paralyzing self-doubt. So desperate for a unique kind of connection, she placed an astronomical amount of importance upon every single relationship she ever had, relationships which were currently restricted to family and friends. Sammy had never had a boyfriend, and that fact haunted her, made her feel like J. Alfred Prufrock, the protagonist of her favorite poem by T.S. Eliot, who was convinced he'd die alone because he could not live up to society's grandiose romantic expectations. She was twenty-one-years old and hadn't been kissed, and she had never felt the warm, gentle and essential pressure of her hand clasped in someone else's. These facts nearly killed her, especially when listed one after the other, and served as explanation enough as to why the male species intrigued her so, especially the handsome, mysterious ones who shared an interest in literature, and sat next to her. A million and one sordid fantasies formed in her writer's mind, each starring the beautiful boy from class, and she entertained every single one of them on the drive home from campus.

Unless Sammy was in class, time passed primarily without incident; a fact which brought with it an unappealing mixture of disappointment and comfort. It was an odd sort of sensation that she simultaneously loathed and loved; that she needed, yet longed to be rid of. The revulsion and attraction to loneliness consistently threatened to trap her and in order to prevent that horrible self-imprisonment, Sammy escaped to a fake, manufactured world. Whether it be the posters of the leading men lining her bedroom walls, or the printed pages she devoured and created, or the romantic movies she had seen a thousand and one times, or the sad songs she found so cathartic, Sammy could use the creative materials as some kind of great leveler. She learned what she could about the elusive ecstasy of romance from others. At night, as she lay in bed, she closed her dark eyes and tried to imagine what a passionate embrace felt like. She had gathered, from her less than scholarly research, that there was a rush of blood, a tensing of the muscles, baited breath, and most importantly, a kind of bliss a person spends his or her whole life trying to recreate. Melodramatic as it may be, love and that singular elation which accompanied it had evaded her for far too long. That's not to say she was depressed and moping around her parents' house with no sort of social life to speak of. Well aware of Sammy's melodramatic predisposition to get locked inside her self-pitying and therefore dangerous mind, Sammy's friend Maeve would call Sammy with plans to go out almost every weekend. The two had become incredibly close incredibly fast during the last academic year. Neither could go a day without talking to the other. So when Sammy politely declined the weekend invitations, as she always did, Maeve would sigh, but continue the conversation ... and inevitably, it would turn to boys. Maeve was dating Mike, another student from school, and was pleased to share his better qualities and fleeting romantic tendencies with Sammy. Sammy gobbled them up, followed each question with another, asked for precise details and though she was genuinely happy for Maeve, she envied her too. Maeve would abate the tension by asking Sammy about men in her life. Ninety-nine times out of one hundred, Sammy had nothing to share, other than Robert Pattinson having a particularly steamy photo shoot in a certain magazine. But when Maeve called after class that day, Sammy got to tell her all about Beautiful Boy.

"His eyes, Maeve, are ... like ... out of this world. They set my soul on fire, you know? And his hair was so perfectly disheveled that it was all I could do to keep from leaping over my desk and running my fingers through it." Sammy sighed contentedly.

Maeve was consistently entertained by Sammy's juvenile dramatics. "Okay, great. Did you talk to him?"

"What?"

This time Maeve sighed, and not so contentedly. "Do you even know his name?"

After a brief pause, allowing herself time to think, Sammy said, "I could always check the sign-in sheet next class."

"Sweet Lord, you are such a creeper," Maeve teased.

"I am not! C'mon Maeve, what do you honestly think someone like him would do if someone like me said 'Hi'?"

"Hi. That's what I honestly think he'd say."

Sammy would then begin a self-deprecating rant, an upsettingly familiar downward spiral Maeve could never save her from. All of Maeve's sage wisdom would fall on deaf ears, and she began to fear that Sammy had fallen in love with her own romanticized loneliness. What other explanation could there be for the declining of invitations, the obsession with romances not her own and the safety net of Hollywood stories? Maeve was not to be deterred. Sure, Sammy felt incomplete; was in desperate need of something she could call her own, something intimate only she understood, and Maeve shuddered to think about how Sammy could sit at a small desk, hunched over an old typewriter she had received as a birthday gift, putting her perversions into print for hours at a time. Sammy's creative endeavors, or at least the few she had allowed Maeve to read, always started off with such promise and potential, but quickly became nothing more than smut. Maeve was a witness as Sammy's severe desperation was plaguing everything. Harsh as it may seem, Sammy would agree. She knew its foul stench was all over the rejection slips from publishers that came in the mail. Sammy dutifully tacked each slip on the wall above her computer, and the monitor of said computer constantly glowed bright with a blank text document. If at first you don't succeed, give 'em hell and keep on trucking.

Class was back in session. Sammy was punctual this time. Hell, she was early, eager to catch a glimpse of the young man she had already placed on some pedestal, built by loneliness that was absurdly adolescent and cinematic notions. The walking dream swept through the door just moments before the professor shut it with a nervy, little cough. The Greek god had a wide, goofy smile and carried himself as if at any minute he was going to turn and share in some real riot of a joke. Dark shades remaining over what Sammy knew to be devastatingly remarkable eyes, he sat beside her for the second class in a row, silently laughing to himself. She soon found herself smiling widely too, though she couldn't exactly say why.

"Did you do the reading?"

Sammy jumped. Twenty minutes into the class session had her bored and daydreaming, and her wandering mind was unprepared for the hushed whisper coming from the guy in shades. Her face burned red. "What?"

"Did you read the first four chapters of The Beautiful and Damned?"

Sammy's mouth had suddenly gone dry. She believed a beer, or any other cold, stiff drink, could alleviate her sudden affliction; offer some liquid courage, so to speak. "Um, yeah, I read it." She paused for a moment, still struggling to understand why he was talking to her. She'd never been in a situation like this before; the only classmates who talked to her asked for a pen and then called it a day. Curious, she asked, "Why?"

Nonchalantly, he shrugged and impressively stretched his grin wider. "I was just wondering, I guess."

"Did you?"

"Did I what?"

"Um, did you read?" All of Sammy's adolescent insecurities came rushing back, like a fat kid going for seconds in the buffet line. He had to be staring at her love handles, or that mole above her eye, or the acne near the temples of her forehead. Suddenly, she realized she should have gotten braces years ago.

"Of course; I love Fitzgerald."

"Me too," she barely responded. Her words were a croaked whisper.

He laughed softly. Speaking from the corner of his mouth as he idly wrote in his notebook, not looking at her, he said, "But not as much as Stephen King."

"Excuse me?"

He slightly inclined his head to her bag on the floor, decorated in cover art from King's novels. She had purchased it in Maine on a trip to stalk Mr. King, a trip that had been thinly disguised as a summer vacation. Protectively, she slid her bag under her chair. He still smiled. "The other day in class, I saw you reading The Stand when Professor Windbag over there went off on one of his tangents."

"That novel's my favorite," Sammy quickly mumbled with her eyes locked on the desk.

"I prefer IT myself. The idea of being an integral part of something bigger, while retaining your childhood to be a complete, whole adult is really remarkable and reassuring. There's real optimism in that." He still hadn't looked at her and was now mindlessly chewing on his pen cap. Sammy, however, was shamelessly gawking at her conversational partner, the desk becoming increasingly less interesting.

"You read King?" She had found her soul mate.

"Of course; horror is my genre of choice. I guess it's yours, too?"

Not trusting herself to speak, Sammy nodded silently. The conversation appeared to end there, as the young man smiled and turned more fully to the professor and away from her, now clearly focused on the lesson. She was elated nonetheless. When class ended and the young man hurried out the door, Sammy watched him go with a real sense of regret. Yes, they had talked, and that was all well and good, but she hadn't even learned his name. Was their entire relationship to be based on hushed, rushed dialogue in a class that only lasted, like, fourteen weeks? What was the point? He didn't even look back to her. Discouragement was a fast-acting poison, and her face fell as she straightened up and made for the exit.

"Ah, excuse me, Miss Thogode? Excuse me?"

Fuck.

Shit.

Balls.

Slowly, wincing, Sammy turned to face her narcissistic, little bastard of a professor. His smile was sickly sweet and strained. "I was hoping you had a moment to discuss your chronic lateness?" She hoped his dark hair would thin in awkward patches, and that his dark eyes would be swallowed up by wrinkles, and that he'd have a huge gut that hung over his belt. She wanted his future to be as weak as she currently felt. Sammy knew she was being spiteful and that she was kind of in the wrong, but she didn't care, and that was essentially Sammy.

Nervously, she fumbled with the strap of her bag. "Actually, I have something important to … do."

The professor continued as if Sammy hadn't said a word. He made it easy to hate him. "I was going to simply drop your grade from an A to a C, but Dr. Nicosia and Dr. Bronson came to your aid and convinced me I was being harsh."

"Wow … really?" Sammy paused to revel in the fact that she had professors in her corner, and to silently curse the academics for not teaching the current class. She wouldn't be having all these problems if it was someone else standing at the podium. At least, she hoped that was true and that she wasn't losing her scholarly edge. Palms nearly sweating, she said, "I'm extremely grateful, and –"

"However, they agreed something needed to be done, and both are in full agreement that an extra assignment would be in order."

"What?"

The professor's smile slowly became more genuine. "By the end of the semester, I expect a fictitious manuscript thirty pages in length."

"Did you say thirty pages?" Sammy's jaw dropped. "Excuse me, sir, but this isn't a creative writing class."

Straightening his stylishly pretentious glasses, the professor leveled his gaze at Sammy. "I am well aware of what this class is not. Nowhere on the syllabus, which I wrote, is this course described as silent, sustained reading," he eyed the battered-looking King novel clutched in her hand, "or speed dating." Sammy started. What the hell was that about? She always paid attention, always handed in assignments on time and completed them to the professor's satisfaction- her only issue was lateness. Her heart skipped a couple of beats when she realized the professor's latter dig must be a reference to the beautiful student who had sat beside her again today. Did he think they were flirting, and if so, on what grounds? She was about to ask for some clarification and for some specifics when he continued his condescending speech Sammy was now really listening to, but for the wrong reason. "I must admit I'm fairly surprised by your resistance. Professors Nicosia and Bronson informed me of your aspiration to be a writer, and I assumed you'd simply jump at the chance to write and receive feedback from a published author such as myself."

"Of course, sir, it's just —"

"It's settled then. The last formal class session, you will present to me a thirty-page manuscript of fiction. Good evening." He turned from Sammy, busily straightening his papers to better tuck them neatly away in his briefcase. Blood boiling and stomach churning, Sammy exited the room with as much dignity as she could muster, but it wasn't as much as she would have liked. Leaving the stifling box of a classroom, Sammy texted Maeve and demanded to know where she was. She wanted to vent and as luck would have it, Maeve was catching a late dinner in the pizzeria on campus. The pizzeria was located on the bottom floor of the Student Center. The front of the building was always crowded with people, especially when the weather permitted it. Before descending the ramp to the right of the stairs that served as the most direct path to the pizzeria, she took a moment to calm herself, and appreciate that she was a part of something as, for lack of a better term, cool as college. She had always loved school, had always been good at it, and the immersion the campus provided made her nerdy little heart swell.

Ten minutes later, Maeve's mouth was full of mozzarella cheese while Sammy's was full of angry, angry words- so much for trying to stay calm and not infuriated. The high stools they were seated upon were uncomfortable, and the place had been packed as the last classes of the day were letting out so ordering and actually receiving food had taken forever, and only made Sammy angrier and more crotchety. "So the douche bag gives me this huge extra assignment because I miss his grand entrance every week. What could he possibly teach in the first five minutes of class that's so important anyway?"

Maeve shrugged. "Maybe he's teaching everyone how to get dates." A teasing smirk stretched her lips.

"Don't be mean," Sammy said as she smiled in spite of herself.

"I'm sorry your day sucked." Maeve wiped her mouth after offering her condolences.

"Eh, it wasn't all bad. I was in a really good mood earlier, but now I can't remember why." Suddenly, Sammy's face lit up. "Oh! That beautiful boy I was telling you about initiated contact!"

Maeve beamed. "Tell me all about it." Sammy launched into a fanciful retelling of the class, making sure to emphasize the suaveness that exuded from his pores, and how he came in smiling and how that made life better. Maeve laughed in all the right places, widening her eyes every time a bit of dialogue was revealed and smiled the entire time. It wasn't the first time she'd seen Sammy gush over a stranger but she was pleased that the stranger was made of flesh and bone, rather than ink and paper, so she would gladly suck it up and indulge her friend because it made Sammy happy, and it was a small price to pay to see a smile lift the corners of Sammy's lips and eyes. Her shoulders relaxed slightly and her stance slacked just a smidge, but it was enough to make her look at ease, and that put Maeve at ease.

The next day was Sammy's last day of classes for the week. Her schedule allowed her a late lunch. Venturing to the Student Center, she was seated alone, as usual, in a secluded corner of the largest cafeteria on campus, mindlessly shoving chicken fingers in her mouth. The room was vast, with several ceiling fans slowly and idly rotating above. The overall color scheme was gray – gray, plastic tables with gray, felt-covered chairs that were flimsy in construction, and complete with arm rests that were really too thin to be effective. As a result, her elbows were on the table, and she was trying to hurry up and finish *The Beautiful and Damned* so she could continue onward to *The Sun Also Rises* by Hemingway. If she were to complete her stupid, fucking extra assignment to her professor's stupid, fucking standards, she couldn't afford to fall behind on the reading or to miss any notes during lecture. The more Sammy thought about it, the more she realized that this added stress via an extra assignment was really the absolute last thing she needed. It wasn't like she didn't have any other classes to worry about or anything; actually, she had several other classes, and how dare that big, old bag of douche –

"Remember to tell me what you think about the last line. I'm thinking about getting it tattooed somewhere on my body. It's that good, I promise."

The book flew from Sammy's hands and she had to swallow a scream. Turning toward the startling and yet somehow seductive voice, Sammy watched with fascination as the vision of perfection from class took a seat beside her for the third time in recent memory. Again, he was displaying a goofy, infectious grin. "Sorry. I didn't mean to scare you."

Struggling to regulate her breathing, Sammy offered a queasy smile. "It's okay," she said, sliding her things to the empty chair nearest her, making room for his tray of food. "It was probably more the book than you."

He raised an eyebrow in disbelief. It was just visible over his familiar dark, square shades. "Hmm, I didn't know Fitzgerald was scary."

"He absolutely can be," Sammy insisted. "I'm at the part where Amory thinks he sees the Devil and tries to escape it in a crowded city. There are definitely elements of horror there."

"My bad; you're right." He was still smiling.

There was an awkward pause because Sammy didn't know what to say or even what to do with her hands. She couldn't eat in front of him, so her two hands were just twitching nervously on the table. Sammy may not have known how to be entirely engaging or adequately suave, but she did know, with one hundred percent certainty, that she didn't want the conversation to end. "Did you already get to that part?" she asked.

He began to un-wrap a sandwich. "Yes. I've finished the book, actually."

"Oh," Sammy sighed. "You're a fast reader."

"Not really. I just love to read."

Sammy furrowed her brows. He wasn't implying that her love for reading wasn't on par with his own, was he? Or could she infer from his comment that he thought that she was a slow reader? This wasn't going as well as Sammy would have liked, and she was starting to falter. "Well, I do too," she retorted and she knew she sounded combative. Silently cursing her inability to interact normally with other human beings, she tried to soften the blow by adding, "I was just pacing myself until that douche bag gave me an extra assignment for my apparent chronic lateness, which complete bullshit, by the way, because I was freaking early last class." Sammy had wanted to let the beautiful boy know she was just angry at life and he was an innocent bystander, but she did not understand the magnitude of that anger until she realized she had been clenching her fists, and had been doing so hard enough to feel the sting of half-moons being etched into her palms by her fingernails. "Sorry. I'm still angry about it, obviously." She laughed, but it was more of a nervous titter, really.

He laughed softly, and that was a good sign - he found her rage endearing. "It's alright," he said, offering his empathy. "I'd be furious, too. What's the extra assignment? That is, if you don't mind me asking." He took a large bite of his meal before regarding Sammy with what she thought was real interest, but those damn sunglasses made it hard to be sure. At least he was sort of looking at her this time.

"A thirty-page manuscript of fiction, to be turned in to a published author who thinks I'm lazy, rude, and stupid." Sammy tossed the chicken finger she had been eating aside. Facing the true enormity of the assignment made her lose her appetite. Shrugging, her eyes glazed over as she tried to imagine where to begin. "I'm screwed."

"That sounds pretty awesome, actually. You get to have your work read by someone in the field, and because of how he feels about you, you know that he'll definitely be brutally honest." He grinned widely, but noticed that Sammy was still looking defeated, still staring out into nothing. He cleared his throat and quickly added, "I mean, I don't think he hates you, but even if he does, now's your chance to prove him wrong. It'll be a little overwhelming at first, sure, but still awesome. Do you have any ideas yet?"

Sammy shook her head.

He wiped his mouth clean with the back of his hand before wiping that same hand clean with a napkin. It was a completely thoughtless gesture that Sammy found inexplicably and incredibly sexy. Embarrassed, she looked away from him as he spoke. "What do you normally write?" Completely unperturbed by her awkward body language, he drank from his cup while patiently awaiting a response. This was normal for him, and the absurd and abnormal

Sammy was not changing that fact- another good sign? Sammy silently prayed that it was.

"Horror," Sammy said, answering his question after a small delay. She laughed because the response was well received; the Beautiful Boy from English Class was smiling warmly.

"I should have guessed. Is it in the tradition of Mr. King, by any chance?"

"He's a big influence, yeah. But my inspiration mainly comes from music." Forgetting herself, Sammy turned her body fully to Beautiful Boy with an easy confidence she had never known before. The absurdity and abnormality dissipated as the conversation kept the normally aggressive doubts and melodramatic questions at bay.

Beautiful Boy, oblivious to all the infantile inner turmoil that twisted Sammy's intestines into knots, drank again from his cup. Cool and collected, he continued the conversation with another question. "Are there any particularly inspiring artists?"

"I'll listen to anyone, but I find Springsteen, Seger, and Brand New very inspirational." Unconsciously, Sammy was leaning closer to him. Later that day, when she would realize just how close she was sitting to Beautiful Boy, as she replayed the scene over and over again while listening to soft rock radio, she would rationalize her actions by insisting she only wanted to be sure she heard him over the dull roar of the crowded cafeteria. Whether or not she convinced herself is debatable.

"Can I make a suggestion?"

"Please," Sammy pleaded, only she hoped it sounded more polite than pleading.

"Go home and make a playlist with all of your favorite songs by these artists, then burn it onto a CD, and drive to the end of Longhill Road. Bring a notebook and a pen. I think something will come to you." Grinning, he picked up his tray and books, and walked away to the nearest exit with a garbage can. When it became clear he wasn't returning to bid a proper adieu, Sammy panicked.

"Wait!" She called out, rising to her feet. "What's your name?" This conversation had to be more progressive than the last.

Turning and walking backwards with a grace Sammy had never seen exude from anyone before, he yelled, "Eliot! It was a pleasure meeting you!" Then he disappeared into the throng of students. Sammy slowly sank into her chair. She picked at her bottom lip, smiling wide enough to cause her eyes to disappear into her cheeks. Eliot ... a beautiful name for a beautiful boy; it was all very fitting.

Chapter Two
Beers, Bars and Boys

*"Love is just a hoax so forget everything
that you have heard."* ~ The Spill Canvas

Sammy drove home in the softly falling rain of an idle weekday evening. Tired and sore, she was anxious to get home and sleep. As she was not really much of an athlete, Sammy wasn't sure why she was so sore. Laughing to herself, she considered it might be from oversleeping on a mattress that was too soft. Following that logic, she was more overtired than plain tired, and the dreary weather wasn't helping. The mist was lulling her to sleep, and she decided homework and all other obligations could wait. More than anything, Sammy wanted to just relax and let her mind drift. She wanted, if only for a moment, to stop worrying about obligations and situations beyond her control. She wanted to think about more pleasant opportunities, like Eliot and romance and writing and being successful at writing and holding a book signing. Sammy found life much easier to handle if, every now and again, she took the time to be completely unrealistic and just accept it. Whether it was in the middle of a particularly boring lecture, during her lunch break at her summer job, or alone in a bathroom and near tears, she made it a point to revisit her dreams. On the bad days, she feared her dreams were all she really had.

And here she was again, locked inside her mind. Rolling to a smooth and complete stop at a red light, Sammy turned on the radio and twisted the knob, searching for a soothing, relaxing kind of melody. Bob Seger was sensually singing, "We've Got Tonight" and that was perfect. She listened to Seger imploring his lady friend to stay and would have shut her eyes and drifted away to a scene developing in her mind had she not needed her attention elsewhere, like the road. To have a man, and a man's man at that, be vulnerable because of the love of a woman ... well, that was something she wanted to know, and needed to become acquainted with. The song ended, and left her feeling nostalgic.

Pulling into her parents' driveway, Sammy's cell phone rang. As she parked before the whitewashed garage, she fumbled to answer the phone before she missed the call. "Hello?"

"Hey, girl, hey!"

"Hey Maeve," Sammy smiled. "What's up?"

"Nothing's really going on over here, and that's an issue. That is also why I'm calling. Are you going to be around later? We should head over the bridge and check out the bars over there, like around nine o'clock. Does that interest you at all?" she asked.

Sammy paused a moment to consider. She was tired, but was emboldened by the conversation with Eliot from earlier in the week, when he had invited himself to lunch. Maybe going out would be fun. Maybe another beautiful boy would initiate a conversation, invite himself into Sammy's social circle, which was certainly lacking members, particularly of the male persuasion. Maybe this new sense of confidence would help her even do the inviting. Who knew? Smiling widely, Sammy said, "Sure. I'll be ready."

"What?"

"I said I'll go."

"Really, or are you trying to be funny?"

Sammy laughed. "Really; I'll go."

Maeve was surprised – shocked, even. They'd been having this same conversation every weekend for about a year. Sammy had declined every invitation until this one, but Maeve had kept at it all the same. Loyal and determined, Maeve promised Sammy many a night that she'd have Sammy out of her so-called "rut" before they could call themselves college graduates. Time was running out, though. Time in college moved double time and with each passing semester, Maeve worried Sammy was losing faith and losing her grip. Needless to say, Maeve's worries were eased by Sammy's eagerness to go out, and Maeve knew Sammy could hold on for just a little longer.

Maeve picked her up later that night. The rain had finally tapered off and it had warmed up a bit to make the night incredibly dreamy. Possibilities seemed endless and life seemed to be unlimited. To be young, to be alive, and to be optimistic was almost enough to feel sane and whole; to feel complete. The young women rode in the car with the windows down, yelling and laughing over the blaring radio. As Sammy fought to keep her hair from whipping about her face, she was struck by the sudden realization that she was still lonely. Optimism turned to dust and was carried away by the warm summer winds that swooped in and out of the windows as quickly as they came. As great as talking with Beautiful Boy had been, and as much fun as Maeve and her had together, she strongly felt that something was missing from the night, something like a beautiful boy reaching for her hand from across the great expanse of the center console in a flat bed Ford. That would be something worth writing about.

That would be perfect.

"What are you thinking about? Don't get weird on me!" Maeve yelled.

"Just a story idea," Sammy said, smiling softly.

The bar was crowded with plenty of familiar faces. It seemed as if every student from the college was in attendance. It was the typical Irish pub – dark wooden tables, chairs and booths, stained glass decorative windows, and dim lighting. There were no tablecloths, a hard wooden floor and technically, there were three bars; one right inside the entrance with the others on either side of the place. The bar to the left was not as mobbed and the girls sought drinks there. Maeve and Sammy, armed with beers, turned to face the swarm of bodies. Maeve tapped Sammy on the arm and put her mouth by her ear. "Wait right here. I'm going to see if I can find Mike."

Frowning, Sammy kept Maeve from rushing off by grabbing her arm. "Whoa, wait! You didn't tell me you invited Mike."

"Since when do you have a problem with my boyfriend?" Maeve asked, puzzled. "You guys get along great."

Sammy shook her head impatiently. "That's not it. I have nothing against Mike. I have something against being the third wheel, though."

"It's not going to be like that! It never is," Maeve argued, rolling her eyes and thereby dismissing what she believed to be a ludicrous complaint from Sammy. "I'll be right back," was all she said before disappearing into the crowd. Sammy turned back to the bar and took a large swig from her bottle. She was dreading another awkward, lonely night.

"I like a girl with a healthy thirst," said someone beside her. Sammy turned to the right and saw a decent-looking man in a pressed, white shirt, smiling kindly at her. She returned the smile, although her expression was definitely more sarcastic than his.

"I'm sure you can find a lot of girls with a healthy thirst at a bar." She waved her hand around to indicate the myriad of drunken co-eds surrounding them. Sammy locked her gaze on an indeterminate object before her and made a mental note to sip her beer rather than chug it. Chugging beer was the key to attracting creepers, apparently.

The sarcasm was not lost on Mr. White Shirt, but he would not give up so easily, it seemed. Still smiling, he leaned closer and said, "A healthy thirst isn't all I'm looking for."

Avoiding eye contact, Sammy began to pick at the label on her bottle. She couldn't bring herself to be a total bitch, not to a boy willing to have a conversation, so she not-so reluctantly encouraged him by asking, "Is that so?"

"Definitely," he said, and his renewed confidence was evident. "I like a girl who can cook and clean, too." Jaw nearly cracking against the bar, Sammy was shocked and appalled by the chauvinistic sleaze next to her. She turned to enter into a tirade and only stopped when she saw him shaking with mirth. "I'm sorry, but I just wanted to see what you'd do. Your face was totally worth it." He was laughing heartily, obviously very pleased with himself.

Though she shook her head in disdain, Sammy laughed in spite of herself. "Glad I could amuse you." She paused only for a moment, to collect her drink from the bar, and then said, "Goodnight!" She tried to slide further down the bar, but he gently touched her arm to keep her still. It worked; she turned back.

"Come on, don't be like that. I didn't say anything repulsive, right? Did I make any gross sexual gestures or references?"

Sammy thought, reviewed the dialogue, and realized that he hadn't been gross. She admitted, "No, you didn't."

His smile widened and Sammy noticed the way it lit up his whole face. "Then let me buy you a drink."

Sammy raised her bottle with the tiniest twinge of regret. "I'm all set. Thanks though."

"Let's do a shot, then." His tenacity was to be commended. Sammy opened her mouth to politely decline, but he cut her off at the pass. "Look, I had a real shitty day and I need to get wasted, so I'm taking this shot with or without you. A little company would be nice, is all."

Sammy thought of later that night when she would return home. In the moment her head hit the pillow, would her face be sore from smiling, or from fighting back tears? Could she face another night being the last person anyone thought of? She didn't think she could. A small smile on her thick lips, Sammy agreed. "All right, I'm in."

"Great! What do you want?"

"You had the shitty day, so you decide. Besides, you're the one who's paying - not me."

He appraised her with smiling eyes. "I just might have to buy you two shots." He turned to flag down the bartender and while he was occupied, Sammy's eyes roamed the bar for Maeve or Mike. She assumed finding one would lead to the other, but alas – there was no sign of the pair. The young man turned back, glasses in hand. "Here you are …?"

"Sammy." She supplied her first name and took the shot from his hand. "And you are?"

He gave her what he believed to be a seductive smile. She'd take it. "Rob."

"And this is …?" she asked, raising her glass.

"That would be my good friend Jack Daniels." Rob knocked his glass against the one in Sammy's hand. "Here's to shitty days!" They drank in unison, slamming the drained glasses on the bar at nearly the same time. Sammy felt her liver recoil and grimaced. She chased the shot by chugging the majority of her beer. Rob laughed and patted her on the back. "You're chasing Jack with a beer? I'm a fan!"

Nearly three hours had passed since Maeve left to go find her boy, but Sammy was completely unaware. Rob had kept her thoroughly entertained. The most recent round of shots and laughter was subsiding and Sammy had thoughtlessly placed her hand upon Rob's shoulder. He inched closer, but Sammy was buzzed and feeling good, and less perceptive. Rob moved his mouth close to her ear to ask what he thought was an obvious and expected question. "Are you seeing anyone, Sammy?"

Fuck.

Shit.

Balls.

Sammy panicked. She should just tell him the truth, right? But if honesty was the best policy, how honest should she get? Telling him she'd never ever been seeing anyone was unnecessary; too much information ... right? Suddenly sober, Sammy nervously cleared her throat. "Actually, I ..." Her breath cut short and her eyes felt like they doubled in size. Behind Rob, leaning against the far wall and eyeing the dance floor was Eliot, the Beautiful Boy from English class. There was no mistaking those intense, burning brown eyes that, dear Lord, suddenly stared back at her. Eliot was definitely staring this time. His hands gripped an icy bottle that dripped condensation. Though people passed before him, brushing against him and muttering pardons, Eliot's eyes were boring into Sammy's. Drunken sluts grinded against entranced dates on the floor, the bass beat loud enough to be felt against the rib cage, but all went unnoticed by either Sammy or Eliot. Her face grew hot when he winked at her. What the hell was that supposed to mean? Shutting her eyes, Sammy shook her head quickly to clear it. When she looked again, Eliot the Beautiful Boy was gone, completely gone.

Had he ever really been there?

Sammy remembered Rob's question. Her eyes met his, still patiently focused on her. They were light-colored eyes. She wasn't sure why that mattered, or why it had to be noted, only that it did. "Sorry. I actually thought I was just seeing someone I knew, but I was wrong." She eyed her drink warily. "Maybe I should slow down."

Rob laughed. "Want to step outside for some fresh air? I could use a cigarette."

Cringing in mock embarrassment, Sammy said, "Please tell me you see the stupidity in what you just said."

"Shut up," Rob smiled as he slipped an arm around her waist, "and let's go." Sammy allowed Rob to steer her to the parking lot.

Once the night breeze sailed along their skin, Rob released Sammy, but with a lingering hesitation that did not go unnoticed. Thankful for the cover of night, Sammy's cheeks burned red. Rob spoke first. "So, let me try my previous question again." Rob pulled a long, white cigarette from his battered-looking pack. "Do you have a boyfriend?" Never taking his eyes from hers, he held the cigarette between his pale lips and struck a match with his thumbnail. It was all so suave and debonair. It was all so impressive.

Unable not to, Sammy smiled. "I do not have a boyfriend." She was impressed by Rob, for sure, but she was thankful that he had simplified the question. Just because Sammy didn't currently have a man on her arm didn't mean that she never did, so Rob had unknowingly helped Sammy avoid a can of worms most definitely best left unopened.

Rob took a long drag of his newly lit cigarette. Exhaling smoke slowly, he took a step closer. Sammy's blood was pounding in her ears, so much so that she could barely hear Rob's shoes crunch against the pavement. The lack of auditory ability was frustrating - she had to hear whatever he said next. "Would you be opposed to giving me your number, then?"

Grinning like an idiot, Sammy said, "Not at all." She rattled off digits and watched Rob program them into his cell phone, her heart racing. This was all strange, exciting and new. That shot hadn't been a bad idea after all.

"I assume this means I can give you a call?" Rob took another drag of his cigarette and Sammy had a sudden, strong image of James Dean. It wasn't nearly as romantic as all that, it was all really unremarkable, but her flair for the dramatic would not rest.

"Of course; anytime," she breathed, doing her best impression of Marilyn Monroe, which naturally meant it was awful.

"Sammy! There you are!" Maeve's voice sounded across the parking lot. She was hurrying over. "I'm starving! Do you want to grab something to eat at the diner?"

Sammy wanted to turn her down. She really wanted to stay with Rob. Mediocre mozzarella sticks were no substitute for romance. However, her hazy mind slurred something about playing hard to get and she turned to Rob. "I'm going to head out. Thanks for the drinks." She turned and did her best to calmly walk to her friend's side. Sammy was gushing, and by the cheesy excitement on Maeve's face, Maeve could tell. Maeve certainly knew the reason for all the gushing and giggling and girlish indulgence. Arm in arm, suppressing the aforementioned giggles, the two young women headed for the car.

"You better pick up when I call!" Rob called after Sammy. He was beaming as he headed back inside, wiping the corners of his lips with his thumb.

Composure completely dissolving once inside the car, Sammy cracked up and covered her face. Maeve joined in the merriment as she buckled her seatbelt. "So, tell me Miss Sammy - who was that?"

"That was what happens when you ditch me in a bar," Sammy reprimanded her friend as she buckled herself in. "What the hell happened to you?"

"I did not ditch you, bitch." Maeve was still laughing as she turned the key in the ignition. "I found Mike. We went back to find you, but you had found someone else ... so much for being a third wheel." Watching her friend blush like a little girl from the corners of her eyes, Maeve pulled out of the parking spot and left the bar. "What's his name?"

"Rob." Sammy loved the way his name felt in her mouth. In love with the night, she rolled down her window to get closer to it.

"Did you get his number?"

"No, but he got mine." Sammy smiled at Maeve's ensuing catcalls. She turned the radio on and she turned the volume up to drown out Maeve's playful teasing. She also hoped to drown out any more questions because Rob was all hers, something personal and private, and she wanted to keep it that way for as long as possible. She went as far as to hope Mike would make an appearance at the diner and keep Maeve distracted. Sammy turned to face the wind and felt it lift her hair all around her. A fire was burning in her veins. Her stomach was pleasantly unsettled and for the first time in her existence, Sammy was sure that when her head hit the pillow, someone would at least be thinking of her, and it was worth living for. Hell, it was even worth dying for.

"Come on, Sammy, spill it! I want to know everything," Maeve demanded. Sammy found it hard to take Maeve's order seriously when Maeve had marinara sauce smeared all over her mouth. Laughing, Sammy handed Maeve a napkin.

"His name is Rob. He bought me a few drinks and we talked for a while. I gave him my number and that's it." Realizing she was hungrier than she thought, Sammy began to devour the plate of fries she had ordered, loaded with salt and ketchup. Briefly, in between bites, she marveled at how greasy food managed to soak up alcohol. Catching a second wind of sobriety would be awesome, so as to avoid stumbling through the front door of her parents' house. She wouldn't be in trouble, but she'd feel awful if she woke them up. Nine times out of ten, though, her dad would be lightly napping on the couch in the living room, right by the front door. He liked to wait up for her, make sure she was okay, and then he'd head to bed. Though she longed to move out, living at home had its underappreciated advantages.

Maeve brought Sammy back to the present when she asked, "What did you talk about?"

Sammy's face must have betrayed her irritation with Maeve and Maeve's persistence. She opened her mouth to answer, and the answer would have been short – maybe even curt – but Mike spoke instead. "Hon, leave her alone," he said to Maeve. "Let her enjoy it in peace," Mike advised, and then smiled at Sammy before tearing into his burger.

Sammy grinned widely at Mike. She thanked him for intervening before concentrating on her fries, while Maeve gave a detailed account of her trip through the bar to find Mike, which was filled with comedic mishaps and guest appearances from the people they knew. Kate, an old roommate, had been waiting for her fiancé, Ryan, outside the men's room as Ryan proudly declared, loud enough for most to hear, that he was taking a shit. Ally, a classmate, had been seen having a romantic dinner with a professor (someone in the biology department) and Maeve couldn't wait to tell everyone, even though Mike thought she was making it up. Maeve didn't particularly care what Mike thought, seeing as how it was his fault she had to turn the bar inside out looking for him. After all, what kind of idiot leaves their I.D. in their other pants, at home, when invited to a bar? Blushing lightly, Mike smiled and admitted his own stupidity. Maeve told Sammy it was a good thing Mike was cute and blah, blah, blah. The conversation continued in that fashion until the check came an hour later. Sammy dug through her purse to round up some cash, and was startled when her cell phone buzzed loudly across the table. Who would be calling so late? Was it her dad, annoyed and wanting to go to sleep in his own room? Throwing ten dollars in the center of the table, Sammy then checked her phone. It was a text message from an unfamiliar number. It read: "This better be your real number."

It had to be Rob. Laughing out loud, Sammy quickly replied that it was the right number. She asked how the bar scene was treating Rob now that she'd gone. The texts continued in a flirtatious manner the whole ride home and only ended when Sammy could keep her eyes open no longer. Rob promised to call her soon and suggested they get coffee. It was something perfect. It was something to write about.

Rob called two days later. The conversation lasted for hours. They made more concrete plans for coffee, and Sammy found out that Rob was an assistant manager in an office that sold something or other, that he had really wanted to be the lead singer of a rock band (even though he couldn't sing), that he had two younger sisters, that he owned every Frank Sinatra album ever made, and that his favorite movie of all time was "The Departed." Intelligent, charming and sincere, Rob asked as many questions as he answered, and repeatedly announced his excitement for the date (yes, he said date!). After hanging up, Sammy screamed with elation into her pillow. When another rejection slip from another publisher arrived, she scribbled Rob's name all over it, complete with tiny hearts.

The day of the date, Sammy sat in the coffee shop, drumming her fingernails against the table. The coffee shop was just indie enough to be cool and was on the main highway in town, highly populated and very popular. Anxiously, she chewed her bottom lip. Would Rob show up? He wasn't late, but he hadn't been early. Was that some sort of signal? Sammy had no clue. All of this was bizarre. Her heart was beating fast enough to break. It was too much, all too much, and Sammy had decided a million and one times that she was just going to get up and leave. She bent to pick up her purse when the bell above the door jingled to announce a new arrival. Rob walked in.

He looked beautiful. His short, black hair was gelled with a careless sense of consideration. His blue, button-down shirt and khaki pants screamed professional casualness. As he stood near the entrance, nonchalantly looking this way and that for Sammy, she marveled at his light eyes, expressive mouth and strong chin. It dawned on her that the handsome man at the front of the coffee shop was looking for her. Afraid to disturb the perfect scene she'd helped create, Sammy slowly rose to her feet and called out Rob's name. He turned toward the sound almost instantly, broke into a radiant smile, and headed over.

"Hey! You look beautiful," Rob greeted. Sammy blushed, looking down at the thin, purple dress she had bought with Maeve the day before, for this very occasion. She had been worried the summer dress bought on clearance would be out of place this time of year and that she would look like an idiot, but Maeve assured

Sammy she'd look great as long as she dressed it up with leggings, a black cardigan, and some shiny new black flats. Sammy had listened, Maeve had been right, and Sammy was happy Rob thought that she looked nice. Sammy looked back to Rob, and he enveloped her in his strong arms. It was the first time Sammy had felt such a warm, comfortable weight against her and she returned it eagerly. She stepped back and smiled.

"You look great too. I really like your hair." Inside, she cringed. The compliment sounded so lame. It sounded forced and not genuine. Rob still beamed, all the same.

"Thank you very much. Have you ordered yet?"

"No, I was waiting for you."

Rob's smiled widened to show his pearly whites. "You're quite the lady. What can I get you?"

"Oh, no, you don't have to do that. I could easily ...," Sammy faltered.

"Don't worry about it. I asked you out, now I'm paying. It's all standard operating procedure."

Sammy looked down at her shoes. The shiny black flats sent back her reflection, and Sammy thought she looked dumb. "I'll have a frozen cappuccino," she mumbled.

"Alright, a frozen cappuccino it is. Have a seat, and I'll be right back."

"You don't want me to come with you?"

"I'll only be a second. Take a load off." With that easy smile, Rob walked up to the counter. Sammy sank into her chair like a deflating balloon. He hadn't wanted her to wait with him. That was weird, right? Lines were the ultimate, universal stage for public displays of affection, golden opportunities to make those around you irritable with envy. Maybe Rob didn't want to be affectionate with her. If that was true, then what the hell was she doing there? Was she really on a date? That's not where she belonged. She was resolving to leave yet again when Rob returned.

"Here you are, Sammy." He handed her the frozen drink. "I also thought we could share a brownie." Rob slid the monstrous dessert on the table before reclaiming his seat. "Please don't tell me you're watching your weight or say it's too much. I'm hoping you'll take it as it was intended; as a delicious surprise. That's why I had you wait here, so you couldn't say no."

Sammy smiled. "Thank you." She eyed Rob's drink. "What are you having?"

"I ordered the same thing I always do; just a cup of black coffee. I'm boring, I know."

"I wasn't going to say anything," Sammy chuckled.

The date was amazing. The two talked for hours, again, until the gray light of the late-October day turned to the royal purple of dusk. Rob had taken Sammy's hand in his, had run his thumb across her smooth skin and sat close enough for Sammy to smell his cigarettes and soap. He walked her to her car, where they agreed to hang out at the bar again. Rob encouraged her to invite Maeve and Mike, and make it a double date. Rob moved to open her door for her, and Sammy meant to thank him, but a solitary figure standing on the corner stopped her. He was looking up at the traffic light, waiting for it to change from green to red. It was Eliot leaning against the thick, steel pole, and his flannel shirt hung open and flapped slightly in the breeze. His hands were tucked carelessly in his back pockets, and his dark sunglasses were superfluous in the fading light of the day.

Slowly, Eliot lowered his head and lifted his shades. He winked and smiled at Sammy. Her heart scrambled into her throat.

"Sammy?" Rob called. He placed a tentative hand upon her shoulder. "Are you still with us?" He breathed a shaky laugh.

"Oh, yeah, I'm sorry." She blinked a couple of times before returning her gaze to Rob. "I just thought I saw someone I knew standing by the traffic light."

Rob turned in the direction Sammy indicated. "Where did you see someone?" he called over his shoulder.

"I saw him leaning against the pole. He's a kid in my American Literature class."

"He's not there now."

"What?" Sammy moved to stand beside Rob. There wasn't a soul on the street corner.

"I think you're seeing things. That's too much drinking and not enough thinking." Rob had an uncomplicated, glorious smile.

Sammy was staring, and when she finally realized she had been staring at Rob, she cast her eyes elsewhere, anywhere else, and mumbled, "Sorry. But … uh … so, can I call you tonight?"

"Absolutely you can. I look forward to it." They exchanged farewells and Rob watched Sammy drive off, smiling so widely that his face was sore.

MANDI BEAN

Chapter Three
The Benediction

*"I believe that lovers should be chained together, thrown into a
fire with their songs and letters, left there to burn, left there to
burn in their arrogance."* ~ Bright Eyes

Running from the parking garage and up the stupid monster of
a hill, Sammy was just barely on time for her least favorite class.
She was able to claim her usual seat in the back, but found the seat
beside her vacant. Was Eliot absent? Her eyes scanned the
classroom, and found him in the front making hushed conversation
with another girl. The girl's straight, dark hair, over-sized
sunglasses and over-sized, crocheted hat made her exactly like
every other female on the campus. Chewing her bottom lip,
Sammy tried to figure out how the action defined Eliot's character.
The whole mysterious thing was totally sexy at first, but now that
it was over, Sammy found the revelation to be disappointing. Eliot
had just been a nice guy - no chance for romance there. Sammy
cursed herself silently for being so naive. Class began shortly after,
and Sammy was glad. She could use the distraction.

Time ticked by and Sammy was all packed up just as class was
dismissed. She left the building quickly and upon entering her

battered car, Sammy placed her bag beside her on the passenger
seat and waited for the engine to turn over and start. She let it idle
for five minutes, letting the old girl warm up, before she pulled out
of the lot. The CD she had made to inspire herself, the CD she had
made under Eliot's advisement, was sitting in the player. She
turned it on, turned the volume up, and instead of heading home,
she made a left towards Longhill Road. That particular stretch of
pavement was essentially deserted. Streetlights were few and far
between, and as the road twisted on the houses that were hidden
back on hills and behind hedges and trees began to disappear as
well. Dark clusters of bushes lined the road, and the trees that
covered the residences so well crept forward to meet the road until
they blocked everything else from view. Sammy couldn't see the
dim glow of headlights from cars passing on adjacent roads, and
Sammy couldn't see any lights ahead in the distance. She turned
her bright lights on; the progressing lack of civilization made for
beautiful scenery, but it also made Sammy uneasy. Just as she
wondered when the asphalt would end, it did, and it did so in the
form of a scenic overlook. The lights of the city winked at her,
encouraging her to leave the car. The light that had evaded her for
the last ten minutes of the drive had relocated altogether at the end
of the pavement, and it was striking. The allure of electricity and
the voyeuristic gratification of watching a whole city full of people
undetected were enthralling. Smiling in awe, Sammy put the car in
park and killed the engine, but left the lights and the radio on. The
rubber soles of her cheap sneakers treaded silently across the soft
dirt as she walked to the edge of the drop. Looking down, foliage
gave way to urban sprawl and the contradiction was breath-taking.
A gentle breeze picked up, and Sammy shut her eyes. Words and
images filled her mind as the earthy smell of dirt filled her nostrils.
It was a moment in which she thanked God for her breath of life.
Sammy believed it was a shame that so many people let these
moments simply pass them by. The scene did not only inspire her
to write about living; it inspired her to do it. As the Boss crooned

about Mary's dress waving in the light wind, Sammy opened her eyes and felt blessed, refreshed. She retrieved her notebook from the car, sat cross-legged on the hard ground, and wrote. She wrote until her fingers were stiff and sore, until the ink nearly ran dry, and until her car battery almost died.

Class was back in session. Armed with a frozen mocha (she hadn't been able to stop drinking frozen coffee since the date with Rob); Sammy was waiting for the professor to show up, along with the rest of the class. Ever since he had assaulted her with that extra assignment, she had tried to be obnoxiously early, and she was enjoying her first successful attempt at doing so. She was busily writing since Eliot's advice had proved to be extremely helpful. Sammy was planning on going back to that scenic overlook at the end of Longhill Road as soon as possible ... maybe even tonight ... And maybe Rob could join her, and she could show him some of her writing. She'd never ever done that before; it was an act of the most severe intimacy and it scared the shit out of her. While her heart skipped a beat at the thought of Rob reading her work, Sammy's brain, always the optimist despite the pessimism which was the very essence of her soul, entertained several romantic interludes (especially if she let Rob read the smuttier stuff) as students drifted into the classroom. There were still about ten minutes before class was scheduled to start, and there were still many vacant seats, so Sammy was surprised when Eliot strolled in and seated himself beside her. She thought he'd return to his seat from last week, next to the leggy hipster he'd been chatting up. Watching him settle into his claimed seat out of the corner of her eye, Sammy wondered if she should say hello. The headphones tucked discreetly in Eliot's ears told her trying to start a conversation would probably be more trouble than it was worth. She resumed writing until the professor arrived and class started.

Eliot tossed his notebook on top of Sammy's halfway through the lecture. She wasn't expecting it, as the droning professor had lulled her into a soporific state, and she gasped loudly. A few heads turned, but the professor continued to ramble, and Sammy was able to breathe easy. The last thing she desired was to have Professor Prick reprimand her in front of the class like a kindergartener for not paying attention. Looking down to the notebook, she saw writing across the top. "Hi." With something like skepticism, Sammy wrote, "Hello." She passed the notebook back with what she hoped was a cool indifference.

A few moments passed by before the notebook found its way back to her desk. "How are you?"

"I'm good, and yourself?"

"I'm well, thanks. Did you take my advice and take a trip down Longhill Road?"

The politeness of what they were writing was absurd, as was the need for both to be grammatically correct. What else could you expect from notes from English majors? Sammy smiled as she scrawled her response. "Yeah, and it turned out really well. Thanks." As Sammy passed the notebook back, she tried to catch Eliot's eye to offer a conspiratorial grin, but he was careful not to look at her. What the hell was that about? She pondered the implications until the notebook was plopped back on her desk, complete with a response.

"I'm glad I could help. Was your weekend as productive?"

"Not really. I was writing before class, though. It's definitely coming along."

"I'm glad to hear that."

Not wanting the written conversation to end, but unsure of what to say, Sammy anxiously chewed her thumbnail. She decided to play it safe and ask about his weekend. Eliot had spent it in Maine, visiting his parents. He explained how they lived on the same property as the mental institution they were administrators of, and that each visit was usually pretty crazy, no pun intended. Eliot asked the obvious question next, which naturally, was to inquire how Sammy spent her weekend; asking for more specifics since she had not spent it hunched over a notebook or computer keyboard. The notebook was again stopped on Sammy's desk as she debated the best way to respond. Should she tell him about Rob? She decided not to, remembering her resolve to keep him all to herself for as long as possible. Putting it in print could ruin everything. The only thing she knew for sure was that not telling Eliot about how she saw him places he wasn't was a brilliant idea. Not wanting to be too specific, she wrote, "I went out with some friends. It was a lot of fun."

"Glad you had fun. Man, this class puts me to sleep."

Sammy laughed conspiratorially. "Yeah … why aren't you sitting next to your girlfriend?" Passing the notebook back to Eliot, Sammy unabashedly and eagerly scrutinized Eliot's face for a reaction. His eyebrows furrowed together almost imperceptibly. Sammy grinned.

"What are you talking about?"

"Last class, you were talking with some girl in the front. It seemed pretty serious." Again, Sammy observed Eliot closely and was surprised when he snorted dismissively at her response. She nearly snatched the notebook from him when he was done writing.

"I asked her for a pen – that was it."

"I think she likes you. She may even be in love with you." She thought her jeering response would be an awkward end to their conversation, and it disappointed her. Suddenly, class was over and people were leaving the classroom in small crowds. Eliot was in such a crowd, not bothering to look back over his shoulder at Sammy. She was slow to leave, guilt and curiosity delaying the whole process. He sat next to her and had been flirtatious, but she was seeing Rob for another date. The crush on Eliot had been juvenile, albeit entertaining, but it was over now- it had to be, because it was difficult enough for Sammy to be normal with Rob. She didn't have the ability to be normal with Eliot, too. Some more experienced young woman could have coped accordingly, but Sammy was decidedly inexperienced and emotionally stunted. One beautiful boy was enough.

Sammy was in Maeve's bedroom, getting ready for the double date, and about to change her shirt for the thousandth time. She was determining the proper amount of cleavage to show. It was a fine line between sexy and slutty, a line that Sammy was having trouble navigating. Stepping out into the hallway, Sammy yelled, "Maeve! Does this look okay?"

Maeve's voice came muffled from the living room. "The last three looked fine! Can you hurry, please?"

"It's practically my first date ever, Maeve. Give me a break!"

A deep sigh from the living room meant Maeve was acquiescing, slowly getting to her feet and shuffling into the hall. She gave Sammy a weary but genuine smile. "You look great – honest."

Sammy smiled. "Do you think Rob will think so?"

"If he doesn't, then he isn't worth your time."

Sammy nodded, smoothed her pants and turned off the bedroom light. "Let's go."

The ride to the bar was uneventful. Sammy was too nervous to say much, terrified that if she opened her mouth, she would vomit. Maeve was kind enough to crank the volume in the car and place the verbal burden on no one but the Boss. Bruce Springsteen had been one of the first things Maeve and Sammy talked about. Maeve came in wearing an early tour tee shirt, and Sammy had complimented her on it, and before long, they were arguing which album was the best of all time. Maeve really liked "Born to Run" but Sammy thought "Darkness on the Edge of Town" was a real masterpiece. They debated all the way to their cars, had found each other on Facebook, and that was all she wrote, as the saying goes. Being friends with Maeve had been effortless, but this whole dating thing was just the opposite. Parking in the designated lot, Sammy almost refused to get out of the car. Though Maeve thought the whole spectacle was ridiculous, she waited with Sammy in the car until she felt comfortable enough to enter the bar. Being fashionably late never hurt, so Maeve wasn't too enraged. The girls walked in together, with Sammy doing breathing exercises to try and stay calm, and easily found Mike. Rob was a different story, and after about twelve seconds, Sammy texted him, asking if he had arrived yet. After another twelve seconds passed with no response from Rob, Sammy convinced herself he had stood her up. About to retreat to the ladies' room, she turned and was halted by Rob. He was exuding joy from every pore of his body. "Wow," he breathed. "You look amazing."

He showed up. How about them apples? Sammy's smile was radiant. "You look amazing as well, sir!" Rob hesitated awkwardly for a moment before enveloping her in his arms. The embrace was brief, but long enough to make Sammy develop a renewed confidence. She stepped back, surveying the man before her. His dark hair, light eyes that looked the way uncontrollable laughter sounded, and perfect lips were enough to make her stomach flip over in a not-so-uncomfortable way.

Rob rested his hand on the small of her back and began to lead her to the bar. "So, where are Maeve and Mike?"

Introductions went really well. A round of shots was ordered for the group, and then they hit the dance floor. Rob's hands remained gripping Sammy's hips as they turned and twisted to the beat. Sammy's hands, meanwhile, held firmly to Rob's strong, broad shoulders, and when the songs slowed down now and then there wasn't an inch of daylight between them. More drinks in and Maeve was surprised by how well Sammy was doing. Her social inequities and awkwardness had yet to make an appearance in front of Rob, and luckily for Sammy and Rob, Rob never left her side. He kept leaning close to whisper in Sammy's ear and grinded against her on the dance floor as eagerly as she grinded against him. Maeve was not surprised when Sammy told her she was joining Rob outside while he smoked a cigarette. As she watched them leave, arms wrapped around each other, Maeve slipped her hand into Mike's and let a tiny smile curl her lips.

Rob and Sammy stepped out of the bar and onto the pavement, laughing and panting from the effort of making their way through the crowd. Rob fell silent, but Sammy was oblivious to his change in demeanor as she shut her eyes in the cool night air to keep the world from spinning. Raising her face to the nighttime sky, Sammy finally gained what composure she could and opened her eyes to find Rob quiet and still, eyes intensely focused on her. Suddenly self-conscious as her liquid courage drained, Sammy lowered her eyes to somewhere near Rob's knees and tucked her hair behind her ears, which now felt swollen and enormous. "What?" she asked, with the drunken humor from before still evident in her voice.

"You really do look beautiful."

Sammy's eyes, still averted from Rob's, widened. "Thank you. That's sweet. I meant it before, too. You look great."

Rob laughed gently, kindly. "Sammy, why aren't you looking at me?"

She snorted laughter. "I don't think I could handle that right now."

"Please look at me."

Little by little, Sammy raised her eyes to Rob's eyes. She felt awkward and dumb. With nothing else in her arsenal, she said, "Hi."

Rob stepped closer and cupped Sammy's cheek in his palm. "There's nowhere else I'd rather be right now, Sammy."

"Rob, no one's ever ... I mean, this is the first time a guy has, um ...." Sammy felt the onslaught of new tears and was powerless against them. She tried blinking them back. "I'm very new at this."

"It's okay. If any of this makes you uncomfortable, just let me know and I'll stop. I promise." Rob slinked his arm around her waist and pulled her close against him.

"Okay," Sammy said, releasing a shaky breath. Trembling hands rested upon Rob's smooth, firm chest. She could feel his warm breath against her face and feared she'd go cross-eyed.

Rob leaned closer, his lips taunting Sammy's from mere inches away. "Can I kiss you, Sammy?"

"Absolutely you can."

Smiling wide, Rob pressed his lips firmly against Sammy's. Both parties shut their eyes. Colors exploded against the insides of Sammy's eyelids, a smattering of deep shades of red and purple. Her hands slid to Rob's shoulders as his hand slipped gracefully from her cheek to the back of her neck. Pulling away, Rob's eyes searched Sammy's face. "How was that?"

"That was my first kiss."

Rob smirked. "Was it now?"

Nodding, Sammy looked back at Rob as intently as he looked at her.

"Can I give you your first *real* kiss?"

Confused by the question, Sammy was about to ask for clarification when Rob crushed her mouth with his. He pressed against her until her back was against the brick wall of the bar. It was the return of that comfortable weight, a delicious kind of pressure. Together, Rob and Sammy explored the dark, soft recesses of each other's mouths. She never knew the taste of beer and cigarettes could be a benediction. Sammy marveled at how fast her heart could beat when time slowed so impossibly.

Eventually, they made their way back inside, fingers entwined and wearing identical expressions. Stopping at the bar for more drinks, the new couple moved to join their friends on the dance floor. With Rob close against her, Sammy thanked God for the return of that comfortable weight and delicious pressure. Rob lowered his lips to her neck and Sammy thought her heart would burst. Rob's heart swelled as well, as he loved the way her dark hair curled slightly and hung down the middle of her back, and as he loved her long eyelashes painted black with mascara, and as he loved her thick, red lips. She was a beauty and she was smart. Listening to her talk about all the different books she'd read and loved impressed Rob – it really did. He had never met anyone quite like Sammy, someone so smart but so uncertain of everything. It was endearing and frustrating all at the same time, and that terrible confusion was essentially Sammy, and it was also extremely appealing to Rob. He opened his mouth to tell her so, but she surprised him with a sweet and simple kiss. Returning it, Rob felt deep in his bones and flowing blood that this was special. This was going to work.

"Okay. So I'll take Sammy home, and we'll see you soon," Maeve said. They had been the last ones out of the bar, had "shut the place down;" Mike yelled the news of that unlikely victory to any unfortunate passerby. Now they stood in a circle in the nearly vacant lot, the boys opposite the girls, saying goodbye. Maeve had offered to take Sammy back for a selfish, ulterior motive: to get dirt on Rob. She wanted to know absolutely every little thing about Sammy's first kiss and her first boyfriend. However, Rob had an ulterior motive of his own.

"Actually, Maeve, I was hoping I could take Sammy home … if that's okay with her, of course." He turned from Maeve to Sammy with slightly pleading eyes. Sammy's heart melted, and she felt it bleed out her fingertips – they were warm and tingling. How could she ever say no when all he had to do was look at her to make her insides freak out and malfunction?

"I'd like that very much," Sammy smiled. Rob reached for her hand, and she gave it to him willingly, eagerly. She said goodbye to Maeve and Mike from over her shoulder as Rob led her to his car. Climbing in, they rode with the radio off. The cozy space in the car was filled with their happy voices describing their pasts, anticipating their futures, and exposing their true selves to one another. Sitting in a parked car outside of a Dunkin Donuts, coffees in hand, with the radio now playing Bob Seger softly,

Sammy and Rob talked until the sky turned from an inky black to a rich and reddish orange.

When he finally took her home, Rob parked outside, and, after a very physical goodbye, Rob asked her to dinner on Wednesday. Sammy agreed without thinking. Grinning like a toddler caught with his hand in the cookie jar, Rob climbed out of the car to rush to the passenger side and open Sammy's door. He was such a gentleman, and Sammy honestly didn't believe it was happening, didn't understand how she could deserve all of this. Rob kissed the center of her forehead with a delicate sweetness. "I'll call you later, okay?"

She kissed his lips. "Absolutely you will – you better." Sammy gave his hand a quick squeeze before turning to walk inside. Rob watched her go, an odd altercation of satisfaction and longing brewing in his stomach.

"Sammy!" He suddenly called out; he felt that he had to.

She paused at her front door, looking back over her shoulder. "What?"

Rob faltered. A deep blush assaulted his cheeks. "You're great."

Tears rushed to the front of Sammy's eyes as if they were eager to see the person responsible for the summons. When she responded, her voice cracked. "You're great too. Goodnight." She unlocked the door and rushed in quickly, shutting it behind her. She had to shove her first in her mouth to stifle the happy sobs and screams that charged to the front lines of her lips. It was amazing, this night. She'd never ever forget it. Hearing her squeals, her dad groggily opened his eyes, smiled and mumbled he was glad she had fun. Then he promptly collected his pillow and blanket and shuffled down the hallway to his bedroom. If he hadn't been so visibly exhausted, Sammy would have assaulted him with the details of the evening and would have forced him to suffer through her almost manic happiness. But Sammy realized this was the kind of happiness she had been searching for, and she would keep it secret and keep it safe ... for now.

Rob had asked Sammy what her favorite kind of food was, and she had readily responded, "Seafood." Rob went quiet on the other end of the line for a moment, before instructing her to be at his apartment by 7:30PM on Thursday, and when Thursday rolled around, Sammy pulled into Rob's driveway at 7:28PM. Smiling as she put the car in park, Sammy found humor in her new found punctuality when it came to males. Maybe she could write a short story about it, and call it "Penis Punctuality" or something just as clever. Giggling at her wit, Sammy climbed out of her car and shut the door behind her. It echoed loudly in the brisk, emptiness of the early November night. She shivered and pulled her sweater tighter around her. She wondered if the warmth the action provided was worth the way it made her look – like a fat sausage. Frowning, she paused outside the front door to try and lose ten pounds before ringing the doorbell. Resigning herself to jumping jacks, Sammy was about to begin when the front door opened. Rob smiled, clearly amused. "What are you doing, crazy?"

"What?"

"Why didn't you ring the bell? Or knock?"

Sammy raised an eyebrow. "How did you know I was here?"

Rob leaned against the doorjamb, suavely crossing his arms over his chest. "I was sitting by the window, waiting and watching for you. I've never been this excited for dinner before." He grinned.

Sammy's face was on fire. She could roast a marshmallow on her cheeks. "That's cute."

"You're welcome." He stepped out onto his porch and kissed her lips. "Will you come in?" He took her hand in his and led her inside.

Rob's house was immaculate. The brave man had white carpeting in the living room, which was the first room one could enter. A hallway led off to the right, to what Sammy supposed was the way to the bedrooms and the bathroom, while the combined kitchen and dining room were ahead and slightly to the left. The rooms were only separated by décor and the color of the walls; the house was very open, with wide doorways and few pieces of furniture. The living room only offered one large sectional, situated across from a gas fireplace with the television hanging above it. It was quaint and reminded Sammy of her parents' one story ranch. Mindful of the carpeting, Sammy slid her feet out of her black flats and prayed that they didn't smell, prayed like a whore in church ... or was the expression sweating like a whore in church? Speaking of sweating, were her feet sweaty? She was sweating thinking about the possibility of sweating as Rob blabbed on and on about the kung fu movies proudly displayed on the shelves of the entertainment center assembled around the fireplace. He was giving her a grand tour of sorts; just the living room and kitchen and bathroom for tonight. He smirked when he explained that seeing the bedroom was a privilege she had to earn. Giggling like a fifth grader at the innuendo, Sammy followed Rob into the dining room and lost her breath.

The table was beautifully set, and a lobster dinner awaited the pair. Sammy turned back to Rob, flustered and faltering. "This is too much, much too much. Rob, you didn't have to do all of this for me. Some popcorn shrimp would have been fine, really."

He laughed and pulled her chair out for her. "Did you say popcorn shrimp? Please. Sammy, this is our third date. I've got to step it up." Nodding toward the chair, Rob clearly wanted Sammy to sit. Sammy walked over, but still felt unsure of how to further proceed. She resolved to sit, and Rob pushed her chair in and continued to the opposite side of the table, smiling at her all the while. After taking his own seat, he said, "I hope you like it. I worked really hard on everything."

Sammy's jaw dropped. "You made this?"

"Did you know lobsters are bitches to get into the pot? Well, they are for me, anyway." He winked at her.

"I don't ... I can't ..."

"What would you like to drink?"

A few glasses of wine made the luxurious meal not such a big deal. Sammy felt more comfortable and Rob's humorous anecdotes about his family and co-workers kept her more than mildly entertained. Rob was a real riot – tears gathered in her eyes and she had to gasp to catch her breath in between stories. He looked pleased with himself, and Sammy liked that best of all. She wanted to make Rob happy just as much as Rob wanted to do the same for her. It was a healthy balance. She had never had one of those before, and she wanted to keep it for as long as possible. "So how was everything?"

"Absolutely delicious; my compliments to the chef," Sammy smiled.

"This chef doesn't accept compliments of the verbal variety, if you know what I'm saying," Rob grinned wide enough to force his eyes to close and Sammy cracked up.

"I think I understand," Sammy said as she slid her chair back and stood. Slowly, but smoothly, she walked over to Rob, who was seated and looking at her with a bemused expression. Bending her head to his, she chastely kissed his lips. "Thank you so much for a wonderful evening, Rob."

Rob pulled Sammy onto his lap with his strong arms. Surprised, but pleasantly so, Sammy laughed until Rob's lips met hers, and no magazine she had ever read, no testimonial she had ever heard, no cinematic production she had ever paid good money to see, and no scene she had ever created prepared her for the sensuality of the moment. Intimate didn't just mean smut; it meant stolen moments of happiness and precious caresses. Sammy loved each and every one of them and couldn't wait for more, and by the way Rob's hands were freely entangling themselves in her hair, Sammy believed he felt the same. A few impassioned embraces later, and Rob was walking Sammy to the door like a true gentleman.

"Next Thursday, dinner at my place, okay?"

Rob kissed her lips. "I wouldn't miss it for the world."

Sammy kissed his lips. "What's your favorite food?"

Smirking, Rob kissed her lips again. "This is pretty tasty."

Laughing, Sammy lightly slapped his arm. "That's not on the menu, jackass."

"Surprise me. I'll love whatever it is."

"Do you have any food allergies? It'd be a buzz kill if you died during a romantic dinner."

Throwing his head back in laughter, Rob kissed her forehead when he could catch his breath. "No food allergies, I promise. Sitting across the table from you is the way to go, though."

Sammy smiled, but shivered. "Alright, let's not talk about this anymore. It's giving me the creeps." She kissed his lips and hurried down the porch steps. "I'll see you Thursday."

"See you Thursday." Rob waved and watched as Sammy climbed in her car and revved the engine. A sudden urge to leave her with something special overcame Rob. "Goodnight, Sammy!" Rob yelled. Though it came muffled through the car door, its impact was as great as intended. Sammy smiled and drove off with her heart pounding. It was unfortunate it'd be the last time Sammy would ever hear his voice.

Chapter Four
Bad News

"Never gonna fall for modern love." ~ David Bowie

The weekend came suddenly. Between all the reading and all the writing she had been doing, Sammy hadn't been able to spare a moment and realize it was Friday night. When that time of the week rolled around, Sammy was usually doing her laundry – the tedious but quintessential part of the single lady's weekend. She had hoped being with Rob would change all that, but of course, the one weekend she wanted to shake off the baggage from her lonely existence and celebrate this newfound companionship, Rob was gone. He was gallivanting in South Carolina, visiting with family and old friends. He hadn't called, had texted her sparingly, and Sammy was missing Rob something awful. She had just lugged her mound of dirty clothes into her parents' laundry room, which was really just a glorified pantry with a cold, tile floor and too many shelves, when her phone sounded off loudly from the kitchen. A smile broke across her face like dawn on the horizon after a fierce storm. Rob was calling – finally! She sprinted to the table and scooped the phone up in her hands … only to discover that the caller was Maeve and not Rob. Fuck. Shit. Balls ... and all that good stuff.

"Hey Maeve," Sammy greeted, unable to disguise the disappointment in her tone.

"Don't sound too excited to talk to me, douche bag." Maeve laughed playfully on the other end. "What's going on?"

"Rob hasn't called at all. Isn't that weird?"

"Dude – you just started dating. He's out of state with his family. Relax, Sammy; everything's okay."

Sammy sighed. "I know that. I'm just lonely and bored."

"Me too," Maeve commiserated. "Mike's working late. Want to come over? We'll have a girls' night in. You can sleep over! We'll order food and watch movies! Come on, it'll be fun!"

Sammy eyed the dirty articles of clothing in the off-white basket, yellowed with age. She paused to listen to the silent house. Her parents and little brother had gone to the movies, and her sister was staying at school for the weekend. She could put in the load of laundry, then retreat to her room and listen to sad songs, writing smutty scene after smutty scene and relive the pains of old rejection slips. Or she could pack a bag and her laundry and spend the night with her best friend. It was a no-brainer. Sammy couldn't even fathom why solitude would even be an option, and that was a marked change in Sammy. Only a few weeks prior, she would have argued solitude was the only option, and that she had to be alone because no one wanted to be with her, or because no one understood her. What Maeve had worked so tirelessly at for semesters, and what Rob had managed to do in a couple of weeks, was to help Sammy realize that friendships and relationships didn't have to be like a movie or a book to be worth the effort. As long as those relationships were real, they were perfect. Oblivious to her own personal breakthrough, Sammy agreed to head over, and asked, "I can do my laundry over there, right?"

On the other end, Maeve rolled her eyes. "Of course; just get here soon. This is going to be awesome!"

Sammy smiled. "I'll call you when I get there."

Sammy stood before another washing machine, this one slightly more dilapidated. Maeve had seated herself upon the folding table across the dingy room and seemed content to swing her legs back forth as she discussed Mike, his roommates, Mike, what movie they were going to watch, Mike, television, Mike, other girls, and of course, Mike. Sammy had listened patiently, leaning back against the machine to watch Maeve's expressions change as often as the topic of conversation. Each time she would mention Mike's name, her eyes would widen slightly, a breathless quality would assault her tone of voice, but most importantly, she'd smile. She'd smile wide and without pretense – it was genuine, the real deal. Sammy wondered if she looked that way talking about Rob.

"What are you thinking about?" Maeve asked suddenly.

"Nothing," Sammy lied. "I was listening."

"Liar," Maeve accused with a good-natured smile. "Are you thinking about your boy?"

Sammy nodded.

Grinning, Maeve asked, "How are things with Rob? How was dinner?"

"Oh Maeve, everything's perfect!" Sammy rushed to her friend's side. "I mean, I know it's clichéd, and in the beginning I'll see the world in rose-colored glasses and blah, blah, blah, but I'm really happy, Maeve. He's... ugh, he's just amazing." Beaming and giggling, Sammy hopped next to Maeve on the folding table.

"I knew it must be good, seeing as how you haven't mentioned Beautiful Boy in days."

"Beautiful Boy?" Sammy was momentarily confused until the reference was remembered. "Oh! That's Eliot from American Literature."

"What?"

"His name is Eliot. Beautiful Boy is Eliot from class."

"Eliot? Eliot who?" Maeve's legs had stopped joyfully swinging and her knuckles whitened as she strengthened her grip on the edge of the folding table.

"I don't know. He didn't tell me his last name." Sammy eyed the young woman beside her warily. "Is everything alright? You seem jumpy."

"Everything's fine," Maeve said. "I just can't believe you found out his name and didn't tell me."

"It wasn't a big deal, really. We had lunch together, where he gave me some really great writing advice. He told me to make a CD of my favorite songs and then drive to the end of Longhill Road and –"

"Longhill Road?" Maeve repeated, interrupting. "What about Longhill Road?"

Sammy shrugged. "It's inspirational, I guess. Have you ever been there?"

"Of course I have. Have you?"

Maeve's changing moods were making Sammy's head spin. "Yeah, I took a drive over there a few days ago."

"You took a drive with Eliot?"

Exasperated, Sammy got to her feet. "What is your deal? Why is all of this so important?"

Maeve smoothed her hair, tucking the flyaway strands behind her ears. "Hip, trendy college couples go to Longhill Road with a blanket and a bottle of wine and do one thing, Sammy. I don't want you to be used like that."

"I went by myself and got some writing done. Eliot didn't even try to come along." Sammy walked back over to the washing machine that had just finished its cycle. "You know I'm not like that, Maeve."

Sammy was offended and alarmed, and Maeve knew she had to do some damage control. "Yeah, I do. I'm sorry. I'm in a weird mood, that's all." Maeve climbed to her feet as well and walked to her friend, offering to help chuck the damp clothing into a working dryer, of which there was only one. Sammy stepped back to survey Maeve's tensed muscles and shifting eyes. Something had upset her. Sammy couldn't think of what possible cause there could be. Maeve didn't know Eliot, didn't know they had talked. Maybe that was it; maybe Maeve was affronted because Sammy hadn't confided in her about that detail. Or maybe it was just like Maeve said, and Maeve was just out of sorts.

Whatever was up with the bizarre reactions to the conversation about Eliot, it was forgotten when Chinese food came and *Never Been Kissed* started. Both girls were definitely in better spirits by the time the credits rolled. The glasses of wine may have had something to do with it, but when the girls curled up to go to bed both were happy and didn't feel so lonely anymore.

The next day, Sammy woke, packed up her laundry, and headed home. Mike was coming back for breakfast, and Sammy decided she had to get out of there. As much as she loved Maeve and as much as she enjoyed Mike's company, she was missing Rob too much to be satisfied with being the third wheel. Her ultimate desire was to get in touch with Rob and bask in the perfection that Rob embodied, and his selfless act of sharing it with her. No such luck; there was one text message in the morning where Rob apologized for not responding, and that was it. He was due home in a few days, so Sammy just had to wait. Patience was never one of Sammy's strongest suits, and she needed a distraction. So after dinner with the family, she grabbed a notebook, a bottle of water, and her favorite sweatshirt and packed them in her car. She was going to drive down Longhill Road again and she was going to write. Rob hadn't called, but Sammy knew that he was busy and knew that she was being silly and over the top with the dramatics, but if her and Rob didn't last, the memories would, and she would liberate that elation onto paper and make it immortal, make damn sure the memories did last and for her, that could be enough. She had been living with and through the printed word for years. What was a few more?

The drive was shorter than she remembered, but probably because she was no longer anticipating an unknown destination, and because she was preoccupied with Rob. Rob, Rob, Rob, Rob – she'd never get tired of tumbling each precious syllable from her mouth, letting the name dangle precariously from her lips. Maybe if she kept repeating his name, he'd call. Hell, maybe he'd even text. She didn't want to seem needy, obsessed, or dependent, so once three messages had been sent without a response, she had given up. Her mind was completely focused on her boyfriend, her beau, her boo, her Rob, so that it took her a moment as she parked to notice another car. She was more than ready to throw her car into reverse and head back home, but a familiar face was illuminated by her headlights. Eliot gave a little wave, and Sammy relaxed, killing the engine. She hopped out of the car. "Imagine seeing you here."

Eliot grinned. "Yeah, how about that? Pure coincidence, I assure you."

Sammy smiled, but it faded shortly thereafter. She was remembering all the places she had thought she had seen Eliot lately, and now here he was again. This time was real, no doubt about that, and she wondered now if the other times had been real too. His use of the word "coincidence" was intriguing, was it not? Looking away, fearful of the consequences of her question, Sammy asked, "Have you been following me?"

"What?" Eliot asked. Her question had definitely surprised him.

Sammy cleared her throat, shifted uneasily to her other side, and spoke again. "I thought I saw you at the bar like two weeks ago, and then again outside the coffee shop like a week ago, and now you're here."

Eliot took a hesitant step towards Sammy. "I definitely was not at the bar. My friends are all back at home in Maine, so I rarely go out and when I do, believe me when I say it's much tamer than the local watering hole for the college kids." He laughed, and Sammy wasn't entirely sure if Eliot was thumbing his nose at such activities, or trying to hide his true feelings of longing. Either way, Eliot continued on. "As for the coffee shop, I could have been there, but I don't remember going. And as for now, I did tell you about this place, so I don't think you seeing me here is completely bizarre or unreasonable, right?" He smiled kindly, albeit awkwardly, and added, "Maybe it's mostly a lot of wishful thinking on your part."

Relaxing slightly, Sammy smirked. "It was definitely not wishful thinking- clearly, they're horrible hallucinations."

Eliot feigned offense. "Did you say horrible?"

"I wouldn't have been so harsh if you had tried some modesty there." She eyed Eliot coolly, believe it or not, and leaned back against the hood of her car, her arms at her sides. "You were right about one thing, though: you did tell me about this place. I couldn't expect to steal it from you."

Eliot laughed, and said, "I don't think you're capable of stealing anything from anyone. You're not that basic." A silence commenced to fall upon the two. It was awkward as much as it was necessary- an opportunity to change the subject and avoid addressing the implications in Eliot's last remark. Sammy would have ordinarily loved to probe deeper, to have Eliot admit it was a loaded statement, but the effortless conversation and harmless flirtation was fun, much preferred over former habits. Sammy opened her mouth to continue things just as they were, but Eliot beat her to the punch and asked, "Did you come here to write? I could leave if you'd rather…"

"No, no, don't be silly," Sammy insisted. "You were here first, so if anything, I'll be the one to leave." She rose from her relaxed position and shuffled to the side to take a hesitant step backwards, ready to make good on her offer and leave if Eliot would rather the solitude. "Did you come here to write?" Her question was dangerous because if he admitted he'd rather be alone, regardless if it was to write, he'd be choosing silence over Sammy, and she wasn't prepared for what that would feel like. Trying to ease the lines of her face that wanted to tense and expose the inner workings of her brain, Sammy waited for Eliot's answer.

Eliot rubbed the back of his neck, exhaling deeply. He was taking his time, almost as if he understood Sammy's misgivings, and that scared Sammy more than the rejection. When he finally did respond to the question, Sammy had almost forgotten what it was she had asked. "I'm trying. I'm not feeling particularly inspired, though," Eliot said, shrugging.

Sammy smiled widely, thrilled that she had not been rejected and thrilled because she had a way to ingratiate herself further into Eliot's creative process. "I think I have something that might help to inspire you." Walking backwards again, she moved to her car door and opened it, grabbing the CD Eliot had advised her to make for this very purpose. She walked to Eliot and handed over the music compilation she was so proud of. "Maybe try listening to this. It works for me."

Eliot eyed the young woman before him with playful skepticism before taking the CD. "You took my advice?"

Sammy was confused by Eliot's surprise. "Yeah; why wouldn't I?"

Eliot's eyes widened, perhaps perceiving Sammy's confusion as anger or frustration. "No, I didn't mean that it's weird or anything like that. I just never had anyone take my advice before, you know? I give it all the time, whether or not anyone's asking for it." He laughed anxiously, hoping the self-depreciative humor would go over well. Sammy was smiling, but she had been smiling for a while now and if anything, that smile looked strained. "I talk a lot, but it's- whatever." Abruptly ending his speech, Eliot strolled back to his car and began to play the offered inspirational tool. As Bruce Springsteen began to fill the scenic silence of the overlook, Sammy walked over to be closer to the music. Eliot nodded at her, impressed. "Not bad." He leaned against his car, crossing his arms over his chest. "You weren't kidding when you said you liked the Boss."

Sammy was about to offer up a witty response when she realized the Boss was in the middle of sensually growling "I'm On Fire." Sammy squealed in delight. "Oh man, this is my favorite song ever!"

Eliot turned to look at the radio and CD player in the car. "Do you want me to start it over?"

"Yes, please! Can you turn the volume up?"

Amused, Eliot said, "Of course; whatever you want." He took a second to look back at Sammy before doing as she asked, and as soon as the song restarted Sammy forgot all about Eliot as she soundlessly moved her lips to form the lyrics she held so dear and considered genius. Eliot resumed reclining against his car, and observed Sammy with a special kind of interest. He saw her long, dark hair fly about her face in soft tendrils in the sighing breeze picking up around her. Her eyes were closed, and her lashes were full and reminded him that she couldn't see him, that she didn't need to or even want to. Sammy's complete disregard for his presence was something new and alluring. Though he had teased about Sammy wanting him to be places where she was, Eliot knew she found him attractive and was well aware that he flustered her. He also knew that Sammy did her best to disguise those truths and, while it was flattering, for Eliot, it was expected and trite. He much preferred this; Sammy's ears straining for another voice as his ceased to matter, even if it was for just a few minutes, and her full, pink lips were not working to inform or impress him. In the moment they told of bad desires, and Eliot didn't give a damn if the words weren't her own. Watching the deceptively simple words with the lascivious implications escape a pretty and innocent mouth was almost more than he could stand; he considered turning the song off when her tongue darted out to wet her lips during the instrumental break to avoid feeling like a voyeur, to avoid feeling perverted, and it was then that Eliot understood he was witnessing something private, that in some abstract way that was hard to explain, Sammy was exposing more of herself than he deserved, maybe more than she ever intended, and that was why he felt so uncomfortable. When the song ended and Sammy opened her eyes to meet his, Eliot clenched his fists to remind himself where he was.

"Sorry," Sammy said. "You probably think I'm really weird, but I really do love that song. It's so sexy, but there's still so much longing, you know? Springsteen is a genius. It's like everything I've ever wanted to write about, he already did and did it the best."

Eliot smiled. "It's a good song."

Sammy agreed and said, "And that is why it is on my inspirational playlist."

"If all the songs are as good as that one, I'd like a copy," Eliot said, making the humble request to his shoes, avoiding Sammy's eyes as a means of avoiding only the possibility of an adverse reaction.

Clearly, Eliot didn't really know Sammy. "Sure." The response was immediate and instinctive.

Eliot, relaxing more and more as Sammy did the same, ventured to ask, "What does that song make you want to write about? How does it inspire you?"

Sammy's eyes glazed over as she thought it over. "It makes me want to write about ... just, um, something about a boy and girl being in love." Idly, she picked at the denim of her faded jeans, careful to avoid eye contact. Eliot had certainly brought this conversation to a whole new place. Sammy believed writing was an extension of the writer, and that made it very personal. For Sammy, asking what she wrote about was like asking what she dreamed about and what she longed for; and of course it came back to love. She added, "That's what I always write about."

Eliot's eyes squinted. "Why?"

Sammy hesitated. How much honesty was too much? "I love the idea of love. I'm fascinated by it, so it finds a way into everything I write. I'm in love with being in love, obsessed by the mere idea of it." She cleared her throat nervously. "Hopefully it's just a phase."

"What do you mean?" he asked.

Man! What was with this kid and the questions? Sammy couldn't get overwhelmed- she had to be careful here; the footing could be treacherous. "Um, just that I hope to tackle other emotions in my writing." Sammy was tempted to pat herself on the back; it had been a nice save.

Eliot leaned closer to Sammy, no longer leaning against his car. Now he was standing fairly close, giving her his full attention. He said, "E.M. Forrester's epigraph to Howard's End reads, 'Only connect.' I believe the whole point of human existence is to form relationships with others, and it is those bonds that keep us tethered to life, keep us waking up for the new day. Love makes all the bullshit in between worthwhile."

"That's beautiful," Sammy said. Her voice cracked and she hoped Eliot didn't notice, or if he did that he'd be kind enough to disregard it.

Eliot shrugged the compliment off, leaning back as if he were retreating into himself. Had he just had a moment of too much honesty? Sammy watched with interest, and listened closely when he said, "Don't feel like you have to defend yourself for writing about love. Every writer does in one way or another." Eliot spoke in earnest. "Don't defend yourself to anyone. You are who you are and ..." Eliot faltered, not entirely sure of what he was saying, or why he was saying it. He ended with, "I guess I'm saying you shouldn't be so willing to please others, you know? To hell with what anyone else thinks."

Rob did not call or text Sammy before they were scheduled to have dinner at her house after class. Checking her phone every two seconds during lectures did not offer any relief – there were no messages, and she began to believe that there would never be any messages. She was also beginning to worry that she had ruined everything. Had he gotten sick of her so quickly? The day of their dinner date dawned dreary and did little to improve her souring mood. The chilling wind and constant rainfall created the perfect backdrop of misery. All she had to look forward to was that damn dinner with Rob, but he had been missing in action. Sammy was cranky as she sat upon a bench outside of the Student Center. The day was gray and miserable, very chilled, and campus was essentially deserted – and all that suited Sammy just fine because if she did happen to bump into somebody she'd be mean just because she could, and because it might make her feel better. Desperate for something to go right, Sammy's trepidation increased when her cell phone rang to announce an unfamiliar caller; the screen displayed an unknown number. The caller greeted, "Hello? Is this Sammy Thogode?"

Sammy's mouth went dry. "Yes, this is Sammy." Heartbeat accelerating, Sammy believed she'd be sick any minute. Sammy put her bag on her shoulder and stood. The sinking suspicion that she was going to have to leave campus settled over her. It was a horrifying premonition and she prayed it was just a result of the melancholy weather and her dejected mood. "I'm sorry, but who is this?" she asked.

There was a heavy sigh on the other end of the line. "I'm sorry, ma'am. This is Detective Taylor with the Essex County police department. Do you think you could make it down to the station today?"

"Why?" Sammy's bag slipped from her shoulder. "What's wrong?"

"Were you acquainted with a young man named Rob Hall?"

The oxygen in her lungs was on fire. It seared her throat, and her eyes watered from the pain. "We had been seeing each other, yeah, but, I mean, is everything okay?"

The man on the other end paused. "I hate to be the one to tell you this, ma'am, but Rob Hall is dead."

Colors swirled and the earth titled forward. Struggling to remain standing, Sammy found it harder and harder to breathe, with that incendiary element plaguing her organs as she was desperately gasping between sobs. "What? That's impossible. He was in South Carolina until this morning. Is he even back yet?"

"He came back to New Jersey late last night to surprise you, according to his mother." The detective sighed heavily. "Miss Thogode, there are questions I need to ask you that would be better to address in person. I will also be able to answer questions that you may have. When can you be at the station?"

"I can be there in twenty minutes."

"Okay. Just tell them your name, and that Detective Taylor is expecting you."

"Okay."

"Do you need a cruiser to come pick you up?"

"No. No, that's okay. I'll find a ride."

"Okay then. I'll see you shortly, Miss Thogode."

There was no goodbye. The line simply went dead. Sprinting to the nearest garbage can, Sammy's insides emptied themselves. She was pale. Sweat coated her body, and no matter how hard she tried Sammy couldn't keep from shaking. Sobs seared her lungs. It didn't make any sense for Rob to be dead.

A compassionate passerby stopped and asked if she was okay. As calmly as possible, Sammy assured the young woman that no, she was not okay. Sliding to the concrete ground, Sammy asked the passerby to hand her the discarded bag a few yards away and, if it wasn't too much trouble, to call a student named Maeve from Sammy's phone within the bag, tell Maeve to meet Sammy in the quad, and that it was an emergency. Without complaint, the stranger did all that was asked of her and even waited with Sammy until Maeve showed up. Had Sammy possessed the proper presence of mind, she would have asked the young woman for her name and sent her something like a fruit basket, or some other kind of offering of thanks.

When she arrived, Maeve was greatly bothered by Sammy's weak frame slumped against a filthy trash receptacle. She was practically forced to carry Sammy to her car, placing together bits of information through Sammy's broken sobs. Rob was dead, and they had questions for Sammy. Was she a suspect? Did that mean Rob was murdered? Maeve hurried to get her friend to the police station.

When Rob told his mother he was cutting the vacation short, and that he planned to drive back to New Jersey to surprise the new girl in his life, she had some trepidation. Voicing her motherly concerns, she said, "That's an awful long drive to make by yourself, sweetie. What if you get tired?" She had momentarily stopped washing the dishes from the night's dinner to face her son and see if he was being serious. Sometimes Rob got ideas in his head, wonderful ideas with the best of intentions, and he would hold those ideas until they either came to fruition or shattered into tiny pieces of disappointment. Being her only son, Mrs. Hall never wanted Rob to feel any pain, even a pain as common as disappointment. She had to be the Pessimistic Patty to his rampant optimism so his feet could stay on the ground, and she had slipped into the role quite easily this time around. She didn't know this girl, couldn't assess if she was worth the effort of returning home and ending a vacation early and hoped Rob would consider that a possibility- that this girl wouldn't appreciate his return trip as much as his mother would appreciate him staying.

No such luck; Rob rolled his eyes and said, "I'm not dumb, Ma. If I get tired, I'll stop at a hotel. The point is to surprise Sammy, not to get killed." He laughed and grabbed another cookie from the plate in the middle of the kitchen table. He had made himself quite comfortable before informing his mother of his plans, well aware that it could take quite some time for her to see it his way, and to be at peace with it. It was never his style to leave anything unresolved. He could see his mother was still not entirely convinced, so he added, "It's only twelve hours, mom. I'll go to bed early tonight, leave early tomorrow morning, and be back in Jersey in the evening."

Mrs. Hall, avoiding eye contact with her son, fidgeted with the wedding ring on her left hand. "I just don't like the idea of you travelling alone," she said quietly. With her carefully pressed khaki slacks, and smart-looking white polo that was impeccably clean, Mrs. Hall looked the part of the quintessential Mrs. Cleaver- and she was every bit as doting. It was a blessing and a curse; while the Halls were a tight-knit, loving family, it sometimes became too much, and her efforts to be the ultimate matriarch were underappreciated or warped into something akin to meddling. She could see such an occurrence beginning now, as her son flippantly snorted at her genuine concern.

He said, "Please, Ma. You were fine with me driving down to meet you guys here." Though Rob was smiling kindly, his eyes were stern. She was being unreasonable, and she knew it, so there was no logical reason as to why the behavior should continue. He hadn't introduced the woman in his life to the other woman in his life, and didn't have any plans to as things were going smoothly, so it wasn't like his mother could disapprove of Sammy, and he just pointed out how ridiculous her concerns about the trip were. How could he be allowed to traverse states alone a few days prior, and suddenly encounter such resistance to do the same thing? His mother had to give in and be the one to compromise; it was only fair.

Mrs. Hall watched her son's face closely, noting the changes in expression as his thoughts progressed. Deep down, she knew he was right and that it would be unfair to make Rob feel guilty for wanting to surprise his new girlfriend. With a heavy sigh, but a sweet smile, Mrs. Hall said, "You can leave tomorrow morning after I've made you some breakfast."

Rob rose from his seat and kissed his mother quickly on the cheek. Life was good.

The trip back to the Garden State had been no big deal, just as Rob had predicted. Aside from stopping for food, gas, and to relieve himself, the ride was peaceful with limited interruptions.

He watched the sun set from the Garden State Parkway, the heater in the car humming loudly in competition with the radio and the glowing orb hanging low in the sky, sinking slowly, burned a deep orange. The light filtered in the cab of the truck and seemed to set everything aflame. In contrast, the surrounding sky outside of the truck was an inky kind of violet, and the first few evening stars were making their appearance. By the time he reached his exit, night had fallen completely, and a bright winter moon illuminated the landscape and aided in giving everything in sight a crisper feel. The silver moonlight slipped into the cab in shifting slants, emphasized by the total blackness of the night. Rob had never stopped to notice the weather or the sky before and thought his heightened awareness and sudden appreciation were direct results of Sammy. He knew she noticed things like that and he wanted to impress her with his ability to do the same. When he arrived at her home with flowers, he wanted to comment on the beautiful night and how it made life beautiful and all that Thoreau business he had tried to comprehend in high school. More than matching intelligence, Rob just wanted to be with her. She made him feel important; made him feel wanted and made him feel great. What more could anyone ask for? He wanted to make sure Sammy felt the same, so here he was, making a surprise trip. Showing up empty handed would be lame, and Rob pulled into the first gas station he saw. He'd bring her flowers and candy; she'd appreciate that, right? All girls liked that. Pulling beside a pump, he told the attendant to fill it with regular gas, and headed inside.

He found what he wanted to purchase quickly and was walking back outside in a manner of minutes. He passed the attendant on the way out, who had mumbled something in passing about a malfunction with the pump and that it'd only be a moment. Half-listening, Rob nodded and pulled his cell phone from his back pocket. He was going to text Sammy and make sure she was home. Granted it would have been wiser to confirm her location earlier, but this spur of the moment stuff was exhilarating; he wanted to live spontaneously for the rest of his life. He added Sammy as the recipient of the text from his contacts and had composed a vague greeting when something strong grabbed hold of his neck. The cell phone dropped from his hand as his body went stiff momentarily, shocked by the sudden hostile force assaulting it. Comprehending that something awful and unnatural was going on, Rob brought his hands to the arm around his neck and pulled and pulled. It was instinctive; he had to breathe to live, and the arm was not letting him breathe. Thus, if he wanted to live, the arm had to be removed. Rob was struggling for his life and was alarmed at how much of a struggle it was; the arm would not be removed. Indeed, its grip seemed to strengthen the more he writhed and yanked. Rob tried to stagger closer to his truck, thinking he could slam the owner of the arm against it and start to make some progress, but a sharp and intense pain near his stomach consumed his mind and his body, as the pain ebbed out all over. He went to scream, despite having his air cut off, but the arm wrapped around his neck moved to cover his mouth and muffled the awful moan escaping Rob's bruised, crushed throat. The attacker's other arm had done something cruel and serious, and Rob realized he was going to die unless he did something drastic. Rob was panicking though, didn't know what to do, and then the free arm returned to the neck with something cold and metallic and Rob felt the beginning of a never-ending slice. The arm hadn't let go until the fight and life had left Rob.

Rob Hall was found by the attendant some ten minutes later outside the gas station, which was about a mile from Sammy's home. He had filled his car with gas, purchased a bouquet of roses and some peanut butter cups. The flowers were found beside the body, the plastic wrapping tainted with tiny crimson droplets of the liquid that had, until very recently, sustained Rob's life. The area was neat, as far as crime scenes go. No money was missing from the wallet. His keys were still in his pocket. His cell phone was on and lay on the ground beside the body, displaying an unfinished text message with Sammy listed as the recipient. Detective Taylor was indeed interested to meet with her, especially since no one else had seen or heard anything. Not one soul had come forward with information and the secrecy greatly troubled Detective Taylor. His steely blue eyes, usually squinted in pensive thought, had widened when they surveyed the brutality of the attack. Hall's throat had been slit and he had been stabbed in the torso area around ten times, as if it had been for good measure. Whoever the attacker was, he or she had wanted to be sure Hall was dead.

In speaking with Sammy, Detective Taylor kept the details discreet, on a need to know basis. Still, Sammy was at the station for a little over an hour. Her alibi checked out, and she had little information to offer. Maeve was relieved to see Sammy had calmed down considerably. She supposed the initial shock had sent Sammy reeling. Exhausted, Sammy slept the whole way back to campus. Maeve was hesitant to let Sammy drive home. Together they stood in the parking lot, eying each other warily, unsure of what to say. Maeve asked the same question again. "Are you sure you're okay?" Before Sammy could answer, Maeve added, "Let's get something to eat."

Sammy wiped her ever-weeping eyes and shook her head slowly. "I'm not going to make you miss your class," she said.

Maeve gently reached out to touch Sammy's arm. Assuring Sammy getting food would not be an issue, she explained, "I don't have class tonight, remember? Come on, you haven't eaten anything all day and I know you're not going to class. What's stopping you?"

Sighing, Sammy turned to lead the way to the Student Center in the center of campus. "I'm okay. You don't have to do this," Sammy practically growled. She was annoyed because she wanted to be alone, to wallow in the loss and despair, but deep down inside, she knew this was better, healthier behavior. And then again, she didn't want to be alone. Truth be told, she wanted to be with Rob, but Rob was dead, dead and gone, and Maeve would have to do for now. Vaguely aware of her cruelty and bitterness,

Sammy felt guilty but felt angry for being made to feel guilty and just felt sad. Emotions were raging inside her, and she gladly let herself be swept away by that tide. She didn't have the strength to fight it off.

Maeve told Sammy to stop acting like she was being a burden and told her to quit being ridiculous. They entered the pizzeria on the first floor, and Maeve's maternal instinct kicked in. She had Sammy sit while she ordered their meals, and brought Sammy a large cup of water. Sammy was sitting alone, mindlessly sipping her water and wondering what Rob had wanted to say to her. She sighed and rubbed her eyes. It was too much; all too much. Eventually, Maeve returned from the line. She slid two plates onto the table and eyed Sammy with genuine sympathy. "Do you need anything else?" Maeve asked as she sat beside Sammy and waited patiently for a response. Pulling her hair back, Sammy was resolved to staring at the chicken parmesan dinner before her, trying to convince herself that she was ravenous, even though she wasn't hungry; if anything, she was nauseous. Students formed a line at the counter Maeve had just returned from that was long enough to meander through the tables. A hundred different conversations among the patient patrons, and those gathered among the condiment counter against the wall opposite the door, made the perfect white noise amid the metallic clatter of the food preparation. Sammy could easily be lost, could easily be allowed to be swallowed up by the carefree co-eds around her. It was easier than acknowledging the pain, the haunting questions of why someone would want to kill Rob, and what he had wanted to say to her.

During her musings, Sammy vaguely remembered that Maeve had asked a question. "Fine; never better," Sammy said. Her answer probably didn't make sense, but she didn't give a shit. She couldn't even remember what Maeve had asked.

Maeve's face fell. She warned, "Don't shut down, Sammy …"

"Maeve, this is horrible," Sammy mumbled from trembling lips. The sudden rush of blood to her head was pounding in her ears loudly, so loudly that she couldn't even hear herself breathing. Had she stopped filling and expanding her lungs? Had it come to that? She tried to focus her eyes on something, and she found the chicken on the cheap, plastic plate, and decided it looked like a hunk of flesh brutally torn from some poor, unsuspecting young man who had only been trying to send some poor, unsuspecting young woman a text message and surprise her with flowers and candy. The marinara sauce resembled pooling blood, and Sammy shut her eyes tight against the culinary nightmare before her. Sliding the plate away, she swallowed hard against the rising bile.

Maeve was growing seriously alarmed. She stared at Sammy anxiously. "I know this is horrible, but you've got to talk about it and let it out. You know all that Lifetime movie, girl chat crap. Okay? I'll get ice cream if I have to," Maeve encouraged Sammy, rubbing her back. She tried to make a joke to lighten the mood, but it was lame, and everyone knew it.

"I don't want you to ..." Sammy's voice trailed off, almost as if she were standing up and leaving, leaving Maeve alone at the table, but that wasn't fair; she didn't want Maeve to be alone, and she didn't want Rob to be cold and alone, dead and murdered. But she didn't want to talk about Rob, didn't need her own quivering lips to send her tumbling into the dark, widening chasm before her, like some broken and bruised Alice in some brutal, merciless Wonderland. She swayed in her seat, and strong hands held her still.

"Sammy, can you hear me?"

"I don't know what I'm supposed to do!" Sammy was slurring, falling.

"You don't look good. Let's try and –"

"Stop!" Sammy pleaded. "I don't want to hear it!"

Boom.

Crash.

Bang.

The bar was empty, and that struck Sammy as incredibly odd. This place was always crowded; the makeup of the crowd and the music blaring within were the only two variables. No drunken, sloppy co-eds were anywhere to be found, nor were there any older women in clothes that were too tight with older men who were anxious to fight and relive their youths. The only other soul in the whole place was Rob. As her footsteps echoed against the floor, Rob turned on the wooden bar stool to welcome Sammy. He seemed to be too pale but Sammy admitted it could just be the lighting in the desolate, damp, dank bar, though she would have previously described it as warm, comfortable and entertaining. Something was wrong in some aspect, and walking over to the handsome, young man who was waving at her, Sammy wondered again, but only briefly, where everyone else was. Dark eyes focusing on Rob, Sammy smiled and he strained to smile back. The stitched skin across his neck split open and blood spilled down his front. Gallons of warm, red liquid splashed to the floor, splattered against everything at knee-level. The amount of life force painting the scene red was impossible; all that blood could not come from one person.

Sammy looked down and suddenly realized she was bleeding, too.

It was warm, incredibly warm, and so soft. She couldn't remember ever being this comfortable in her entire life. Sighing contentedly, Sammy decided that she was never going to open her eyes again. She was going to stay just like this for eternity, until she turned to ash and simply floated away on a breeze. But something was shaking her, calling her name loudly again and again. It made her angry. Wasn't it obvious she didn't want to wake up? Her blood was beginning to boil-

Blood; it had been everywhere, and all over everything. It had been coming from Rob and her.

Sammy's eyes shot open, and then darted from side to side. Her surroundings were completely unfamiliar. The light was dim, inviting and yellow. She was on one of three small beds, covered in a crisp sheet and an itchy blanket. The walls were painted a deep shade of rose, and Sammy suddenly felt anything but relaxed. Her stomach twisted itself into complicated knots, and Sammy felt uneasy. Slowly, she sat up. The blanket she had been covered with pooled around her waist. Maeve was sitting back in a plastic chair, looking slightly relieved.

"Hey," Maeve greeted apprehensively. "How are you feeling?"

Sammy held her head in her hands, averting her gaze from her best friend as Maeve studied her. She was embarrassed and confused. This wasn't Maeve's apartment, so where were they? Did Maeve take Sammy here? Why would she do that? Did she know where they were? Had someone else taken both of them here? Sammy said, "I'm okay. Where am I?"

"This is the Health Center on campus," Maeve answered.

"We have a Health Center?" Sammy asked, confusion lingering but resembling something more like surprise.

Maeve smiled and said, "Duh; it's on the bottom floor of the freshman dorm. Remember? It's like the only building behind the Student Center and before the other parking garages."

Sammy released a shaky breath. "Why am I here?" The questions were never going to end, apparently. Maeve's wearied expression concurred with that assessment.

Rubbing her forehead, Maeve said, "You passed out in the pizzeria. I was able to sort of walk you over here. I wanted to get you out of there without a big scene or production. Hardly anyone really saw anything, I promise."

"I passed out?" Sammy repeated.

Maeve leaned forward and said, "Well, you were fading in and out. I was already holding you steady when you completely blacked out, so it wasn't like you fell to the floor in an emotional heap or anything embarrassing like that. I think it could be chalked up to the Swine Flu."

Sammy nodded and said, "Thank you."

There was a silence Maeve felt compelled to fill. She wanted to offer her condolences. She said, "I'm sorry about Rob."

Sammy nodded again. When she spoke, her voice didn't sound as normal as she had hoped it would. "It's okay," she said. "We had just met, so, it wasn't, like, anything."

"You don't have to diminish it, Sammy," Maeve said quickly, admonishing Sammy's irrational behavior.

Hurriedly, Sammy got to her feet. She spoke just as quickly and said, "It's fine. I'm fine. I have to leave. I have to go home."

"What's the rush?" Maeve asked as she rose from her chair. "You just woke up."

"I have homework. I have to eat. I just ..." Sammy pressed her palms tightly against her eyes and let the silence envelop her.

Maeve waited a moment for Sammy to gain some composure. "Alright, alright; I'll drive you home. Mike can follow us in your car," she said. Maeve turned from Sammy to grab their personal belongings. She said, "Promise me you'll take care of yourself, though. You didn't eat anything before, and that's the only reason I'm taking you home – so you can eat, because you really shouldn't be by yourself and shutting down. You have to let someone in and let someone help you." Maeve turned back to study Sammy closely.

Sammy was standing still, palms pushing against her eyes. "I really appreciate everything you're doing, Maeve. I just want to get home and see my mom." When she spoke, her voice cracked, and she hated herself for it; she didn't want to blubber and cry anymore. She searched for her bag frantically, tossing the blanket aside and scurrying about the small room.

Maeve held Sammy still and said, "I've got it here, Sammy." Breathing deeply, she stepped backwards from Sammy. "This is going to cripple you if you think you have to do it alone."

Shudders assaulted Sammy, and the tears spilled forward, unrelenting. Maeve pulled Sammy close against her and let Sammy shatter, let Sammy fall into the black hole opening before her. Maeve would piece her together, pull her back.

When Sammy shuffled through her front door, her mother and father were both wide awake on the couch. It was late, and she hadn't kept in touch, and now they were furious. They both got to their feet with enraged expressions that dissipated instantly when they saw the broken young woman before them, the young woman that only barely resembled their daughter. Rushing to her side, they pieced together the unfolding tragedy and Sammy fell asleep on the couch, her mother soothing her hair and her father standing guard anxiously nearby. Both insisted that Sammy stay home the next day, and she most willingly agreed. Her mom was really great about the whole thing; when Rob's mother called to ask Sammy about her son's activities with her, Sammy's mom took the phone when it overwhelmed her, and she also had the presence of mind to ask about the funeral arrangements. Waking up with swollen eyes, Sammy vaguely remembered talking to Maeve before getting home and passing out. Stretching towards the ceiling, she yawned at full volume. Her phone beeped loudly in the silence, and she reached to pick it up from her windowsill. Maeve had called about ten times. Sammy would have to call her back. She dialed and waited.

"Hello?" Maeve sounded as if the call had woken her up.

"Hey. How are you?"

"Don't be dumb. You know I'm fine. How are you?"

Sammy pulled her hair back. "My first kiss got his throat cut. My first boyfriend is dead."

"Use his name, Sammy," Maeve advised.

"I miss Rob, Maeve. I don't want him to be dead." Sammy wished her sobs would quickly and completely dissolve. She hated sounding sheepish and weak.

"I know, sweetie."

"I'm sorry. I –"

Maeve interrupted. "Don't apologize when you didn't do anything wrong." There was an awkward pause while Maeve tried to decide what to say next, and Sammy wiped her eyes and sniffed loudly.

Sammy broke the silence and asked, "Will you go to Rob's funeral with me tonight?"

"Of course I will, Sammy." Maeve didn't hesitate in responding. Besides the fact that Sammy obviously didn't want to go alone, Maeve thought she should pay her respects as well because she had met Rob twice and because she felt like she knew him. "When is it?" she asked.

Sammy answered, "Tonight at seven o'clock. Is that okay? I mean, can you still make it?"

Maeve inhaled sharply. None of this was going to be easy and understandably so, but that fact didn't help her any or offer much comfort. She replied, "Of course I can."

Maeve, dressed in an exceedingly simple and modest black dress, stood in front of the full-length mirror in her small bedroom. She was twisting this way and that to better appraise her appearance, but she didn't particularly care about what she looked like. Maybe she was just going through the motions, trying to behave as normally as possible, which was ridiculous because there was nothing normal about attending a funeral for a murder victim who just happened to be your best friend's most recent and only boyfriend ever. What else was there to do? Should she fall to pieces? Should she be brave and strong for Sammy? Was it possible to be a little bit of both? Breathing deeply, Maeve smoothed the front of her dress and stood still. She looked fine, but how did she feel? Did the lines of her face betray her? Would those who saw her know she didn't really want to be there, that it was out of duty to her friendship with Sammy, rather than grief, that she was paying her final respects? Did that make her a horrible person? Maeve brought her hands to her face and felt very much like crying.

Suddenly, Mike's voice came from somewhere behind her. "Babe, you better get moving or you're going to be late." Maeve turned to her boyfriend and found an answer to one of her earlier questions. Upon seeing the troubled expression that was Maeve's face, Mike rushed to her and took her in his arms. "What's wrong, Maeve? Are you okay?"

She hugged him tightly and tried her best not to cry. "I feel horrible that Rob's dead, and I know that Sammy feels worse and that she needs me, but I don't want to go."

Mike kissed Maeve's cheek. "I'm sorry, babe, I really am. If you don't want to go …." His voice trailed off not only because he didn't know what to say, but because his heart wasn't in it. Honestly, Mike didn't think Maeve had any other choice or option- she *had* to go. He tried to articulate his thoughts without making her feel guilty or worse than she already did. "I mean, no one ever *wants* to go to a funeral, but I think you have to." Mike understood it wasn't easy for Maeve. Hell, he was extremely grateful that Sammy hadn't asked him to go. Funerals were miserable experiences, and this one would be rough because Rob had been so young, and it hadn't been a freak accident or a result of a long illness; it had been murder. Still, Mike knew that his presence might be needed all the same and taking a breath to strengthen his resolve, Mike said, "I can go with you, if it'll make it easier." He stepped back to study Maeve's face. The dark clouds that had been lingering there had lightened considerably, but she shook her head.

"I'm not going to ask you to do that." Looking up at Mike, Maeve said, "It wouldn't be fair, especially since I don't even want to go." Maeve shrugged and looked down at the floor at their respective feet. Her hands fidgeted with her dress again, smoothing it here and there. "Just please be here when I get back."

Nodding, Mike took Maeve's hands in his own hands. "Of course; will you tell Sammy I'm thinking about her?"

Feeling his eyes heavy upon her, Maeve looked up and made eye contact with her boyfriend. She offered him half of a smile and said, "Of course; she'll appreciate that very much." Maeve kissed the corner of Mike's mouth quickly, reached behind him to grab her purse from the bed, and turned to leave the bedroom. Mike asked another question.

"Do you think Sammy will be okay?"

Maeve, halfway out of her bedroom door, did not stop or even turn around. She only shrugged, said "I really don't know," and continued on her way.

That was not at all the response Mike had been expecting. He thought Maeve would retain the half-smile and tell him that yeah, sure, Sammy would be fine, that healing took time and other clichés she learned in her psychology classes. Mike wondered if the answer had been a result of anger; anger at him for not insisting on going, anger at Sammy for asking Maeve to go, anger at herself for feeling so conflicted about the whole tragic situation. Or was Maeve really worried about Sammy? Was Sammy so distraught and damaged that recovery might not be imminent? Whatever the reason, Mike was worried and longed to know what to do to help Maeve, to be a good boyfriend, and to be a good friend to Sammy. Lost in these thoughts, Mike didn't leave his girlfriend's bedroom until long after the apartment door shut behind Maeve when she left. When he finally came back to himself, he hurried and flopped onto the couch for some mindless television. He had decided the answers would come when the moment was right, and that simple, instinctive responses would be best.

Rob's mother was very nice, as was his father. Sammy could see Rob's strong chin and dark hair when she looked to his father, and Rob's kind eyes and sweet smile had most definitely come from his mother. They had hugged Sammy; Rob's father was reserved, functioning on some other plane of existence where pain was temporary and Rob was alive, and everything was an awful, horrible dream. Rob's mother, on the other hand, had broken in

Sammy's arms, dealing with the reality head on, being absorbed in it to the point where it might actually kill her. Sobbing and wailing, she asked incoherent questions about why this had to happen, and how Sammy was coping. It was gut wrenching and honestly embarrassing for Sammy, who did her best to rub the woman's back and empathize with her lack of answers and insurmountable amount of questions. Eventually, Rob's father realized what was going on and gathered his wife in his arms. Together, they moved to a secluded corner of the funeral parlor and tried to get it together. Trembling, Sammy turned to find Maeve, but instead faced Rob's little sisters. They were calmer, although still terribly upset, and were eager to ask Sammy questions. They were thrilled to know that Rob had told Sammy all about them, and it was a bittersweet moment when Sammy guessed their names correctly based solely on Rob's delicate and detailed descriptions. The sisters also retreated somewhere private, presumably to digest what was happening, and to discuss the young woman their brother had been murdered trying to visit. Sammy found Maeve, and when she did, she grabbed Maeve's hand tightly and clammed up, becoming silent and stoic. She didn't want any more public scenes, didn't want to be introduced to mourning members of Rob's family, and she didn't want to face another grieving friend.

When the service started, Rob's mother, now barely composed, insisted that Sammy and Maeve sit with the family in the first row. The two interlopers sat at the very end, beside the sisters. In her simple black dress, continuing to tightly grip Maeve's hand in her own, Sammy cried softly. Her dark eyes were locked on the casket. She said her last goodbyes to the first boy to hold her hand and to kiss her. The first man to make her feel valuable was dead and gone. When his casket was being led to its final resting place, somewhere green and far from where he was needed, Maeve and Sammy snuck back to Maeve's car – Sammy had had enough. Travelling around the front of Maeve's car to the passenger side, something caught Sammy's eye, and she stopped. She was surprised by a little white piece of paper folded neatly beneath one of the windshield wiper blades. Careful not to rip it, she unfolded it and read, "I'm sorry." She showed the note to Maeve, who immediately began to search her car for any signs of damage. Everything seemed to be in order, and the note was forgotten.

Sammy's mom told Sammy she could take another day off if she needed to, but Sammy declined as her father looked on anxiously. Her mom also looked nervous, but her dad cleared his throat and cleared his clouded expression to support the decision. He knew that Sammy staying alone in her room, locked in with no company other than her own maddening thoughts, was the least healthy thing for her. She wasn't letting anyone in, had decided to cope on her own no matter how difficult or painful doing so would become, so he understood that being back on campus with lots of new faces and distractions would be much better for her psyche – just what the doctor ordered, so to speak. Sammy's mother acquiesced, but Sammy could hear her parents talking in hushed voices in the kitchen as she left. She didn't want them to worry. She just wanted everything to go back to the way it had been before Rob.

Upon entering the overly warm classroom for American Literature class, the douche bag of a professor offered Sammy his condolences and inquired about her extra assignment all in the same breath. She was sure the latter remark came from a genuine place, but Sammy had serious doubts about his condolences. Graciously smiling, she accepted them anyway, because it was the thought that counted after all, right? Sammy trudged to her usual seat in the back. The professor still irritating her was the beginning of a return to normalcy. She noticed the seat beside her was empty, and she hoped it looked anything but inviting, because she didn't particularly want to talk to anyone, wanted to return to the days when the only other soul who said anything to her was Maeve. Things had been simpler then; less messy.

Eliot came to class late and sat beside her, but Sammy avoided eye contact and looked busy. Thankfully, by the time Eliot had arrived, the lecture had already started and though he tried to catch Sammy's eyes, she was stalwart in her effort to avoid human contact. She knew she'd have to skillfully avoid Eliot until the class was over, and Sammy raised her eyes to the heavens and thanked God when there wasn't an opportunity for dialogue. Halfway through the class, however, Sammy realized she was being stupid, and that her behavior could be fairly perceived by Eliot as mean and rude. He didn't know who Rob was or that he was dead, or what that meant for Sammy. Why should he be punished for his ignorance? Maybe she should at least say hello, especially since their last conversation at Longhill Road had been so pleasant. Word choices filled her brain and she worried she'd seem odd or too distant, and she feared Eliot would ask if something was wrong. She knew that if she tried to deny anything was the matter, her voice would crack and her bottom lip would quiver and she'd be crying. She was frustrated with herself; greeting someone who had been enjoyable previously shouldn't be so arduous a task. The words should come easily and be simple, but genuine- all of this Sammy understood, but she obsessed over the many possible results of the conversation, as she always did. Maybe reverting to old habits, as awful as they were, was a good sign. As briefly as she had known Rob, he had embodied the promise she was constantly searching for and the possibility that something other than loneliness was ... well, possible. But when class was dismissed, Eliot hurried out, and Sammy released a deep breath she had only been vaguely aware of holding in.

Sammy slowly walked to her car, passing beneath fluorescent light after fluorescent light. Her mind was preoccupied and unhappily so. It was not until she reached the Buick that she noticed Eliot had parked his car beside her car. He seemed to be cleaning out the back seat, and Sammy smiled slightly. She slowed her pace to a crawl, her eyes bouncing back and forth between Eliot and the pavement. "Hey," was all she said; how lame.

"Hey," Eliot greeted, straightening up. "How are you? You were pretty quiet during class."

Sammy shrugged and pulled her coat tightly around her. It wasn't terribly cold, but she felt as if she needed something to do. She was flustered, though she couldn't exactly say why. Was that wrong? Was it an insult to Rob to be so flustered by Eliot? "I'm ... um, I'm ... well, I guess I'm okay. Thank you for asking. Uh, how are you?"

Eliot grinned, rubbing the back of his neck thoughtlessly. "I really can't complain. You missed one hell of a class last week."

"Seriously?" Sammy asked, suddenly anxious.

Eliot grinned. "No. It was really boring actually."

Sammy swallowed hard and barked a humorless laugh. "Figures; that professor is such a tool." She met his eyes and felt her face flush.

"I hope you were doing something better," Eliot said, stepping closer. "Were you out and about, gallivanting and whatnot?"

"What?"

"I'm sorry," Eliot said, color sprinting from his face. "I tried to make a joke and discreetly ask what you had been doing. I just ..." He took another few steps forward, cautiously, and nervously rubbed his hands together. "I am just bad at conversation, clearly." He smiled.

Sammy looked at him, chewing ferociously on her bottom lip. She crossed her arms over her chest and furrowed her brow. She didn't quite know what to say or what to make of Eliot. "I was at a funeral," she said. She knew the words would plummet and just sit there, but better they sit elsewhere than heavy on her heart and mind. She wanted to be unburdened, and poor Eliot had offered himself unwittingly.

"Oh, I'm such an asshole," Eliot said and reached out and gently, instinctively, touched Sammy's arm. "I'm sorry, really and truly sorry. Are you okay?"

She nodded. "I'm okay."

Eliot cleared his throat. "If there's anything you ever need, don't hesitate to ask."

The smile Sammy presented was genuine and felt wonderful upon her face. "Thanks." She paused to let the expected awkward silence descend. "Well... you have a good night, Eliot."

"Goodnight."

Chapter Five
Moving On, Starting Over, and Other Clichés

"I read with every broken heart, we should become more adventurous. And if you banish me from your prophets, and if I get banished from the kingdom up above, I'd sacrifice money and heaven all for love. Let me be loved. Let me be loved."~ Rilo Kiley

Days passed indiscriminately. Sammy ate meals with Maeve and Mike or with her family. She wrote little, as most of it was too melodramatic and too macabre to be enjoyable. She stopped crying herself to sleep, but the loneliness returned with a vengeance. Sad songs, mumbled apologies, and smudged eyeliner were all Sammy had to offer. She embraced the loneliness like an old friend and let it consume her and overwhelm her willingly. Maeve suffered through Sammy's self-pity and dramatics, and, surprisingly, so did Eliot. He was charming and as talkative as ever. He encouraged Sammy to keep writing, shared ideas through passed notes during lectures, and occasionally walked Sammy to her car after class, using his best lines to try and get a smile on Sammy's face. With Eliot's intensified presence in her life, it probably shouldn't have, but when Eliot invited Sammy to dinner, it shocked her. Her friend, loneliness, couldn't possibly be leaving already- they had barely gotten reacquainted with one another. She didn't reply to Eliot's invitation right away, and over breakfast the morning after the invitation had been made Sammy sought Maeve's wisdom.

The two girls were seated in a booth in the back corner of the diner on campus. It was a lot of chrome and red leather, inspiring a nostalgic atmosphere. The food was good and cheap, so it was usually busy, but the two girls must have just missed the breakfast crowd and been too early for the brunch crowd; the diner was something of a ghost town. Other than dim sounds of metal on metal, the occasional bark of an order, and footfalls against the tile floor, the only sounds came from Maeve and Sammy. This made Sammy somewhat uncomfortable, especially since she already felt like a dork for regressing to a high school freshman- she was about to ask Maeve's advice for something as simple as dinner? Disgusted with herself, Sammy sipped gingerly from her steaming mug of coffee. "So, what do you think: should I have dinner with Eliot or not?"

Maeve let her shoulders rise and fall in an indeterminate kind of shrug. In between mouthfuls of egg, she said, "It's totally up to you. Why not go?"

Sammy sighed, placing her mug on the table. She pulled her hair back tight against her head, and then let it fall. Her food was relatively untouched, and she wasn't looking at Maeve any longer. "I know it's not a big deal, and I'm well aware I'm being silly. It's just ... I don't want to be weird with him. I don't want to make it more than it is."

"Too late," Maeve said with a laugh. Sammy didn't smile. Dismayed, Maeve quickly added, "You won't make more of this than what it is as long as you don't use Eliot to fill the void Rob left. Even if Eliot's intentions are of the romantic variety, Eliot can't replace Rob; that's a lot of pressure to put on it right at the beginning. Besides, you can survive being alone again."

Sammy released a shaky breath. She could feel her bottom lip twitching dangerously, and she was worried that she would cry.

"But I don't want to go back to being lonely and desperate and all that. I hate the way I am now, Maeve. It's worse than who I was before. I don't want to keep sliding back."

Maeve nodded and smiled sadly, concerned for her friend. "No one wants that." She paused before deciding to simply give Sammy what she wanted; a straight answer. "Go to dinner with Eliot, Sammy. I think it's a good idea. It'll help get you back to normal. Eliot can say something that'll open your eyes, or you two could just have fun together. I want you to go, Sammy."

Trepidation marring her complexion, Sammy simply looked at Maeve and blinked. Maeve bit her tongue and looked away, frustrated. Sammy was so emotionally stunted and so self-involved that everything, absolutely everything, about being her friend was difficult. It was useless to confront Sammy about it, as she would forever be the victim and Maeve forever the aggressor, so Maeve had learned to smile, regroup, and change the subject. For example, as she lightly spread butter on a piece of toast, she asked Sammy for her thoughts on the latest horror movie that had been released. Sammy began giving an in-depth analysis, and all else was forgotten. Maeve was satisfied.

It was time for class with Eliot. Sammy paused briefly outside the open door, releasing a deep, tremulous breath. She wanted to tell him yes; she would love to go to dinner with him. After all, Maeve had seemed to think it was for the best to accept the invitation and Maeve had never steered her wrong before. However, she didn't want to sound too excited or too disinterested, as she was once again trying to find a healthy balance and was once again having difficulty in doing so. Sammy was considering the very real possibility that there was nothing healthy or balanced about her as she walked into the classroom, chewing her bottom lip. She made for her usual seat in the back corner of the room. Eliot was already there. She hoped his eyes, aflame, weren't even looking at her. The very thought of the interaction made her mouth go dry. Running a nervous hand through her tangled locks, Sammy sat beside Eliot. Careful to remain distracted and avoid eye contact, Sammy dug through her cluttered bag for her notebook and said, "Hi."

Eliot's cheerful voice returned the greeting. "Hey, Sammy, how are you?"

Sammy's bag thudded to her feet as she let it drop to the floor carelessly. She appeared to be very involved with arranging the books just so on her desk, so without looking at Eliot, she said, "I'm doing well, and you?"

Eliot was smiling brightly, but Sammy was still not looking at him. She was also being politely cold, like they were meeting for the first time. Confusion crept onto his face. "I'm great."

"I thought about your dinner invitation," Sammy said and flipped open her notebook, pen poised and ready to mar the white innocence of the blank pages before her. She felt sick and nervous and wanted to leave the room. She was spiraling out of control with her emotions and that was weak, coquettish and foolish. Why couldn't she just be normal?

Eliot straightened up in his seat beside Sammy. "You did? Did you make a decision?" Eliot asked with the anxiety of anticipation hidden poorly in his tone. He leaned closer to Sammy.

She leaned away from him, smiling politely but laughing nervously. "The truth is that I, um … Eliot, I would –"

The professor walked in and both parties diverted their attention to the front of the room. Sammy's face burned and she cursed herself silently. All she had to do was say yes. Why was it so hard? Why was she perpetually fifteen-years-old?

"Please read at least the first three chapters of <u>One Flew over the Cuckoo's Nest</u> over the weekend. Oh! Miss Thogode, do you have a moment?"

Damn it. Sammy walked to the front of the room, dragging her feet and leaving her bag and books behind to be gathered later. What could Professor Windbag want now? She paused before his desk. "You asked to see me, sir?"

"How's the extra assignment coming along?"

Fuck.

Shit.

Balls.

Sammy's face fell. "Um, it's turning out really great."

The professor smirked humorlessly, almost as if he had expected this. It made Sammy's blood boil. Smugly, the professor said, "You haven't given it a single thought, have you?"

"Of course I have!" Sammy was indignant. She had been writing; as to whether or not her lurid fantasies would satisfy the requirements of the assignment, she did not know. "I was writing just the other night."

The professor leaned against his desk. "Do tell." He crossed his arms over his thin chest, over his stupid sweater vest that he probably thought was appropriately academically stylish. Everything he did and everything he wore was just what someone would expect, and Sammy hated him for it. She hated him for other things, but also because he adequately assumed every stereotype there was about young, male, English professors. He was a walking caricature of himself, and it seemed like he had no idea. In that, Sammy found some courage and began to answer his question.

"Uh, there's a boy and girl who develop a relationship against the backdrop of … a … well, um … of a …" Sammy tried to force a moment of literary genius, but she could only think of Eliot and homework … homework … she had it! Sammy finally finished her sentence. "They develop a romance against the backdrop of an asylum, maybe in the tradition of Ken Kesey."

The professor narrowed his eyes. He knew Miss Thogode had pulled that out of her ass, but what good would it do to call her out on it? She had been having a rough time, and he had asked the question to invite her to have a conversation, to maybe lighten her load, but she was too annoyed with him to realize his intentions. Sighing, the professor said, "I look forward to reading it. Good evening." He dismissed Sammy by promptly ignoring her to fuss with his briefcase. Able to take the hint, Sammy went back for her bag and books, and then hurried out, a mumbled goodbye expiring on her lips. Eliot was leaning against the wall opposite the ending of the long, carpeted hallway. His muscular arms were crossed over his firm chest. Those thin lips were curled into a confident, easy smile and Sammy inhaled sharply through her teeth as she walked up to him.

"Did you wait for me?" she asked. Still angry, the question came out fiercer than Sammy had intended, so she smiled warmly.

"You wanted to tell me something, right?" Eliot asked as his smile widened and his arms slid to hang at his sides.

"I did." One more moment of uncertainty, one last pause before Sammy said, "Eliot, I would love to go to dinner with you." Suddenly embarrassed, Sammy spun to the left in the most deliberate of exits. She was off in her march to the door nearest the parking lot. Eliot followed, quickening his pace to catch up.

"That's great! When are you free?" he asked, slipping into an easy stroll beside Sammy, who had slowed down in spite of her burning desire to get the hell out of there before things went south as they inevitably did whenever she was involved.

She answered, "Um, I guess Thursday night would be best." Their conversation, if it could be called that, carried them outside. Sammy shivered against the burst of icy evening winds most particular to October nights. Eliot was not so easily distracted by the weather, and he stepped in front of Sammy, forcing her fleeing to a halt.

"Okay, Thursday night it is!" Beaming, he asked "What's your address so I know where to pick you up?"

Sammy's face twisted with discomfort. She didn't want Eliot to pick her up at her house because she didn't want her parents to give either of them the third degree. With a pinched expression, she asked, "How about we meet on campus?"

Eliot's smile dimmed. Did Sammy not trust him? He made his face as blank as possible and agreed. "Oh, yeah, sure; I'll meet you in this parking lot around seven o'clock?"

Sammy began to breathe easier. "Perfect. I'll see you then." Picking up her knees, Sammy hurried to her car. Eliot watched her leave, brows furrowed but still in good spirits. Sammy was odd, but in an endearing sort of way.

It was Thursday evening, just a few minutes past seven o'clock. Sammy parked her car in the lot and stepped out onto the pavement. There was no sign of Eliot anywhere and she nervously began to bounce from foot to foot. The bouncing helped to keep her warm in the bitterly cold night and served as a means of expelling her nervous energy and anxiety. She realized she wouldn't be so stressed if Eliot was an Ellen or an Eliza; then she could have proceeded thoughtlessly on instinct, but because Eliot was a member of the male persuasion, that mysterious and attractive group that had been so elusive to her for so long, she was freaking out. She couldn't remember the last time a boy had wanted to take her to dinner or the last time a boy had singled her out to talk to. Well, Rob had done all that. How could she possibly forget that? Sammy paused to painfully miss the brilliant, beautiful young man before resuming the search for Eliot. Looking for the new boy was easier than grieving the lost boy. Her eyes roamed the crowded parking lot until short, friendly blasts from a horn stole her attention. Gracefully, Eliot pulled his car alongside Sammy and rolled down the window. "Hop in," he called. Sammy took one last look at her car and entertained one final moment of hesitation before climbing in.

Later, the pair was seated at one of those trendy, high-top tales at a nearby restaurant that was part of a national chain, and the restaurant clearly did not care who knew that fact, as it proudly offered waiters and waitresses with buttons and pins galore on simple yet unflattering black vests who wandered from section to section, sometimes clapping and signing along to what was supposed to be a humorous and clever rendition of "Happy Birthday." It was typical. It was to be expected, and that helped Sammy to relax. Eliot ordered two beers and ordered boneless hot wings for an appetizer. Marveling at the polite and devastatingly handsome specimen opposite her, Sammy wondered how he knew she was a sucker for the boneless hot wings. Once the waiter returned with the bottles and left, Eliot asked if that was okay, and Sammy asked for clarification as to what he meant. He explained, "Most girls hate it when I order for them. It's an old habit and you know what they say about those."

Kindly, Sammy said, "No one's ever ordered for me before. I like it."

Eliot smiled with a hint of nostalgia about his squinted eyes. "I had you pegged as a beer and hot wings kind of girl from the first moment we talked."

"What gave it away?" Sammy asked, sheepishly grinning.

Eliot considered the question. "I don't know if it was really one specific thing. Maybe it was the Seger and the Springsteen, but who knows?"

Laughing softly, Sammy asked, "What you're really saying is that you're a connoisseur of the interests of forty-year-old women."

Eliot didn't miss a beat and cleverly replied, "Lucky for me I found one who looks so young."

Sammy did her best to continue the joke and said, "I may be old-fashioned in my likes and dislikes but don't worry; I promise I'm still emotionally unstable enough to be interesting." She drank deeply from her bottle. "Also, I'm emotionally unstable enough to make you feel better about yourself."

"So it begins; the self-deprecating humor!" Eliot said and leaned back in his seat, smiling ruefully.

"It's what I know," Sammy replied. Later, she would congratulate herself on the witty repartee she was able to engage in.

"What else do you know?"

This time, Sammy leaned forward and spoke softly. "I know myself, but that is all."

"Beautiful," Eliot exclaimed, nearly choking on his beer. "You finished The Beautiful and Damned. What did you think?"

"Eh; it was okay. I don't believe anything could ever be greater than Gatsby."

"Hence the title, right?" Eliot grinned. Sammy opened her mouth to add something, but the waiter had arrived to deliver the appetizers. Eliot asked for another beer for the lady and ordered two sirloin steaks with steamed vegetables and garlic mashed potatoes, all with Sammy's approval. Once the server had departed, Sammy beamed at Eliot. An adorable blush crept across his cheeks and he averted his burning eyes to the table. "Are you a Jay Gatsby?" he asked.

Humor left Sammy's round face. She seriously considered the question, which was odd but so was Sammy, so she was eager to answer it. Jay Gatsby had reinvented himself to be what he thought the girl of his dreams, Daisy Buchanan, wanted and maybe what she even needed. It had been his obsession for years, had become his new life, and he abandoned all that had been his old life, but the kick in the pants was that it was all a lie. Gatsby had been wrong about everything about Daisy and had died as result. After a few moments of thought, she said, "I don't know. I must be, because there's no way in hell I'm Daisy Buchanan. I could never be a beautiful little fool."

Eliot piled Sammy's plate with hot wings, and said, "I respect that." He handed Sammy's plate back to her, and she received it with sincere gratitude. She then asked Eliot if he was Jay Gatsby. His eyes met hers and held them.

"I'd like to think I'm charming, suave, and romantic, but I'd hate to think it was all for naught."

Sammy, with captivated eyes, said, "Me too; I know exactly how you feel."

Two more beers, one entrée, and half a desert later, Sammy was being led by Eliot out to his car. She wasn't drunk or obnoxious or anything so embarrassing; she just felt good. Amused, Eliot watched as Sammy buckled her seat belt and smiled from ear to ear for no apparent reason. She was much more relaxed than earlier and certainly seemed happier. Eliot hoped the beers weren't due all the credit. He liked to hold himself partially responsible for Sammy's improved mood and demeanor. He encouraged Sammy as she made idle chatter on the ride home. Eliot gladly answered all the incredibly random questions Sammy asked of him, questions like: did he like the summer better than the fall? Had he ever been skinny dipping? Would he ever shave his head? As arbitrary as the line of questioning was, it was entertaining, and Eliot answered each question happily, even eagerly. He wanted to ask some questions of his own, but Sammy wouldn't let him get a word in edgewise, and Eliot felt to do so would be to take advantage of Sammy's vulnerability. The beers had nothing to do with the vulnerability; it was crucially a part of Sammy, and Rob's passing had a lot to do with it. So Eliot didn't probe, and when they arrived back on campus Eliot was disappointed that the trip was over. There also seemed to be reluctance to Sammy's movements as she unbuckled her seat belt and opened the door. "I had a lot of fun, Eliot. Thanks again for inviting me out."

He offered a friendly smile. "Hopefully we can do it again real soon."

Silence was building, and it was of the awkward variety. Sammy was just going to bail and let Eliot deal with all of the feelings and all of their implications and consequences all on his own, but then she felt his warm hand upon her arm. Finally, it was the return of that delicious pressure, of another's touch. At any moment, she'd feel his lips against hers and all would be right with the world. Anticipation building, Sammy turned back to the beautiful boy beside her. He only wished her goodnight. Sammy mumbled "goodnight" in response before fleeing from the vehicle.

Being in such close proximity to Eliot after so humiliating a blow was unbearable, and Sammy was certain that if she had stayed even a moment longer, she would have died, would have suffocated, and all would be lost, and then there'd be no point. She'd be Gatsby.

Maeve didn't think the lack of a physical display of affection was catastrophic. As a matter of fact, she thought it showed maturity and praised Eliot highly as the belt of the treadmill moved round and round as she ran and ran. Sammy, battling the elliptical machine beside Maeve, listened patiently. Sammy realized she had been doing quite a bit of eating lately, eating the feelings for comfort and whatnot, so she had decided to come with Maeve to the beautiful and expensive recreation center on campus, which was one of the few buildings behind the Student Center, perched mightily on its own incline. The full-length glass windows showed twinkling lights of a surrounding, affluent neighborhood. It was pretty, but not enough of a distraction. Sweat sticking her bangs to her forehead, face flushed, Sammy debated how to approach Eliot next class and then debated whether or not it was even debatable. She took a swig from her water bottle and asked Maeve how things were with Mike. Gladly, Maeve indulged her friend in changing the subject. Things were great; Mike had surprised her with decent tickets to a play on Broadway that had been described as "psychologically scintillating;" right up Maeve's alley. They'd eaten sushi at some hipster dive closer to campus before heading into the city. Mike had started secretly planning some pretty epic events lately, and Maeve wasn't sure of the intentions or what all this was leading to, and she didn't want to know anything. What if she were wrong? The disappointment would be bitter especially since, as Maeve humbly pointed out, she was never wrong- at least when it came to knowing people.

Sammy longed for Maeve's confidence, or even her alleged in-depth knowledge of human nature, when she saw Eliot in the dining hall the next day. Covertly, she tried to duck behind the mass of students waiting in the sandwich line, but Eliot's eyes were more perceptive than she had hoped. Smiling, he walked over and greeted, "Hey. Were you just trying to avoid me?"

Sammy's face burned. "No, of course not; why would I do that?"

Eliot shrugged. "Maybe because you're mad I didn't kiss you the other night."

Her heart began to pound inside her ears and her mouth went dry. "What? That doesn't even … that never would have … what?"

Eliot pulled Sammy aside from the line. "I'm a very perceptive person, Sammy. I know that you're attracted to me." He grinned like an idiot, like he knew some big secret and suddenly, Sammy wanted to maim that flawless face; maybe blacken an eye or send a tooth spiraling to the floor.

Sammy's anger made her incredibly flustered and she sighed deeply, trying to muster what little dignity she could. She laughed without much humor, stepped back onto the line, and averted her gaze from Eliot. "Who says I'm attracted to you?"

"Why wouldn't you be?"

"Oh, you've got to be –"

Interrupting, Eliot barked a laugh. "Look at the facts, okay? You stare at me in class. You get all flustered whenever I talk to you. You wanted me to kiss you, and when I didn't you acted like none of it bothered you, even though all of it did."

What was with this guy? Sammy snapped, "So?" She had reached the front of the line and was fumbling with her student identification card. "None of that means anything. I liked you because you were nice to me; big deal." Finally succeeding in her battle with the card, Sammy practically chucked it at the server behind the counter. Feeling badly, she mumbled apologies, humbly ordered, and tossed her hair. Sammy was more than prepared to ignore Eliot completely, as he had thoroughly annoyed her. Even though his eyes burned into the back of her, her resolve was strong, and she did not turn around.

Discovering glaring to be unsuccessful, Eliot decided he'd have to speak, have to pull out the big guns, as it were. He asked, "The fact that I noticed those things, that I was actively looking for those things, doesn't mean anything to you?"

The question's effect was as powerful as intended. Sammy was stunned. Though she had hesitantly toyed with the idea of romance with Eliot, she had never thought it could be even remotely accurate. Things like that didn't happen; not to her, at least. Eliot was too beautiful and mysterious to be a part of some loser's wildly desperate romantic dreams. Sometimes Sammy thought Eliot was too beautiful and mysterious to be real period. Slowly, Sammy turned to Eliot. "I don't know," was her response. She had wanted to say more, something truly epic, but had nothing. She was flabbergasted, and besides, her order was up, and she had to turn back around anyway. Tucking her long hair behind her ears, Sammy took her tray and headed over to the line of soda fountains. She didn't care whether or not Eliot followed, honestly, but she released a breath when she heard the rubber soles of his sneakers bouncing against the tile floor. The ice seemed to crash loudly to the bottom of the plastic cup. Her mind contemplated the consequences of choosing root beer over raspberry lemonade, but Eliot's breath was warm against her ear, preventing her from committing to either beverage, because he was preventing her from thinking at all. Beverages, books, eating ... it all flew right out of her ear from her brain and into some nebulous floating above them. Softly, his lips grazed her ear as he whispered, "Well, Sammy, all of those things mean something to me." His hand slid to her elbow and he kept it there, waiting for Sammy to turn around and finally acknowledge his presence. He repeated the action with his other hand in an attempt to stop the tremors suddenly assaulting her body.

Sammy's breath was caught in her throat. Her words came out harsh; the tone was all wrong. She sounded like she was dying, not like she was being saved. "What do they mean to you? And what should they mean to me?"

Eliot laughed and, stepping backwards, took Sammy's hand in his. "Come on," he said. "Let's go eat."

Blushing and anxious, Sammy did as she was told. As she followed Eliot to an empty and secluded table, she inhaled deeply. Black coffee, burning wood, and sleepless nights made up Eliot's scent, and it intoxicated her completely. Sitting beside him, Sammy appraised Eliot. "So …?"

"So?" was Eliot's simple response.

Maeve regarded Sammy with some skepticism. "Dinner went well, so you're going out again. What's the big deal?"

"I don't know. We ended up eating lunch together the next two days, too. Things are … things are good." Sammy said. She was studying a camisole she had picked up from the rack. She rolled her eyes and hung the top back among its brethren. "Things are weird, too. I mean, I guess I'm happy, but I still miss Rob."

Maeve smiled sadly. "I'm happy that you're happy, and I'm sure Rob would be, too. Of course you're still going to miss Rob- that's perfectly normal and natural, so don't let that make things weird."

Sammy nodded slightly in Maeve's direction. "I want you to meet Eliot and let me know what the hell it is I'm doing." Sammy's voice cracked as she made the request. She didn't want to need help and didn't want to rely on Maeve as readily as she was.

Maeve stiffened and said, "Oh?"

Maeve was being distant suddenly, giving more attention to the merchandise before them than the conversation. Perplexed, Sammy thought maybe the way she had introduced the idea had been all wrong- too Eliot-centric. She laughed and added, "Do you want to double date? It'll be something right out of a John Hughes movie!"

Maeve rolled her eyes and moved to another clothing display. "You know, you can't compare everything to a movie or a book. Nothing is ever as dramatic as you make it, Sammy." Her tone was harsh, and Sammy was offended. A scowl descended upon her face, and she followed Maeve to the clothing rack.

"What is your deal? Why are you such a bitch all of a sudden?" Sammy realized she was escalating the situation rather than diffusing it, essentially proving Maeve's insult to be true, but her feelings were hurt, and she felt like lashing out.

Maeve sighed and rubbed her eyes. "I'm sorry, Sammy. It's just I begged you for almost a year to hang out, and you shot me down every single time until this Eliot kid started talking to you. It makes me feel like an idiot, you know?"

Sammy was confused, because she couldn't understand where the hostility towards Eliot was coming from. Just the other day, Maeve had been praising him for aiding Sammy in finding normalcy, but now the same Maeve was admonishing the same Eliot for the very act she had so recently admired. Was Maeve upset she hadn't been the one to "save" Sammy? And if so, didn't that make Maeve just as guilty as Sammy in creating useless drama? Crossing her arms over her chest, Sammy said, "I'm sorry if I hurt your feelings or whatever, but I've got to be honest; this doesn't make any sense. Are you mad because I invited you and Mike out with me and Eliot? Are you angry because I'm changing and becoming less socially awkward?"

Maeve's face reddened and her brows furrowed together threateningly. She was furious or, Sammy wondered, she was ashamed because something Sammy had said had hit a little too close to home. "Sammy, all I want is for you to be happy, honest. I just want you to be sensible about things too, though."

Still confused, Sammy wanted clarification and asked, "What do you mean?"

With another heavy sigh, Maeve softened the expression on her face. "Forget it, okay? All that matters is that I want to meet Eliot, and I'd be ecstatic to double date." In an effort to soften the earlier blows even further, Maeve added, "After spending so much time with you, Mike and I will be quite refreshing for Eliot. A return to normalcy will do him some good."

Sammy smiled, but it didn't come naturally. "Okay. It's a date, then." The false smile faded quickly, and Sammy lowered her gaze to her feet. Whatever Maeve had meant would have to be brought to light sooner or later, or else it would hang over everything, dripping doubts and bitterness all over everything else and thereby maiming it. Sammy wished it could be now and was going to ask Maeve about the sudden change in her mood, but Maeve was the first to break the silence and asked Sammy if she had told Eliot about Rob. Puzzled by the unexpected question, Sammy said, "I haven't told him about Rob. Is that wrong?"

"I don't think it's wrong," Maeve said. "Rob was great and amazing, and he hasn't been forgotten. You're still missing him, and while he doesn't have to be a huge part of this new relationship, I think Eliot has the right to know where you're coming from." Maeve paused for a moment and looked at Sammy earnestly. "As your best friend, I'm supposed to think clearly while you see the world in your rose-colored glasses and enjoy Eliot and whatever it is he has to offer. So I'll let you know if things get weird and immediately advise you to cut and run."

Sammy lowered her arms to hang limply at her sides. This conversation had turned bizarre and Sammy couldn't understand why. "Maeve, is everything okay? You're giving me two totally different pieces of advice."

Maeve looked deflated and defeated. Exhausted, Maeve seemed somehow smaller and more fragile. This revelation caused Sammy to wonder if she had been too harsh, that maybe something was going on with Maeve and Mike and she was feeling low. Sammy was changing, but maybe Maeve was too. Were they growing apart? Sammy swatted at the clothes hanging nearby and cleared her throat. She spoke to change the subject, and said, "I'm not finding anything in here. Do you want to get lunch and then try again?"

"Sure," Maeve agreed, and followed Sammy out of the store and into the crowded shopping mall. Parents chased and called after restless toddlers. Juvenile boys and girls in ripped flannel with facial piercings lingered outside Hot Topic. Senior citizens in pastel-colored sweat suits walked swiftly past the busy storefronts and through the hordes of harried customers. Sammy observed the spectacle of consumerism and the resulting, fairly amusing aspects of human nature before her, walking in silence beside Maeve as Maeve stared straight ahead, gazing into some far off distance. Sammy assumed Maeve was replaying their argument and trying to make heads or tails of it, just like Sammy was. Sammy had been elated that Maeve had been supporting whatever it was she was doing with Eliot, but things were different now. Recalling the sleepover, and the conversation in the laundry room, Sammy remembered that the first mention of Eliot had made Maeve uneasy, and that same uneasiness had reappeared today. Maeve didn't know Eliot, didn't know that Eliot was amazing, and Sammy had tried to rectify that with her invitation so there would be no future uneasiness. Sammy was painfully self-aware that she had placed Eliot on a pedestal already, and maybe that bothered Maeve because Sammy was falling into her old habits, forsaking the progress she had made; the progress she had obtained with Maeve's help. But she couldn't help herself; any girl like her who had won the interest of a guy like Eliot would do the same. Well, maybe not Maeve because she was so level-headed. She balanced Sammy nicely and Sammy knew she'd be fucked without Maeve. Maybe Sammy had been unappreciative towards Maeve, been too self-involved and selfish. Turning to regard Maeve warmly, the pair entered the food court and they found a table near the end of the last row. Setting down her bags, Maeve asked Sammy if she'd sit with their things while she ordered the food. Agreeing, Sammy took a seat, and, before Maeve departed, she apologized. Maeve smiled, and admitted some of the blame was hers to claim as well. For now, things were okay. When Maeve left, Sammy flipped her cell phone open, deciding to keep busy and occupied, and not look so alone, by fiddling around with the little flip phone. There were no missed calls or any new text messages, so Sammy scrolled idly through her inbox. Her heart refused to beat when her eyes rested on the last text she had ever received from Rob. *"Goodnight Sammy. I can't wait to see you again."* She raised a trembling hand to her mouth. He had wanted to say more to her, had died doing so, had been murdered doing so.

"Sammy, is everything okay?"

Startled, she looked up to see Eliot. Sammy was confused by his sudden appearance. "Eliot, what are you doing here?"

Eliot also looked alarmed. He said, "I needed to pick up a few things. I was walking out from the Gap and saw you sitting here, alone, and looking like you're about to cry." He sat beside her. "Are you all right?"

"Yeah," Sammy nodded. "Maeve's here with me, getting food. We were shopping. I, um, was just going through my texts." She closed her inbox.

Eliot smiled. "Reading a text message makes you cry?"

Becoming very tired very quickly, Sammy rubbed her forehead furiously and closed her eyes. She placed her phone on the table beside her and tried to answer Eliot's question. She said, "What? No, not usually, but … Eliot, there's something I never told you."

Eliot nodded slowly and brought his hands together on his lap. Sammy did the same. Abruptly, the atmosphere had turned tense, even awkward. Like a toddler accidentally releasing a beloved balloon, Sammy felt her dreamlike romance with Eliot was beginning to float out of reach. She wracked her brain for a way to get the conversation back on track, to jump up and grab the string of her shiny balloon before the sky claimed it as its own, to get things back to normal. Sammy was so focused that she didn't notice Maeve's return.

"And who is this young man?" Maeve asked. Eliot awkwardly rose to his feet.

"I'm Eliot. You must be Maeve." Eliot extended his hand, and Maeve shook it.

"Are you going to be joining us?" Maeve asked.

Eliot turned to Sammy and paled slightly. "I wish I could, but I have some more shopping to do. I saw Sammy and just thought I'd say hello. It's a pleasure to meet you, though." Eliot lowered his mouth to Sammy's ear. "Call me later, okay?" he asked in a hushed voice. Something about the implications in the husky tone made Sammy's hands go numb. Dazed, she nodded. Eliot snuck a quick kiss, politely said goodbye to Maeve and disappeared. Sitting down to eat, Maeve handed Sammy her food and began assessing Eliot's physical appearance. Sammy responded amicably enough, chiming in here and there with a girlish sigh, but Sammy really wanted to ask Maeve the best way to introduce Eliot to Rob, in a manner of speaking. She wasn't sure what Rob meant to her and Eliot's relationship or if Rob meant anything at all. Was it better to leave the dead buried?

Later that night, Sammy was lying in bed and writing in an old, battered, and tattered journal, feeling lonely. Her twin-sized bed was against the left wall of her bedroom and was simple – just an aged mattress on top of a dilapidated box spring on a cold, wooden floor. The sparseness of it helped her to feel like she was some kind of validated, starving artist. In the center of the room was a square rug badly in need of vacuuming; she was an awful housekeeper. Cluttered minds led to cluttered rooms; Sammy wasn't sure if that was true but was certain it applied in her case. Dust had accumulated on the wooden desk beside the door (which didn't lock – it had once been her older sister's room and her dad had destroyed the lock in a fit of rage during an epic father-daughter battle) and the dusty desk was across from a long window framed by dark curtains; it was under the window that her bed sat. A small closet in disarray was in the wall to the right of the window with a hand-me-down dresser beside it. Against the wall to the left of the window were two bookcases bursting with books, with a bad painting hung between them. The room was simple, but was definitely Sammy. There were reminders tacked on the different walls, along with pictures of Elvis Presley, Robert Pattinson, and a few pictures of friends from high school hung above the desk. Her personality was evident in the room. The room looked lived-in and was thereby quaint and comfortable; Sammy's beloved sanctuary. Currently, Sammy was composing quite the romantic tryst instead of calling Eliot, because she hadn't yet decided how to explain Rob. Was it even something to worry about? Like, what if she brought up Rob, and Eliot thought it was creepy that she was holding on? Or, what if-

Her phone vibrated loudly against her wooden windowsill. Eagerly, she reached for it and was ecstatic to find Eliot calling. Taking a moment or two to decide on the most appropriate greeting, Sammy answered after three rings. "Hey," she said with a kind of relieved disinterest; at least, that was what she was going for.

However Sammy may have sounded, Eliot's tone was definitely strained. "Hey, Sammy; I thought you were going to call?"

Grimacing, Sammy slapped her palm against her forehead. "I know, and I was going to. I just was trying to think about what I was going to say and the best way to say it."

Eliot hesitated a moment before responding. "Why? What's going on, Sammy?"

She took a deep, deep breath and wished she'd never have to take another. "Eliot, there's something about my recent past that I think you need to know."

Eliot responded with more hesitation. When he spoke, it was slowly and clearly, as if he were being as careful with his words as Sammy had wanted to be with her words. "Okay. Well, how about you come outside so we can talk face to face?"

"You want me to come outside?" Sammy repeated, confused. Sliding off her bed, she hurried to the window. Her fingers brushed aside the curtains and her eyes immediately found Eliot's car. The interior light was on, so she could see him, cell phone pressed to his ear. Something was kind of bizarre about that, and though she couldn't exactly explain why, Sammy felt nauseous. "Eliot, how did you know where I live?"

"I asked Maeve for your address. I was going to surprise you with dessert and flowers, but you never called. So I drove over as soon as I could, called you, and now I've ruined the surprise." Eliot laughed softly, but it did little to hide the lingering anxiety and doubt plaguing his tone. "But we can still talk, and I still have presents for you if you come outside. Please?" Sammy thought that given the circumstances, Eliot sounded relatively happy and not too freaked out, which was odd because an ominous reference to some past event in his new girlfriend's life should have made him run for the hills, or at least begin an onslaught of questions. Eliot was handling it calmly, which was more than Sammy could say. She was the one who was uneasy, despite being the one with the secret and despite being the one with the information, and she simply stood at the window, staring at Eliot. She wasn't sure if she should run to his side or play sick and postpone the conversation. Suddenly, with a graceful turn of his neck, Eliot's eyes locked on hers. Gasping, Sammy spun out of sight and against the wall. "Sammy?" Eliot called into the receiver. "Are you okay?"

She was okay and realized she was behaving childishly. There was nothing to be scared of or even worried about. Talking about Rob and how she had felt about him, and how she still felt about him, wasn't so bad. Things could be much worse. Her heart was stupid for pounding the way it was, and her stomach was foolish for twisting itself so intricately. Eliot was being sweet and had tried to surprise her with flowers and chocolates. She shouldn't be cowering in her room like some moron. She should be rushing outside, no questions asked. This was a scene she'd dreamed about, had written about, and had recreated over and over again. How could her first instinct be to resist? Maybe it was because Rob had died trying to surprise her. She couldn't think about that now, though. Now was the time for moving on and living like she had always wanted. The melodrama was nonsensical, and Sammy needed to get everything under control. So the unexpected eye contact had been a little unnerving; it was nothing to fall apart over. Sammy steadied her voice and finally answered Eliot, saying, "Yeah, I'm sorry. I'll be right out." She hung up with Eliot, slipped on her boots, and threw a sweatshirt over her head, all the while trying to control her breathing, to slow the hammer in her chest before it cracked her ribs and those shards of broken bone punctured her lungs. She hurried outside, ran to the passenger side of Eliot's car, and slid in. She didn't remember it being so cold outside and couldn't understand how it could be so cold in his car. Hadn't he been driving with the heat on? Shivering, she turned to Eliot and found his face set with a beautiful smile. His eyes were burning, but with a passionate intensity, as if he was setting cities aflame for a valiant, romantic purpose. His hands offered her violets, her favorite flower, and a box of chocolates that would have made Forrest Gump turn green with envy. "Eliot," Sammy began, touched, "you didn't have to do all of this."

Eliot shrugged the sentiment off. "You looked really upset today, so I wanted to cheer you up. And ask you out again, of course." He was staring into her eyes, and she needed him to blink, to break the power of the moment. Sammy had never experienced anything like this, (Rob had tried, but Rob had died – what a morbid, little rhyme) and she had a strong, overwhelming, and inexplicable desire to diminish it.

"This is beautiful, Eliot. Thank you." Quickly, she kissed his cheek. "How did the rest of your shopping go?" Sammy asked. The uneasiness was quickly abating, and she chalked up its momentary presence to her stunted emotional maturity and nothing more.

Eliot laughed, flexing his grip on the steering wheel and looking ahead, out through the windshield. "Riveting; purchasing new sheets can be quite fascinating."

With a small smile on her lips, Sammy likewise averted her eyes and picked at her denim jeans. "I bet. Maeve and I didn't find anything worth buying either, really."

Eliot was looking at Sammy from the corner of his eyes, appraising her and watching her without Sammy's knowledge or permission. "Is Maeve your best friend?"

The question made Sammy smile as strong waves of nostalgia washed over her. Speaking to her still trembling hands, she said, "Absolutely; we're really close."

"Oh," was all Eliot said. Sammy was unsure as to what the response meant, or rather, what it was supposed to mean. Still scrutinizing her hands, turning them over to see her palms, Sammy was not making any effort whatsoever to begin the conversation she had wanted to have. Perhaps Eliot was growing frustrated because he candidly asked, "Is there a reason why you're not looking at me?"

A request for eye contact was implied, but Sammy ignored it. Eyes following the lines of her palms, she said, "Sort of; I don't know how to explain what I need to explain."

Eliot nodded slowly and turned toward Sammy. His eyes were heavy upon her, dutifully noting the way she was sitting, the way she refused to look him in the eyes, and the way her lips were twitching and twisting without making words. She needed a little push to get started, that was all. Indulging Sammy, Eliot said, "I remember you mentioned something today at the mall, and then again on the phone just now, about you having to tell me something. How about you just say it, whatever it is? I promise not to laugh, or freak out, or anything like that, okay?"

Sammy took a deep breath. She seemed to be doing a lot of deep breathing as of late. "Remember that funeral I went to?"

"Yes," Eliot answered.

There was time for one more deep breath before Sammy dove in, head-first, cold water be damned. "Well, his name was Rob, and he was more than a friend."

Eliot's eyes widened slightly as he asked for clarification. "Do you mean he was a boyfriend?"

Sammy nodded and said, "Yeah, he was my first boyfriend … like first boyfriend ever; he gave me my first kiss. He was my first date. And yeah, that all happened about a month ago. I'm real weird when it comes to guys and romance and all that, and there's a good chance I'm not ready for you. There's something you need to understand about me, Eliot: I'm bat shit crazy. Seriously, I obsess over guys, you included." Eliot turned away from Sammy to consider what she had just revealed, and he did so slowly with those eyes, the fire within them no longer raging out of control. The eyes seemed to be dimmed as they returned to their previous past time of staring out of the windshield. He was definitely freaked out now; Sammy had done it this time. One or two tears rolled down Sammy's stricken face. She decided to keep talking, to let it all out. The damage had been done, so what was the difference? Continuing, she said, "Rob and I didn't go out for very long. We dated for like a couple of weeks, maybe, but he was the first guy who ever thought I was something special, you know? So today at the mall, I was re-reading the last text he ever sent me, which was the last text he ever sent anyone, because he was murdered in the middle of sending me another message. He was coming to my house to surprise me, and he was killed, so I'll never know what that last message said, and that keeps me up at night." Sammy wiped her eyes and laughed, though she couldn't point out anything particularly amusing about the situation. "And I know I'm weird, and this is all bizarre, so if this makes you want to stop all of this, I get it. I understand. I won't kill any of your pets and shove their dismembered heads in your mailbox or anything like that, I promise."

Her head fell into her hands, and Eliot turned to watch her shoulders move up and down with muted sobs. Instinctively, Eliot slid closer to Sammy, moved by the honesty and affected by the disdain she used when speaking about herself. He said, "Sammy, I'm glad you told me." Timidly, he rested his hand on her arm. "Honestly, though, it doesn't make a difference. I'm getting to know you, and I'm willing to do that because I am attracted to every part of you, not just the quote, unquote normal ones." Sammy raised her eyes to Eliot's, and he smiled kindly, and Sammy thought her heart would break.

Sammy wiped her eyes and said, "Eliot, I just … I need you to know what you're getting into."

He nodded and said, "Okay, fair enough." Eliot slid his arm around Sammy's waist and closed the inch of space between them. "Sammy," was all he said, and he spoke softly. He lowered his handsome head to taste her lips. "You can tell me anything, okay? I'm not going to run scared. I promise." His mouth met hers, and a sense of urgency was evident. A second first kiss, this one much different than her first, first kiss. Rob had been deliberate and gentle. Eliot was taking as much as he was giving; nearly painfully gripping Sammy's waist and pursuing kiss after kiss with an awe inspiring kind of reckless abandon that frightened and excited Sammy all at the same time. But Sammy wondered if she should stop all of this, if she was moving too fast, but then again, the bothersome thoughts about pace and betraying Rob's memory could all wait, because Eliot's taste and Eliot's scent were all around her, and she was completely satisfied. Sammy could be comfortable with being deeply troubled and neurotic as long as Eliot held her, caressed her, and wanted her. It was shallow and selfish, but she could live with that for a stolen moment in a car on a deserted, residential street.

Sammy untangled herself from Eliot some time later, her lips swollen and wet, her hair a mess. "I should probably head back inside," she said, offering a bittersweet smile. "It's getting late."

Eliot nodded, but kept right on kissing her neck. Sammy laughed softly, but persisted. "We've both got class tomorrow and my dad will freak out if he goes in my room and sees that I'm gone."

Eliot pulled away and asked, "Can we get dinner before class tomorrow?"

Without a moment's hesitation, Sammy responded, "Sure. Will you text me when you get home?"

Eliot quickly kissed Sammy's cheek and was just as agreeable, saying "Sure."

She eyed him warily, and wanted to make sure things were really as good as they seemed. She asked, "Are you okay? Did I ruin everything?"

Eliot let his fingers slide along Sammy's jaw line and said, "Stop thinking so much. If there's a problem, I'll talk to you about it." Eliot pulled Sammy in close and hugged her tightly as he said, "Goodnight."

Briefly, Sammy buried her face in the crook of Eliot's neck and inhaled deeply. She wanted to remember his scent long after he drove off, when she was back in her bedroom. "Goodnight, Eliot," Sammy said before she kissed his lips and bounded inside with an awesome kind of happiness, an emotion that she had missed and that she believed she could get used to, and it was that particular emotion that kept her grinning like a fool and shaking with a nervous kind of excitement. She didn't watch Eliot leave; she had enough self-restraint to keep from jumping at the window like some over-excited puppy.

"You cried? Are you shitting me?" Maeve looked at her friend incredulously.

"I know, I know," Sammy hissed. "But I told him everything, and he was okay with it. That has to count for something, right?" Her eyes flicked from Maeve to the open textbook on the table that was displaying a rather dense section on Marxist literary theory. Sammy had a midterm coming up and had somehow convinced Maeve to join her at the library. Maeve claimed to have a paper due on some renowned mental health professional from New England who was leading and engineering groundbreaking studies about the behaviors of creative types ... or something like that, because the description Maeve offered bored Sammy to tears. It must have bored Maeve too, because only a few notes had been copied into her notebook and she had willingly allowed the discussion to turn to Eliot. Maeve had seemed genuinely interested in the part of the discussion when the main topic pertained to making out in his car, and Sammy had wanted to keep it at just that – maybe in a last attempt to truly keep at least one part of Eliot to herself, but more likely it was a cowardly attempt to keep from witnessing Maeve become increasingly uncomfortable when discussing Eliot. But it was just as uncomfortable keeping things from Maeve; the two told each other everything. Maeve was Sammy's only friend, Eliot excluded- Sammy had told Eliot practically the same thing just last night.

"What else did you talk about?" Maeve asked.

Sammy shrugged, and replied, "It was really just about Rob. It was a pretty intense conversation, and I know it was probably a bad idea to start devouring each other's faces instead of seeing the conversation to its conclusion, but I really needed to tell him that. Aside from you and my family, he's all that I have, you know? And he's mine, something separate and unique." Smiling thoughtfully, Sammy added, "He makes me feel separate and unique and special."

"First of all, thanks for the mental image of you and Eliot eating each other's faces. It's a shame you can't poke out your mind's eye," Maeve said, laughing teasingly. "But seriously, don't you think that conversation puts a lot of pressure on the two of you? I mean, you have your issues, but Eliot didn't really open up to you yet. It's all well and good to feel special, but you need to help each other. He can't save you, or change you, or bring Rob back. Remember that you can't save him or change him, either. I'm sure you both felt great after a heavy duty make-out session, but something real was going on there, too." Maeve spoke with real concern. "Can you handle all of that at once? You don't have to rush in and put everything on the table the first week, Sammy, especially when he hasn't done the same."

Sammy leaned forward and spoke a trifle defensively, saying, "It's been more than a week. It's been a couple of weeks, and I want this Maeve. I thought that you thought that honesty was the best policy."

Rolling her eyes, Maeve said, "It is, but it's also a two-way street, and relationships grow and evolve- they don't happen overnight. He brought you chocolate and flowers, right? Why not enjoy that moment? Heavy stuff can come later, much later if you can manage it."

Sammy nodded, beaming and glowing and exhibiting every other clichéd synonym for radiance, and said, "Yes, he did surprise me with flora and candy. Thank you for that, by the way."

Maeve shook her head slowly, saying, "Don't thank me, it was all Eliot."

Sammy leaned forward even further. Her whispers were urgent and she feared her lips, strained from an ever-present smile, would slur them. She confided, "That's what's so great about him. Does Mike do stuff like that?"

Maeve considered for a moment. She answered, "Sometimes he'll surprise me with a grand gesture, but not all of the time. He used to do it a lot, but not so often now. It's not a bad thing, though. I think the more frequent the gestures, the less meaning they have."

Sammy nodded, saying, "That makes sense."

"My thing is to have fun," Maeve smiled. "All the big emotional stuff will come when it does, and that's fine, but I'm not going to rush it. Like, I still haven't met Mike's mom, but that's okay. We're only here once. Let's enjoy it."

Leaning back in her chair, Sammy pulled her hair tight against her scalp, and then let it fall freely. Maeve was right, and Sammy knew she was making everything in her life a bigger deal than what it was. In fact, Eliot had said almost exactly the same thing last night, had given Sammy practically the same advice. That feeling of being dumb and juvenile settled over her again, now so familiar it was like a security blanket, or the warm embrace of an old friend. She said, "I'll have to remember that the next time I see Eliot. I'm going to his place for dinner and a movie."

Maeve, turning back to the textbook open on the desk before her, said, "Just have fun, Sammy. Enjoy this, okay? I want you to be happy, man."

Sammy nodded, and shut her eyes tight. "Thanks," she whispered before she shot her friend a goofy smile. She added, "I thought the biggest problem in a relationship was missing underwear on your sixteenth birthday or being from opposite sides of the track. There were never any dead boyfriends involved, not even in all the Stephen King I read."

Maeve smiled. "I hate to break it to you, but life isn't a movie, Sammy. It's not a book either. We've had this conversation before, and I won't patronize you with a lecture, but you can't let your grandiose expectations and inevitable devastating disappointments ruin something that could be good for you."

"Eliot is good for me, I think," Sammy said. "He's sweet. When we got dinner before class yesterday, all he did was ask questions about me, and talk about how interesting he found me, and how impressed he was by me. He wants me, Maeve. This is what I've been waiting for."

Maeve's lips thinned almost imperceptibly. Sammy didn't notice and likened the expression to something closer to a smile than a grimace. "See if you're what he's been waiting for. Try getting him to open up before you jump to any conclusions or make any assumptions about this kid." Maeve paused a moment to raise her eyes to Sammy's. There was something lingering there-Maeve was trying to pass Sammy a meaningful look as she added seriously, "Remember that if it turns out he's crazy, you don't have to be so desperate you'd settle for a complete nut job."

Chapter Six
Crying for Normalcy

"Who needs love when there's Southern Comfort?" ~ Amanda
Palmer

Sammy knocked lightly on Eliot's door, hoping she had enough time to vomit before he answered and before the dinner and movie festivities began. Vomiting would help calm her nerves and reduce her caloric intake for the day; it was a win-win situation as far as Sammy could tell. She was in the middle of debating where to deposit her stomach contents so that Eliot would never know she had done so, when the glorious man himself opened the door. "Hey," he smiled easily, like being happy was the most natural thing in the world. Sammy supposed that, for Eliot, it was. The best thing about Eliot's happiness was that it was infectious, and Sammy smiled in spite of herself. "I thought you got lost."

Sammy checked the time on her cell phone, worried. She asked, "I'm not that late, am I? We agreed on 7:00PM, right?"

Grinning, Eliot said, "We did, but I expected you earlier than that, especially since you've been so early to class these last couple of weeks." He laughed and opened the door wider. "You're not very consistent."

"Oh, shut up," Sammy joked, walking inside. "Please don't remind me about that class. It always makes me think of that damn assignment."

"How's it coming along?" Eliot asked as he shut the door behind Sammy.

With a frown, Sammy admitted, "Not so good. I haven't been able to write anything of real substance for weeks, and what's worse, is that I absolutely hate everything I wrote before!" Sammy sighed dramatically and collapsed onto Eliot's couch. He seated himself beside her.

"Do you want to take a ride out to Longhill Road?" he asked. "We could bring dinner there and–"

"No, that's okay," Sammy interrupted, shaking her head. "Tonight is a date night. I don't want to spend it working. I just want to spend it with you." Sammy turned her head and seemed to be studying Eliot, to be looking for the same thought in his tone, or in the cracks and the lines of his face. Holding his breath, Eliot hoped he would pass whatever test Sammy was forcing him to take. Finally, Sammy's expression softened, and Eliot believed the test was over and that he had passed with something akin to flying colors.

Eliot grinned and kissed Sammy's forehead, removing his lips with a genuine reluctance. He asked, "Then what can I do to help?"

Sammy shrugged and honestly answered, "I don't know." Sammy's mind raced around and around in circles, trying to come up with some way to break the tension and change the topic of conversation. She turned to Eliot and surprised both parties by saying, "Let's talk about you."

"What?" Eliot asked, truly astonished.

Sammy tucked her hair neatly behind her ears and said, "I've spilled my guts to you at least three times now. It's your turn. Maybe something in your past will help with my literary future." Nervously, she laughed. She knew the joke was lame and wanted to end her statements with something more substantial, adding, "And besides, I want to get to know you, too. I don't want you to be just a pretty face."

Eliot laughed softly. He began to talk hesitantly, but once he started the words poured out of him. He was born on the frosty morning of the eighteenth day of November to Dr. Ryan Andrews and his wife, Elizabeth. His father's greatest love was his profession in the field of mental health. He had met his wife during work; she was a nurse in the very same asylum he was now the administrator of. Eliot was more of a bonus for the couple, an unexpected plus. Dr. Ryan Andrews was kind to his son, but much too involved elsewhere to be considered "Dad." His mother retired early, when Eliot was six, because she could afford to, as her husband had received quite the promotion (his being totally consumed by his profession paying off). Rather than adorn her only child with gifts and affection, Elizabeth focused on raising him to be a strong and critical individual; a true scholar and professional. She wanted him to be his father and to find a girl just like her. When other young boys were joining little league or playing with action figures, Eliot was inside his home, reading Freud and larger texts. Eventually Eliot realized he was missing out on something, and Eliot rebelled the only conceivable way: he began reading poetry by eight-years-old, writing poetry at thirteen, and at sixteen he knew he was going away to college to become an English major. His friends were like-minded but, according to Eliot, had not had the courage or true passion to leave the small Maine community and pursue what they had discussed for thirty minutes a day at the lunch table. He sighed heavily at the end of his monologue; rubbing the back of his neck and staring down at his feet firmly planted on the floor. Sammy had delicately taken Eliot's nearest hand, his left hand, in hers and had absent-mindedly traced the lines on his palm with her fingers as he spoke. Her dark eyes and her soft fingers followed each line along Eliot's flawless skin. One such path led to an explosion of tinier, shinier lines. During Eliot's pause, she asked, "Are these scars?"

Eliot turned his head slightly and looked down at the palm in question. "Yeah," he answered. "I've had those for a while."

Sammy's eyes met Eliot's, and she asked, "What happened?"

Eliot released a breath and slid further down against the couch, so that both he and Sammy were in similar reclining positions with their legs stretched out far. "It was a really hot summer. I think it might have been the hottest summer ever recorded in Maine, but that could be the creative type in me making shit up, too." He laughed, and Sammy laughed, and then he continued speaking. "I remember begging my parents for about a week straight to take me to the beach. I'd never seen the ocean before, and I wanted to really badly. I wanted to smell the salt of the sea on the breeze and feel the sand squish between my toes, form against the soles of my feet. They kept saying no, insisting there was no time for it between my studies and my father's work. I was beside myself, and had nearly resigned myself to never speaking to either of them ever again when, finally, the temperature hit the triple digits." Eliot was smiling wistfully, looking at some point beyond his palm at something Sammy couldn't see. "They had to take me now, because all of us wanted to be cool and comfortable. We packed up the car and drove for what seemed like hours and hours until we got to the beach. I leapt from the car, leaving my sandals on the floor beneath my seat in the back and felt incredibly alive when the scalding pavement of the parking lot met my bare soles. I ran faster to the sand and was so grateful for the relief on my feet that I dropped to my knees. I was instantly cooler and plunged my hands into the sand, ecstatic to feel it and see it all for the first time." Here, he sighed heavily and his eyes clouded over, his brows furrowed. "When I did that, though, my left palm splayed out against a bottle someone had buried in the sand and for some inexplicable reason, for some reason I still don't fully understand and most likely never will, I gripped the bottle as hard as I could and it shattered in my hand. I felt the pain, could feel the sticky, warm bleed seeping out , but I didn't give a shit. I only squeezed harder and it hurt worse, but I was okay with it. My mom came over and knelt beside me to see how happy the trip had made me. She asked me some inane question and as an answer, I lifted my hand from the sand and she saw the broken bottle and the blood, and she freaked." He chuckled as if he had said something witty, but Sammy didn't think he meant it. She felt slightly uncomfortable and was gaping at Eliot. "My mom made me stand up and march over to my father. I showed him my hand and he started asking me weird, random questions, like my mother had sent me for a psychological evaluation, like he was still at work or something. We all got back in the car, and went right back home." Eliot ended his story with a different tone than he had used at the beginning. As he spoke, his tone became more and more intense and his words rushed together, falling over one another. Sammy caught most of it, if not all of it, and wasn't sure what to say now. Did he need a hug? Was the solution as simple and cheesy as all that? Eliot, breathing tremulously, said, "I'm sorry. That was too much, right? It's just that when I talk with you, I feel like I can be honest." He made eye contact with Sammy. "Can I?" he asked. "Can I be honest with you?"

"Of course," Sammy answered, sitting up straighter. "You can always tell me anything, Eliot." Smiling sadly, albeit sweetly, Sammy thought back on all that Eliot had shared. She heard every word, let it all sink in and, therefore, couldn't help but notice that Eliot had been mum on one subject. "What about girls?" she asked.

Eliot looked up fast and said, "What?"

Smiling ruefully, Sammy said, "You know what I mean. I'm talking about girls, girlfriends ... what about those?"

Eliot looked confused and asked for elucidation from Sammy. "What about them?"

Sammy sat up a little taller again and dared to make direct, intense eye contact with Eliot. "Did you have a lot of girlfriends in high school?" she asked, rephrasing her previous question.

"Does it really matter?" Eliot asked and took the hand Sammy had been so gently caressing and placed it against her warm cheek. The skin there was smooth and soft and yielded to his touch.

Sammy replied, "Not exactly; I guess I'm just curious." Sammy's arms dropped to her lap, where they twitched and picked at one another. Worried, she added, "I'm sorry if it's inappropriate or whatever. We were just talking about being honest, so I thought …"

Eliot's face was serious but still beautiful, still painfully beautiful. "Don't apologize when you've done nothing wrong, Sammy," he said. "You told me about Rob, so it's only fair I tell you about significant others in my past." He sighed heavily before continuing, "I've slept with a lot of girls because I could. I've never really wanted any girl." Eliot slipped his masculine hand behind her head and said, "Until now; I've never wanted any girl until now."

Sammy released an unsteady breath and looked down. She honestly admitted to Eliot that she was speechless, and said, "Eliot, I don't know what to say."

Eliot laughed and said, "You don't have to say anything." He slipped the fingers of his free hand beneath her chin and raised her face so that her eyes met his. Slowly, gently, kindly, and, dare she think it, lovingly, he chastely kissed her shaking mouth. He kissed her forehead, and then moved his lips to hers once more. Time passed imperceptibly to the young couple on the couch. Both Eliot and Sammy were only concerned with the steady rise and fall of chests, roaming fingers and hungry lips. Eventually, Eliot did pull away with an adorable grin upon his face and asked, "What about dinner?"

Sammy smiled and responded, "I'm starving. Man, you just wouldn't shut up!" Eliot laughed soundlessly, and Sammy asked, "What are we having?"

Eliot said, "Since we're both college students who like things cheap, in great quantities, and easy, I thought pasta would be in order. Is that okay?"

"That sounds fantastic," Sammy said.

Eliot peeled himself from the couch. "I'm adding something special to the sauce – a surprise for you," he said. Standing, looking down at Sammy, Eliot winked. "I think you'll like it. And," he dragged the word out as he gracefully strolled to the low table near the door, "I asked the guy at the video store for the scariest movie in the place." He tossed the bag with the DVD to Sammy, who managed to catch it, even if it was an awkward catch. She took it out of the plastic bag and studied the cover before she admitted to Eliot, with surprise in her tone, that she had never ever seen it. Eliot seemed quite pleased with himself, grinning broadly as he exited the small living room into the tiny kitchen, passing through a deceptively narrow archway. Sammy remained sitting on the couch, taking in Eliot's apartment, and soon she realized that, like all good apartments, it was completely neutral so that one could move in as easily as one could move out. Absolutely nothing hinted at Eliot's intelligence, passions, style, or even his acquaintances and friends. Everything was some sort of beige and had likely been in the space longer than either Eliot or Sammy had been alive. The television sat on the carpeted floor directly across from the couch against the opposite wall, with a cheap DVD player lying on top. That was the entire living room – there was no quaint coffee table with matching end tables supporting stylish lamps. The low table by the door was the only surface on which to put anything, and it was too small for a lamp. All the light in the room came from an overhead light that was more garish than anything else. The only redeeming thing about the space was the large, spotlessly clean window in the right wall. Eliot had the yellowed and aged blinds lifted and Sammy really liked that – that *was* Eliot. Sammy slowly got to her feet and shuffled to the window.

The scene was considerably less than stellar. It only offered a nearly empty parking lot illuminated by harsh halogen bulbs tucked inside impossibly high streetlights. Sammy could see other buildings belonging to the complex but none had a window with open blinds. She smiled, and it only began to fade when she looked to the right and the left of the window and saw four photo frames. Two hung on one side, two hung on the other, all were black, all were the same size, and all still had the display photographs in them. It was slightly off-putting and later, when Sammy thought to ask Eliot why he didn't hang photos of his friends and family, or even throw out the frames and hang pieces of art instead, he explained that the models in the pictures were beautiful – truly beautiful people with beautiful lives and beautiful families and friends. He wanted visitors to believe he could be friends with such people and that he could even be related to people like that. It nearly broke Sammy's heart to hear something like that come from Eliot, so she didn't tell him that anyone who gave the frames more than a cursory glances would know he was a liar.

She walked to the start of the linoleum that marked the beginning of the kitchen. Leaning against the archway, Sammy asked, "Is there anything I can do to help?"

Eliot was startled by the verbal intrusion and spun quickly to face Sammy. His back had been towards her as he busied himself at the stove. Releasing breath, he said, "I would say no and tell you to make yourself comfortable, but our earlier … activities took up a lot of time and I would like to eat before midnight." He smiled. "How are you when it comes to making salad?"

Laughing, Sammy replied, "It's not rocket science, right?"

Eliot laughed too. "Alright, smart ass. Everything's in the fridge and the cutting board is already on the counter. You can grab any bowl from the top of the cabinet to your left." Sammy nodded enthusiastically and got to work right away. She retrieved a large, plastic bowl as instructed, and did her best to gather the necessary ingredients from the fridge – the lettuce, cucumbers, tomatoes, onions, peppers – without getting in Eliot's way as he worked to perfect the sauce, but the kitchen was so small that occasional collisions were inevitable. Reaching for an onion and a pepper, Sammy's arm grazed Eliot's sturdy back and she feared her hands would go numb. Their hips met several times as one tried to make room for the other to pass and at first, Eliot tried to apologize but he could only open and close his mouth stupidly. Both decided to enjoy the physical contact and intimacy the cramped quarters provided and both blushed freely when they thought the other could not see. Sammy had finally begun preparing the salad, having finally navigated her way to a suitable workspace, when Eliot said, "I love this, the two of us cooking together, but I have to admit I'm upset your surprise is ruined."

Sammy stopped ripping up the lettuce to turn to Eliot. "What do you mean?"

Frowning slightly, Eliot gently brushed past Sammy to the fridge and brought out a bag of shrimp and a bag of sea scallops. The refrigerator door swung shut loudly in the stunned silence emanating from Sammy. The light in her eyes grew dimmer – another boyfriend making her a seafood dinner? Rob filled her completely and she turned back to the vegetables in need of slicing and dicing, back to the large, plastic bowl that needed to be filled, hoping the menial task would keep Rob at bay. Eliot didn't seem to notice the tensing muscles or sudden scrambling, so he kept talking. "I remembered you love seafood, so I thought this would be great for the sauce, and I was going to add some red pepper flakes to make it nice and spicy, which I also know you enjoy." He laughed nervously and said, "Surprise."

"Thank you."

Her tone was dead. Eliot couldn't see her face, but her voice carried in the absurdly small kitchen just fine. She was holding back, shutting down and clamming up. Eliot's own muscles tensed as he became nervous. Was this the beginning of the end? He couldn't let this moment grow and evolve into something they couldn't recover from. "Is something wrong, Sammy?"

"It's great, Eliot, but you really shouldn't have done all of this." No inflection in her voice, but her steady, brutal chopping of the vegetables punctuated each syllable. Her actions exhibited a startling kind of controlled violence and if for nothing else, Eliot had to get to the bottom of things to save the salad from being mutilated.

"Can you please stop what you're doing and talk to me? Please, Sammy?"

She could not talk to Eliot and risk blubbering on and on about how she had been here before and had survived but she didn't believe in second chances, so she couldn't do it all again and remain unscathed. Rob was dead, murdered, and haunting her – she didn't want him haunting Eliot, too. Sammy pleaded, "Just let me finish the salad."

"The salad's not important right now. Sammy, I need to talk to you." Eliot grew stern – it was no longer a request.

Sammy shrugged to fake indifference, but the gesture wasn't authentic or genuine and thereby looked awkward. "It'll have to wait."

Eliot exclaimed, "Damn it, Sammy!" just as Sammy exclaimed "Ow, shit!" The rising tension between her and Eliot had met with her erratic and frantic chopping and claimed a casualty- Sammy's middle finger of her left hand had been decently sliced and was bleeding freely. Blood stained the cutting board. Sammy grabbed her quivering left hand with her sturdy right hand and pressed it against her stomach to dull the pain. The knife clattered to the floor and Eliot closed the distance between them. "What happened? Are you okay? What's wrong?"

Sammy turned to face him, letting a few tears fall. She was embarrassed more than anything else. "I just cut myself. I wouldn't use that tomato, though; I'm pretty sure I bled on it." She laughed weakly, trying to make light of the situation.

Eliot didn't smile, didn't even come close to smiling. As a matter of fact, Eliot didn't look all that concerned, either. Sammy wondered at the expression on Eliot's face, which was something like passionate intrigue, and she wondered at the new light illuminating his eyes. "Let me see," he commanded. Almost ashamed and feeling inexplicably guilty, Sammy offered her injured digit to Eliot. He held it closer to his eyes, being firm but somewhat gentle, and marveled at the blood. Taking the pointer finger of his right hand, Eliot slid it slowly along the wound, wiping it free of blood. Sammy wondered why Eliot didn't get a rag or even a paper towel, but she only wondered for a moment because, soon enough, Eliot was dragging her to the bathroom, which was down the short hallway and to the right. Struggling to keep up with Eliot, Sammy was very surprised by his pace. Did he think the wound was life threatening? Was the rushing really necessary? She thought about telling Eliot that she truly was fine and that this whole production was wildly inappropriate, but they had reached the bathroom, and she could only think of one thing: the color blue.

It was the ugliest fucking bathroom she had ever seen.

The size left something to be desired, yes, but that was manageable; the overwhelming and only slightly varying shades of blue were not. Though the shades of blue matched one another, technically, the differences between the paint on the walls, the rug on the floor, the porcelain of the toilet, the countertop framing the sink, the sink itself, and the shower curtain were enough to be noticeable and even unsettling- all that blue was overwhelming and suffocating. She felt like she was drowning in a blue sea of bad taste. Sammy felt it'd be best to make a joke about it since, frankly, it was making her sad. "Was all this blue your idea? Kind of depressing, isn't it?"

Eliot offered Sammy half of a grin as he led her to the sink. "It's an apartment, smart ass. I had no choice." He moved to stand behind her after turning the faucet on and letting icy cold water pour forth. "Okay, Bobby Flay, let's clean the cut." Eliot slinked his arms along Sammy's arms and held her wrists, navigating the injured finger beneath the spout. The contact was intimate and wonderful, but was awkward in the blue, blue bathroom. When the cold water hit the injury, Sammy inhaled sharply. Eliot closed what little space remained between them, pinning Sammy's hips against the countertop. "Does it hurt?"

Sammy shrugged. "It stings a little."

Eliot reached forward, pressing tighter against Sammy (which made it harder for her to breathe and made her blush, furiously, but no one was complaining) to turn off the faucet and open the mirrored cabinet above the sink. The two metal shelves were decidedly bare aside from some essentials like toothpaste, shaving cream and aftershave. Eliot grabbed the bottle of rubbing alcohol that Sammy's roving eyes had missed. It stood alone at the bottom of the cabinet. "This is going to sting, too," Eliot advised. Holding Sammy's hand still, Eliot unscrewed the cap of the brown bottle with his free hand and poured about a half of a teaspoon of the clear liquid over the cut. It did indeed sting, and Sammy had to bite her lip to keep from gasping, but the action proved to be unneeded because Eliot's lips were grazing her right ear and that was a mighty distraction. Stinging forgotten, her breathing had changed, as had her mood. Planting soft kisses on Sammy's neck, Eliot returned the cap to the bottle and returned the bottle to the cabinet, and closed said cabinet. As he leaned to the right toward a small, collapsible stack of shelves made of cheap plastic, Sammy twisted around and leaned back against the countertop surrounding the sink. Eliot said, "We'll just put a band aid on it, and you'll live to fight another day." Eliot smiled after retrieving a small box of Band-Aids ... featuring the amazing Spiderman. Sammy began to laugh loud and hard, and Eliot's smile became rueful as he opened the box.

"I don't know if this is adorable or kind of weird," Sammy said.

Delicately, Eliot wrapped a Band-Aid around the wound. He kissed it sweetly to ensure it would heal properly. He left the box on the counter, tossed the trash in the small, metal can near the toilet, and then snaked his arms around Sammy's waist. "I'm sure you find all of this incredibly charming."

Rolling her eyes, Sammy's laughter slowly subsided. "Oh, yeah; totally." She ran her healthy hand along her cheek a few times- a gesture of weariness that bothered Eliot. He remembered the conversation he had been trying to have in the kitchen.

"You know you can tell me anything, right, Sammy?" Eliot tenderly brushed the hair falling in her eyes back and did his best to tuck the bothersome long, layered and dark strands behind her ears. He loved her hair; it was always soft and his heart always stopped when the subtle blonde highlights would catch the sunlight. Her hair was perfect, the way it fell just past her shoulders and hung heavily about her round face. Eliot was taking all of Sammy in at the moment - not just her luscious locks - even though Sammy's round, dark brown eyes were not doing the same of him. Eliot supposed he was used to that, though- Sammy rarely looked in his eyes for more than a moment or two, but that was alright because the way her thick, pink lips would tremble before she spoke to him was enough for Eliot, for now. Sammy's nose, a little large for her face, would twitch sometimes when she tried to think of the right thing to say, as it was now. Sammy sighed heavily.

She answered, "Well, I know that I should know that." She looked into Eliot's eyes, and Eliot was exhilarated. He kissed Sammy deeply, using his hips to pin Sammy and keep her right where she was. Returning the affection, Sammy was just beginning to slide her palms and arms up Eliot's chest and around his neck so she could tangle her fingers in his unruly hair when Eliot stepped back, turned quickly, and headed back toward the kitchen.

"Don't want the sauce to burn," he called over his shoulder. Sammy wondered at the abrupt exit and thought perhaps she had done something wrong. After a moment of reflection, she followed Eliot.

"It smells wonderful," Sammy said, offering a compliment and announcing her arrival.

Eliot grinned. "I don't mean to brag, but I'm a pretty awesome cook." He poured the thin spaghetti into the pot of boiling water and then turned to Sammy. "Are you sure this is okay? I know you were upset before."

Sammy flushed and faltered. "Yeah, of course, but it's just …." She blinked back a few irritating tears and did her best to clear her throat. "Um, Rob made me seafood the last time I ever saw him." She looked at the ceiling and pressed her palms tight against one another. "I'm sorry. I'm trying really hard to, uh, be normal."

Eliot breathed deeply through his nose. He seemed upset. "No, I'm sorry, Sammy. I should have …." His arms flopped down to his sides as words failed him. Turning away from Sammy, back to the pasta, he slammed his hands against the cabinets above his head. Sammy flinched but continued to watch him breathlessly. When he spoke next, it sounded as if he did so through gritted teeth. "I can throw this all out, and we can go somewhere instead."

Sammy took a few steps toward Eliot. "That'd be stupid. I'm fine, Eliot, really." He wasn't looking at her and seemed to be somewhere else entirely. Nervously, Sammy rubbed her palms against her denim-clad thighs. "I've been looking forward to this, and I really, really want to have this dinner with you. Please, Eliot." He stayed stoic. Frustrated, desperate, Sammy moved to stand directly behind him. "I didn't get upset because I miss Rob. I mean, I do miss him, but it scared me more than anything else, because it made me put you in his place. Not that I want you to be Rob or anything like that, not at all because you're incredible, but I can't lose you like I lost him." Eliot still hadn't turned around and Sammy broke. Crying, she said, "I wouldn't survive losing you, Eliot." He spun quickly to face her, his face incredibly pale. Sammy covered her face with her hands, embarrassed. She was always saying too much too fast. Crying harder now, she said, "That was too intense. I'm sorry; I'm just really emotional and wanted you to acknowledge me, to look at me, but not like that."

Eliot took Sammy into his arms, and held her tightly. He mumbled apologies and reassurances against her hair, telling her he was sorry for being a jealous asshole who didn't want to be understanding and promising her that she wouldn't lose him, that Rob's murderer would be found and things could be and would be normal again.

The sauce burned.

The pasta boiled over.

Neither Eliot nor Sammy were in the mood for a horror movie, and as the food had become inedible, Eliot asked timidly, "Can I take you out?" Sammy nodded, and the two wound up at a nearby diner that was open for business 24 hours a day, 7 days a week.

After some classic burgers, fries and milkshakes both felt decidedly better. They had talked about lighter things, had laughed and smiled. Both were impossibly happy when Sammy headed back out to her car, ready to return home. He had kissed her goodnight, and she had to fight back tears when saying goodbye. She wanted to stay, to lie beside him and feel his warmth, to keep laughing in his strong, secure embrace. Sammy wanted to muffle giggles against his firm chest as he told amusing anecdotes. She didn't always want to be vulnerable and she was mortified by her behavior earlier that night.

The next day, Sammy was driving home from the local bookstore, late and alone, on a chilly October night. She couldn't remember the last time she'd been out so late with classes the next morning or if she had ever even done it before. She hoped the surprise change in schedule would make her tired enough to finally have a decent night's sleep so she could not think and not feel, if only for eight hours. Lately, Sammy had trouble sleeping. The old standby of simply tossing and turning had given way to waking with a start at all times of the night, sheets soaked through with sweat and pooled around her waist. Both her heart and her brain would be pounding fit to split; it was only in pain in which the two organs truly seemed to work in unison. Like an eager cheerleader at her first football game under the Friday night lights, Sammy's insides flipped, twirled and tumbled over and over until some ungodly hour when she remembered what it meant to be tired, or rather, absolutely exhausted. Eyelids slipping shut, Sammy would relax enough to lean back on her elbows and find a beautiful moment of peace. She watched moonlight filter through the blinds of her window and create silvery, slanted shafts of light on the cold, wooden bedroom floor, and at that exact moment, when she was finally relaxed enough to lay back against her soft, black pillows, the alarm would ring. Really, it was more annoying than anything else. And it had all started when Rob died.

No – she had better be precise. It had all started when Rob had been murdered.

Turning into her tiny driveway made of white concrete, Sammy noticed the one-story ranch was all dark. Not a single light was on inside. That made sense though – her sister was probably out and about on the town, and her parents and little brother had likely gone to bed hours ago, as was their routine. Sure, it was normal enough, but Sammy wanted someone to be awake so she'd have someone to talk to all about Eliot and what a pleasant and much needed surprise he had been. Walking up to the front door with her keys in hand, Sammy hoped that maybe Mom would just be leaving the bathroom or pouring a glass of water in the kitchen. That way she'd be able to catch her ear when the rush of emotions was fresh in her mind and she'd be better able to describe the way Eliot would wipe his mouth with the back of his hand when he became nervous or anxious. Or explain how his eyes burned so brightly that sweat would gather on her palms, on her eyelids, and in the small of her back whenever he looked at her. Mom would smile and say all the things Sammy wanted to hear, but Sammy had no such luck. The house slept peacefully as she locked the door behind her and made her way to her bedroom.

Weeks passed, and Eliot and Sammy became inseparable. They sat next to each other in class, walked each other to buildings and to their cars, and ate almost every meal together. They were in their own little world, a world that Sammy had only dreamed of. Every Shakespearean sonnet, every Molly Ringwald rant, every episode of "The O.C." seemed more real, more plausible, because it was happening to her. She couldn't remember ever being this happy, not even when her dad bought her tickets to see the Backstreet Boys or when they announced the last Harry Potter book would be made into two movies. All of her lonely, nerdy, desperate fantasies had been realized in the perfect Eliot. Perfect was the most appropriate and fitting definition for Eliot. Sammy thought lovingly of the young man as she stared at her face in the full-length mirror hanging on the back of her bedroom door. The dark circles that lingered beneath her eyes made her worried. She had seen Eliot every day that week, and he had commented on her appearance. Eliot asked if she was getting enough sleep, and, even though she said she was, Eliot knew she was lying and asked the awful but inevitable follow-up question: was she dreaming of Rob? No, she lied, and, facing her reflection, Sammy wasn't sure if she liked lying to Eliot so much. He wanted her to open up, but Sammy kept listening to Maeve and kept mum. Later that night, the window of her bedroom rattled loudly. With each vibration, her eyelids would open and close and flutter. Sammy longed for the pounding to cease and desist, ardently desired to peacefully drift off back to sleep. With closed eyes, she could better see her beautiful, brilliant man and could nearly feel his fingers journeying along her quivering lips, sliding sensually along her smooth neck and hesitating at her breasts. Whether it was Rob or Eliot, Sammy couldn't tell, but her eyes could not remain shut to continue the sordid dreams and fantasies because the rattling only grew louder. Groaning as she sat up, using her elbows, Sammy eyed the window. There stood Eliot. Sammy reached for her cell phone on the desk nearby, and was horrified to discover it was five-thirty in the morning. She climbed out of bed and trudged to the window groggily. "Eliot, what the hell are you doing here?"

"Get dressed and come outside."

"It's five thirty in the morning. The sun isn't even up yet."

"Yeah, but it will be soon, so hurry!"

"Why? What's going on? I thought you wanted me to get more sleep. This is kind of counterproductive, isn't it?"

Eliot leaned in the window to deeply kiss the young woman asking too many questions. "If you're not dressed in five minutes, I'll just grab you and take you as you are."

Sammy smiled. "That might not be so bad."

Eliot grabbed Sammy around the waist and began pulling her out through the window. Laughing, Sammy allowed herself to be dragged into the freezing, early hours. Eliot literally threw her over his shoulder and then deposited her in the passenger seat of his car. Her breath came in small, white puffs of smoke that vanished as quickly as they appeared. Fastening her seat belt, she asked Eliot about her open bedroom window.

"Don't worry about it," he breathed. "We won't be gone for too long." He started the engine and blasted the heat.

"So where are we going?"

Beginning to drive, Eliot kept both eyes on the road but only one hand on the wheel. The other rested on Sammy's thigh and would gently squeeze it in random intervals. "It's a surprise," he told her. Sammy's only response was a nod. She couldn't open her mouth to breathe, let alone speak, because her mouth couldn't be trusted. At any moment, and without warning, it could spew bile or assault Eliot in an embarrassingly desperate manner. His hand, strong and deliberate, slid slightly further up her thigh. "You're awfully quiet. Is everything okay?"

"Yes." She wondered if she could make her answers even shorter.

"Okay." Eliot's hand continued onward, and Sammy's cheeks burned red and hot when she wondered what that appendage would do when it ran out of terrain, when it conquered the offered territory and completed its sinful journey. Excitement consuming her middle and with her breath quickening, she turned to study Eliot's face. Looking very serious, Eliot's set and sturdy features gave no hint as to the thoughts running through his beautiful and brilliant head. He seemed to be completely and totally unaware of the riot he was inciting within the young woman beside him. His hand rested at the crossroads of thigh and hip, right in the crease. If asked at that moment for her name, birthday or social security number, Sammy would have only been able to blink stupidly. "You're going to love it."

"What?" Her tone was unable to be anything else but a husky whisper.

"You're going to love the surprise."

"Eliot."

"What?" He turned his head toward her direction, but only slightly.

"I, um," she swallowed hard, "just, I guess, wanted to say your name." Like an idiot, she laughed too loud.

Eliot smiled. "You're kind of fascinating to me."

"Wait – is this Longhill Road?"

Eliot smiled as he nodded. The rest of the ride was silent until they pulled into the scenic overlook. Eliot rushed out, opened Sammy's door for her, and then was busy at the trunk. Sammy couldn't exactly see what contents he was extracting from its recesses, because every time she got close, he nearly pushed her away. When the trunk finally did slam shut, Eliot walked along the far side of the car, and when Sammy made to follow him, he barked at her to stay still. Surprised by the harshness of Eliot's tone, Sammy froze where she stood. Unsure of what to do, Sammy pondered her situation until Eliot finally proclaimed that he was ready and called for Sammy to come around the front of the car. When she did, she nearly fainted. Eliot had laid out a soft-looking flannel blanket. There was a bottle of champagne, two glasses, and a box of chocolate-covered strawberries. She had to blink quickly and bite her bottom lip. "Since you refuse to get a good night's sleep, I thought that we could watch the sun come up together," Eliot said. He took Sammy's hand in his and together, they walked to the blanket. Sammy sat with her arms wrapped around herself as Eliot poured the champagne into the quaintglasses. A radio Sammy hadn't noticed before was softly playing Bruce Springsteen's greatest hits. With a contented sigh, Eliot sat beside Sammy and drank from his glass. "Have you ever seen the sun rise?"

Sammy snorted. "Not like this." She sipped from her glass. "Watching it by yourself as you finish a paper doesn't count, I don't think."

"But now you're with me, so this counts," Eliot grinned, kissing Sammy's earlobe quickly. The sky behind Eliot was a smoldering red, like the dying embers of a fire. The beautiful irony was a dark and intriguing background for Eliot; it concealed his darker characteristics – like his sturdy brows and strong chin - and infused him with the pre-dawn sky, so that the areas not encompassed by shadows were illuminated to a kind of eerie luminosity. The shadows that played across Eliot's face were the perfect metaphor for the idea of Eliot being concealed or concealing something. Sammy's creative mind made the abstract comparison easily and readily, and duplicity and doubt broke over her like the dawn over the horizon, but she pushed the thoughts away to be considered some other time. If there was one thing she definitely didn't want to do it was ruin the moment.

"Eliot."

"Yes?"

She smiled. "I just wanted to say your name again."

Eliot didn't return the grin or share in the joke. His face became serious as he leaned in to kiss her. Their tongues disco danced as he climbed on top, forcing her onto her back. Sammy's glass spilled against the frosted grass but went unnoticed as her pajama clad legs slid against Eliot's denim covered legs. Collapsing his body, Eliot's hips dug into hers. Her hands wound in his hair as he slid his body impatiently along the front of hers. The rays of the up and coming sun breached the edge of the cliff. The new light burned and blazed, and Sammy turned her head towards it. Her dark eyes burst open and she gasped for air when she felt Eliot's cold hand sneak beneath her shirt. Staring at the sun without fear for her retinas, she felt Eliot grope her breast. Shaking and trembling, she released a breath she didn't know she had been holding. Her muscles relaxed more and more as Eliot's hands focused on holding her, simply embracing her. He kissed her lips quickly, smiling. "Did I miss it?"

"What?" she asked. Sammy squirmed beneath the perfect pressure of his body to get more comfortable.

"Did I miss the sunrise?"

She laughed softly. "You didn't miss anything." They stayed like that, one's weight crushing the other; one's weight supporting the other, with layered smiles and beautifully complex eye contact until the album finished playing, until Bruce Springsteen ran like he was born to do it.

Eliot parked alongside the fenced edge of Sammy's front yard. She held his hand tightly in hers. "Do you want to come in for breakfast?"

Eliot grinned. "How would your parents react?"

Her face fell. "Shit! They don't know I'm gone!" Hurriedly and with a thousand and one possible tortures leveled against her by her parents poking at the corners of her imagination, she quickly kissed Eliot's lips and fled his car. Her bare feet bolted across the iced lawn and helped her to scramble back inside her open bedroom window.

"They better get here soon or I'm leaving."

Maeve rolled her eyes with a heavy, dramatic sigh. "Knock it off. They're, like, two minutes late, Michael. I'm sure they'll be here soon."

"Yeah, but I'm starving," Mike whined.

"You had a sandwich before we left!"

Mike grinned. "So?"

"You're hopeless." Maeve leaned across the table to softly kiss his lips. She went to seat herself again, but Mike kept her standing to kiss her for a second and third time. They were in the middle of their embrace when Sammy and Eliot approached the table.

"Oh, are we interrupting?" Sammy asked, smiling. Maeve's face burned red, and she sat down quickly. Mike, however, was unashamed.

"What do you expect when you keep people waiting for forever?"

Sammy rolled her eyes. "Please, we're like two minutes late, Michael." They laughed together as Mike rose to hug her. After their friendly greeting, Sammy looked back to Eliot who was timidly standing behind her. He was smoothing the front of his shirt for the thousandth time with hands that shook – but only slightly. With an encouraging smirk, Sammy took Eliot's hand in hers and pulled him forward. "Mike, this is Eliot."

Smiling warmly, Mike extended his hand to Eliot, which Eliot took willingly, and they shook. As the grip continued, Mike assessed Eliot. He looked okay, but there was something slightly off about him. As discreet as the smell of spoiled food creeping up the basement stairs or kitchen garbage that needs to be changed, something indiscernible about Eliot instantly made Mike feel uneasy. Maybe it was the impact of Maeve's phone call the other day, in which she complained about never seeing Sammy because Eliot had monopolized all of her time. Or maybe it was because

Maeve also found Eliot inexplicably charming, but Mike didn't think so. Eager to be free of Eliot's hand, Mike sat. He watched as Maeve and Eliot exchanged greetings.

"It's nice to meet you," Eliot said with a grin. He pulled out Sammy's chair and watched her intently as she sat. He pushed Sammy's chair closer to the table before sitting beside her. "I'm sorry we're late. It's my fault. Did you order yet?"

"Of course not," Maeve replied. "We were waiting for you."

Eliot's smile began to fade. "Thank you for waiting. Sammy, would you like a menu?" Turning to his date, Eliot handed her the discussed item. Worried by the paleness creeping near the edges of his face, his beloved face, Sammy gave his hand a quick squeeze beneath the table. She hoped he found it reassuring and encouraging and added a sweet smile just to be sure. Taking the menu with her free hand and thanking Eliot, Sammy helped the idle and polite dinner conversation along. She and Maeve discussed professors, with Mike chiming in every now and then to ask where the waiter was and to announce loudly that he was starving. Eliot was unusually quiet – he seemed to be dining only with Sammy, as he stared at her and looked to her before answering any kind of question. Sammy was oblivious to Eliot's odd behavior – she was completely engaged in what she believed to be an amusing anecdote about one of the younger, more attractive English professors. Mike was observant, though.

"So Eliot, do you work?" He asked the question to draw Eliot out from behind the wall he had built around himself, out of Sammy's admiration.

Eliot's eyes darted to Sammy, but she was still laughing with Maeve about something about someone. "Yes," Eliot said, startled. He looked to Mike.

Mike laughed awkwardly. "What do you do, if you don't mind me asking?" There was an extra quality to Mike's tone that silenced the conversation between the young ladies.

Eliot neatly folded his hands, stealing glances at Sammy in precise intervals. "While I'm at school, I'm a landscaper for a local business. During the winter, spring and summer breaks, I help my parents with the administrative responsibilities of the mental asylum near our home."

Mike leaned forward, resting his forearms on the table. "You work at a mental asylum?"

"Yes. I, uh, help report on the patients and do a lot of paperwork."

"You never told me that," Sammy said.

Eliot turned to her, relief washing over his face. "I didn't want you to think I was crazy."

Mike snorted. "That's funny."

Maeve bit the insides of her cheeks to keep from laughing. "I think Mike means it's silly to think Sammy would think you were crazy just for working at an asylum. I interned at an asylum last summer, but Sammy doesn't think I'm a nut job."

Eliot nodded, looking at Maeve pointedly. "You're probably right, but spend enough time around the insane and you begin to wonder." Silence descended upon the table as Eliot's words slowly sank in. "That was a joke, but I guess it was a bad one. Sorry to have brought the mood down," Eliot said, gulping hard, "so how about I go to the bar and order us all a round of drinks?" He got to his feet, kissing the top of Sammy's head. "The waiter is taking forever, as Mike has informed us many times over. If he comes back while I'm gone, can you order me something, Sammy?"

She nodded. A sincere smile stretched her full lips smooth. "What do you want?"

He winked at her. "Surprise me."

Sammy watched Eliot head to the bar with sickening sweetness in her eyes. When she turned to her friends, the expression changed drastically as both Maeve and Mike began cracking up. Sweetness souring at an alarming rate, all that was left in her eyes was anger, fierce and unrelenting. "What the hell is so funny?"

"I'm sorry," Maeve said, laughter subsiding, "but you two are the weirdest couple ever."

"Why? Because he's beautiful and I'm not?"

"Sammy, don't be like that. It has nothing to do with looks. You throw yourself at him like he's some Greek god, but he's really a nervous wreck," Mike said.

"Yeah," Maeve agreed. "It's cute, really. There's no need to be all defensive."

"I guess I just don't understand why you have to dissect us."

Maeve was getting angry. "What the hell are you talking about? We're trying to have a nice dinner."

"Then what's with the interrogation?"

"Sammy, chill. I just asked him about his work." Mike rested his hand on top of Maeve's, willing her to calm down. "We're sorry we laughed. You know we didn't mean anything by it."

Sammy was pouting like a kid. She knew she had overreacted but didn't really want to apologize. She mumbled that everything was okay. Maeve, however, had not had her say.

"If we saw you more, you'd remember what it was like to kid around."

"What, I can't spend time with Eliot?"

"I'm not saying that, Sammy, and you know it."

"You're allowed to spend all this time with Mike and drag me around, but the second I'm not around to be a third wheel, there's a problem."

"Don't be a bitch."

The raised voices were starting to draw attention. Aware of the eyes slyly turning in the direction of the table, Mike cleared his throat loudly. "Let's calm down. Okay?"

"I brought him here tonight to meet my best friends, not to face a firing squad," Sammy hissed.

"Best friends? That's funny, because once Eliot started coming around we were so easily forgotten."

Mike touched Maeve's arm. "Eliot's buying us all drinks, babe. He'll be back any minute, so all is forgotten, all right?"

Maeve nodded. "Sure. I'll just forget the whole thing." She rolled her eyes to Sammy's.

"That's fine by me."

An uncomfortable silence settled atop the table like a thick, rolling fog. It blocked out the light, and prevented those trapped within it from properly seeing one another. It greeted Eliot coldly when he returned. "I hope everyone enjoys beer." He handed each person a bottle before sitting beside Sammy once again. "What did I miss? Did the waiter come by?"

"No, but thank you very much for the drinks," Sammy said, and she pointedly kissed Eliot on the lips in an almost embarrassing public display of affection. Were Maeve blessed enough to have eyes that could shoot out red hot lasers the couple across the table would have been nice and crispy.

"How long have you been a landscaper?" Mike asked, in an obvious attempt to end the embrace.

"I just started recently, actually. I'm refraining from dipping into my trust fund too much." Eliot laughed, but he was the only one who did.

"Do you come from money?" Maeve asked.

"Yes. I am fortunate enough to have parents who have worked very hard."

"My parents still work hard," Maeve replied quickly.

"No one said that they didn't," Sammy said through gritted teeth.

"Is everything okay?" Eliot asked. "If I have offended, then I sincerely apologize."

"No, you haven't." Sammy's response was clipped. With uncanny timing, that damned waiter finally showed up. He had the audacity to ask if they were ready to order. Mike had half a mind to tell him that they had been ready, and clearly he was the one they were waiting on, but a swift kick under the table from Maeve got him to think only about food. Eliot ordered a steak, rare as it could be, with mashed potatoes and vegetables. Sammy ordered seared salmon with vegetables. Maeve had to special order some fajitas, insisting that the impending deliciousness was worth the current aggravation with the waiter, and Mike also ordered the steak, though he wanted to be sure his was dead. He didn't want to be able to still hear it moo.

Conversation was sporadic and increasingly superficial as they waited for their meals. Drinks were refreshed, but the liquid did little to lubricate the tongues and ease the tension slowly, but surely, mounting. Mike made the best of it, facing Sammy as they heatedly discussed the New York Giants' chance at the playoffs.

"So where have you been hiding Sammy?" Maeve asked, turning to Eliot. Her tone was pleasant enough, but the jest was tainted with truth.

Smiling, Eliot replied, "We went to the movies last night and saw *Shutter Island*. It was really good. Have you seen it?"

"No. Sammy and I were supposed to see it together."

"Oh. Um ...." Eliot faltered.

"All your friends are back in Maine?" Maeve continued.

"Yes, and all of my family is back in Ellsworth as well."

"So Sammy's all you have?"

Eliot turned to bestow a loving glance upon the woman beside him. "You could say that, yes."

"Don't you think that's a lot of pressure on her?"

"What do you mean?"

Maeve leaned back in her seat. "She's not a psychiatrist. She's just Sammy."

Eliot cleared his throat. "I'm well aware of that. I'm not the one advising her to change her behaviors."

"What is that supposed to mean?" Maeve asked, her tone turning deadly.

"Ah, food's here!" Mike said with a grin.

The waiter, with a penguin-looking entourage, delivered each plate to its respective owner. Blood pooled around the slab of meat on Eliot's white china plate. He eyed it hungrily, mumbling to Sammy that it looked delicious. Reaching across the table, he grabbed a golden brown dinner roll, ripped it savagely in half, and began to sop up the crimson liquid. The three other dinner guests watched with expressions trapped somewhere between incredulity and grotesque intrigue as he bit into the roll, soaked through with blood. The juice, because Sammy couldn't call it blood even in her mind, ran from the corner of his lip to his chin. Without thinking, she reached out and wiped the crimson trail. Eliot smiled at her and winked, and Sammy did her best to keep up appearances, smiling back dutifully. However, her attention was drawn to the blood on her thumb. She stared at it, unsure of what it meant and what business it had there, before wiping her thumb clean with a white, linen napkin, which would never be the same again. The white had been distorted and even destroyed by the red. It was tainted; it would always be different from all the other napkins and everyone would notice.

"Sammy? Are you still with us?" Maeve asked. Her penetrating eyes worried Sammy. Had Maeve been able to tell what she had just been thinking?

"Yeah, sorry. I just can't believe how good this all looks." She smiled and dug into her meal. Unsure of what else to say or do, Maeve and Mike followed suit.

As the meal was consumed, Mike couldn't help but believe that Eliot was staring at him. As his white teeth tore apart the meat on his plate, Eliot stayed focused on Mike, almost as if he were sizing him up for some kind of battle. Mike ate just as ravenously, but felt Eliot's burning eyes go dead as they noted how Mike cut his food, sipped from his glass, rubbed his palm across the back of his neck quickly and calmly breathed in and out with any thought. Of course Mike noticed – how could he not? Eliot's eyes were as strong as low-hanging lights in a claustrophobic interrogation room. They radiated head and discomfort.

Check paid, couples parting, Sammy sat in Eliot's car. They were letting the engine run, letting it warm up. Sammy had been checking her lipstick in the rearview mirror when an audible click from beside her made her jump. Eliot had pulled a pocket knife from somewhere and was cleaning his fingernails, and even his teeth, with the shiny blade. Feeling Sammy's eyes upon him, Eliot turned to engage her, winking at her and keeping his eyes locked on her. Sammy couldn't turn away; her breath caught in her throat and a million inarticulate thoughts screamed in her brain, the result being that something felt wrong, really wrong. Noting the distance in demeanor, Eliot put his pocket knife away. "Sorry – it's a habit from country living, I guess. The part of Maine where I live is very rural, and no one would think twice about cleaning their teeth and fingernails with a pocket knife." He sighed, laughing. "I guess I just feel so comfortable with you that I let things slip."

Sammy reached out to touch his leg gently. "Don't feel like you have to be somebody you're not or anything like that."

"I know, I know. I just feel like you have these grandiose expectations for me in your mind and I'd hate to let you down. Maeve told me I'm putting too much pressure on you." Eliot turned his eyes to the air vents in the car, blushing deeply.

"You're not putting pressure on me. What exactly did Maeve say?"

"You can be honest with me, Sammy. If you want some time apart, that's fine."

Bile was rising in Sammy's throat. "What are you talking about? I don't want that, and I never said that I did."

"Well, Maeve seems to be under the impression that I'm making you change and putting too much pressure on you. You have to understand that was never my intention."

Sammy, eyes widening, shook her head frantically from side to side. "She's wrong, Eliot. I never told her anything! I haven't even talked to her in, like, a month."

"Then why would she say something like that?"

Sammy slowed her shaking head. "I don't know. She just doesn't like us spending so much time together. *She* thinks you're changing me, and she's putting words into my mouth to break us up."

"She's your best friend, Sammy. Would she really do that?"

A bitter, biting cold settled over Sammy. She held herself in her arms and squirmed uncomfortably. Just the thought of Maeve plotting some sabotage made her sick to her stomach. Sammy had a fast-acting desire to lie down or maybe gargle some ginger ale and chew on some crackers. "I don't know. I don't know her anymore."

Eliot took her hand in his. "Don't say that. This is just a new situation you both have to get used to." Eliot kissed her lips. "Let's go back to my place and not think about it anymore tonight, okay?"

Sammy kissed his lips. "That sounds like a plan."

Meanwhile, Maeve and Mike had climbed into Mike's car simultaneously. Mike started the engine as Maeve buckled herself in and started her analysis of Sammy and Eliot. "Is it just me, or was that actually physically painful?"

Mike laughed softly. "Well, it wouldn't make the top ten lists of best dinners ever."

Maeve snorted. "Do you think Sammy really didn't see the creepiness of it all when there was actual blood running down his chin? I like you a whole lot Mike, but eating raw meat is most definitely a deal breaker."

Mike turned in his seat to make sure he could back out of the parking space without causing any vehicular damage, pressing his right hand against the headrest of Maeve's seat for leverage. "To be fair, babe, there's a difference between rare and raw. Eliot's eating habits or preferences are whatever; what got under my skin was the way he was staring at me." Mike gracefully reversed the car out of the parking spot and drove towards the lot's exit. "Did you notice?"

"What do you mean by staring?"

"Like, glaring at me, like he was trying to intimidate me or something," Mike said, gripping the steering wheel in pulsating waves as he tried to make himself clear.

Maeve turned towards Mike with her face set very seriously. "Are you threatened by Eliot?"

Mike chanced a quick succession of brief glances at Maeve. "No- I don't think he'd ever try to hurt me or anything, but there's definitely something weird about the kid, and he's working hard to hide it, so hard that it just makes it more obvious, you know? Well, more obvious to everyone except Sammy."

Appraising her significant other as if she were incredibly intrigued, Maeve mindlessly chewed on her pinky nail and mumbled, "Dually noted."

"What did you say?" Mike asked.

Maeve seemingly snapped back to reality, eyes widening, and she shook her head sharply, like her mind could be less cluttered and more attentive that way. "If Sammy refuses to see Eliot for who he really is, then we'll have to be extra vigilant."

Mike's car rolled to a stop smoothly at a red traffic light. "What do you mean, for who he really is? He's just weird, not dangerous." He turned to Maeve, suddenly nervous. "Do you think he's dangerous? Has he done something to Sammy?"

Maeve shook her head more pointedly this time, frustration seeping in at the edges of her frame. "No, I don't think he's dangerous, but you just said you were afraid of him."

"What!" Mike roared in disbelief. "Those words never came out of my mouth! They never even entered my mind! All I said was that he was trying to stare me down at dinner, and that it was weird!"

147

"Michael, why are you yelling?"

Mike's own frustration flooded his frame and saturated his countenance. His face was so red it positively glowed. When he spoke, he tried to be reserved, and his tone was even for the most part. "I don't mean to yell. I'm just trying to be understood."

Traffic was flowing again, and as Mike redirected his attention to the road, Maeve turned to gaze out of the window. "If Eliot makes you this hysterical, I'll change the subject."

"Please," Mike said, barking a humorless laugh. "You were the one who brought him up as soon as he was out of earshot, and you nearly fought Sammy during dinner. If anything, he makes *you* hysterical. Apparently, this dude really gets under *your* skin, not mine, and that's also kind of strange. I mean, what did he ever do to you?"

Maeve snapped her head to glare at Mike. "He took my best friend away from me and is now forcing me to fight with my boyfriend." She paused a moment. "Can we not talk about this anymore?"

"Gladly," Mike consented through gritted teeth. The rest of the ride back to Maeve's apartment was silent.

Mike walked Maeve to her apartment door. The mood was so awkward that it caused the both of them to be physically uncomfortable. Mike cleared his throat and spoke softly. "Alright … well, I'll talk to you tomorrow."

Maeve, pale, stopped unlocking her door to turn fully to Mike. "Aren't you still going to spend the night?"

Shrugging, Mike shoved his hands into the pockets of his pants and casted his glance downward. "I didn't think you'd still want me to."

"Of course I do," Maeve said. She stepped towards Mike with a heavy sigh. "I'm really sorry about what I said in the car. I was looking for a fight and turned my aggression from Sammy to you. That wasn't fair, and it was totally stupid. Sammy and Eliot aren't part of us, and I need to remember that."

Mike freed his hands of his pockets to wrap Maeve in a warm, strong embrace. "I'm sorry too, babe. I shouldn't have yelled and should have understood you were just upset about Sammy." He stepped back, keeping Maeve within his reach to study her face. "Sammy's your best friend, though, and that makes her a part of you, which is obviously a part of us."

"Maybe that's changing." Maeve crossed her thin arms over her chest. "Maybe Sammy and I aren't as good of friends as I thought." Her eyes lost focus and she shrugged coolly. "Whatever; it's late. Let's go to bed, okay?" Maeve turned back to her apartment door and Mike patiently waited to follow her inside. He had no problem with ending the conversation- he hated fighting, especially when no plausible resolution was readily available. It made him feel helpless. He also didn't care to dwell on the odd effect Eliot seemed to have on Maeve – how angry and crazy he made her. He didn't like the way his girlfriend had so readily dismissed Sammy, either; that wasn't like Maeve. Maeve was severely loyal to those she cared about. Mike wondered if maybe Maeve was really just tired and anxious to shy away from the emotionally intense and intellectually heavy issues, at least until the morning. Mike seconded that train of thought and did his best to force his mind to go blank as he followed Maeve inside her apartment, shutting and locking the door behind him.

Dinner with Maeve and Mike had been a bust, and both couples had avoided each other for several days afterward. Maeve and Mike were content to continue onward as they always had been, though Maeve did miss her best friend. When Mike did something especially sweet and charming, or when he was driving her up a wall, she would call Sammy and feel better, no matter what the circumstance. That option was gone now. It was no longer available to her, because Eliot was providing Sammy with everything she believed she wanted and needed. Eliot could give Sammy things Maeve never could, but it still hurt to see how easily Maeve was swept under the rug or placed upon the shelf; so easily forgotten. Mike noticed the toll it was taking on Maeve and wondered if Sammy noticed, or would even care if she had.

Sammy would have cared if she had noticed, but things with Eliot had been so phenomenal. He had dinner with her parents, which went beautifully, much better than the fiasco with Maeve and Mike. Her father, a large and sturdy man with a peppered mustache that covered his thin upper lip, had been overly friendly. Sammy felt her face flush and muscles tense as her father made wildly inappropriate comments about everything from Eliot's appearance to Sammy's fidgeting to his wife's cooking. Sammy's mother was sterner. Pleasant, but removed, she observed Eliot from a calculating distance. With her thin blonde hair and sharp green eyes, Sammy's mother let her pointer finger rest just above her upper lip as she noted Eliot's confidence. This young man was not at all worried about meeting his girlfriend's parents, and that worried his girlfriend's mother. Over fried chicken, mashed potatoes with country gravy, and corn, Sammy's father talked about being raised in the deep South by a frazzled mother and cruel stepfather, and Eliot listened intently. The two women at the table did not speak very much at all; both were watching the interaction, and both were hedging their bets. Once Eliot had gone home, and Sammy's father had praised Eliot, both released a deep breath. Sammy's mother believed her daughter to be in good hands, and Sammy believed Eliot's greatness was not all in her head.

Eliot surprised Sammy with gifts, called regularly, and was just so damn perfect it made her worried that one day she would wake up, and he would be gone. She clung to him all the tighter, and while she did miss Maeve, she needed Eliot now. He was like an IV, and without him giving her sustenance in the form of doting affection and attention, she would surely perish. Sammy wanted to be defined by love, and she was choosing to be defined by Eliot's. Without it she would no longer be a person.

Chapter Seven

Dreams are Lies the Mind Tells

*"There's blood in my mouth 'cause I've been biting
my tongue all week."* ~ Rilo Kiley

Eliot smiled broadly, holding the door to his apartment open wide for Sammy to enter. Amicably, she nodded and continued inside, trying to step lightly and gracefully through the threshold. Her heels clicked lightly against the wooden floor, as did the door when Eliot shut it behind her. "Have a seat, Sammy," Eliot offered. "I just have to grab my jacket and slip on my shoes."

"Okay," she smiled and smoothed her dress against her bottom before she sat. She had been in Eliot's apartment before, plenty of times in fact, but not in such fancy attire. They had been dating for a little over two months now, and Eliot had gotten the notion in his head that it was worth some grand sort of celebration. Though he intended on keeping the festivities a surprise, Sammy surmised they were off to some fancy restaurant where the appetizers would cost as much as the entrees and waiters with violins would stand beside the tables. Why else would he have asked her to wear something so formal? Self-consciously, she picked at the buckle on her heels and offered up another silent prayer, asking to not fall and to not embarrass Eliot.

"All right, let's head out." Eliot had appeared at the end of the hallway. His voice, which she had once found husky and painfully alluring, and which she still did, matched his appearance. He looked like a dream or a gift, or something equally as cliché. He was the image of perfection; dark, brown hair elegantly disheveled in such a way that was reminiscent of the leading men covering her bedroom walls. But Eliot was not made of paper, was not one of her sordid creations of ink. He was made of flesh and blood, and he was standing before her, wanting to take her out. It was not easily believed, and her eyes burned with tears. His unblemished skin, with varying tones of handsome youth playing throughout, would be soft and warm beneath her trembling fingertips. It would yield to her touch, turn into it even. His pale, thin lips would travel where they liked, wherever they saw fit. Rough, calloused hands would tangle in her hair, slide down her back and grip her waist, and it would be physical, but it would be more than that, as it always had been and always would be. Like in the way he knew she was childish and immature and melodramatic and unrealistic, and how he took all of that in stride. It was the way he wasn't perfect, and was willing to be whatever she needed when she needed it. It wasn't the healthiest of relationships, and it wasn't the most logical, but it worked. Eliot held out his hand to Sammy and she took it eagerly, as she had before and as she always would.

Eliot led Sammy outside the apartment building. They hadn't conversed during the short trip down the hallway, down the elevator, or out onto the street. For her part, Sammy had been quiet because she hadn't known what to say. She had been trying to fill up all kinds of silences in her life since she had learned how to talk. It hadn't served her particularly well as it only made her seem awkward, obnoxious, and stupid. She gladly stayed silent. For Eliot's part, he was content to feel the weight of Sammy's hand in his own. He had never had someone reach for his hand, and had never had any reason to take someone else's. This … thing, this force, this phenomenon with Sammy was something entirely new and something Eliot feared he was beginning to need. As a result, he wasn't about to let it go.

Eliot wanted the evening to be special. He had been planning it for about a week to completely sweep Sammy off her feet- she'd never be able to forget it. He had watched her shift nervously from heel to heel as he locked his door, had observed her deep inhales and shaky exhales she no doubt had intended to be discreet. Clearly Sammy was nervous, but Eliot believed she was more excited than nervous, which was perfect and right where Eliot wanted her. In her heightened emotional state, he believed Sammy would be willing to try crazier things and to be more accepting of crazier behaviors. It wasn't until they were in Eliot's car and travelling that Sammy cleared her throat and spoke. "So, uh, where is it that we're going exactly?"

Eliot smirked. "It's a surprise, which is the same answer I gave you the last three times you asked me in my apartment."

Laughing lightly, Sammy ran slightly trembling fingers along her lips. "I know, I know. It's just- shit, you make me nervous and anxious enough when I know what we're doing."

Color crept into Eliot's cheeks, but he turned his face just enough to keep it hidden from Sammy. "It's not like you don't make me nervous."

Sammy began to laugh louder, as she found Eliot's remark utterly ridiculous. "What are you talking about? How could I possibly make you nervous?"

"Well, I want to make you happy, and you've been so unhappy for so long that I think you've become complacent to it, which makes my job harder." Eliot shifted uncomfortably in the driver's seat. He did not want to psychoanalyze Sammy. He did not want to risk a deep, revealing conversation. Smirk returning, Eliot said, "Plus, you're crazy. So I'm nervous I'll wake up one morning and you'll have my liver chilling on ice in a bathtub."

Sammy threw her head back in laughter and clapped once. "You know, it's a good thing you're funny because, really, what else do you have going for you?"

Eliot laughed quietly beside Sammy and reached for her hand. "And this is why I love being with you." He gave Sammy's hand a gentle squeeze, which she returned eagerly.

That night they went dancing. They were the youngest couple there and decidedly out of place, but that made the night all the more special.

Another night they went bowling.

They saw football games.

They watched movies.

They ate dinner.

The point of the matter is that they did everything together.

Standing before the counter against the far wall of the dining hall, Sammy's mind went blank. She knew she hadn't walked all the way over there for no reason. She'd been so scattered lately, and had been having an incredibly hard time staying focused on anything. If it wasn't Rob's face emblazoned upon her eyelids, it was Eliot's face, and neither would let her sleep or concentrate. For God's sake, she was failing at collecting plastic cutlery! Sammy pulled her hair back and turned around fast, knocking the tray of an innocent bystander to the floor and out of his or her hands. Chicken soared up to the sky and then came crashing to the dirty, tiled floor. Fries complete with ketchup splattered against the nearest table, and Styrofoam and plastic fell to the ground. Arm covered in condiments, she immediately began apologizing. "I am so sorry! I'll swipe you more food, whatever you want, dessert too!"

He looked up at her, laughing. "It's okay, really. Just relax, Sammy."

She focused on the young man collecting trash from the floor, kneeling before her. "Mike?" she asked. Her best friend's boyfriend; how had she missed him?

"Duh - what is with you? I was calling your name, and you didn't even turn around. Well, you did, but ...." He laughed again. "Did you just get here?"

"Yeah, I got food and found a table, but then I needed stuff," she rambled. Sammy bent to help Mike pick up the last scattered pieces of chicken and fries.

"Are you sitting with anyone?"

Sammy raised an eyebrow. "No. Why would I be?"

Mike raised an eyebrow of his own. Sammy wasn't behaving normally. Not that Mike would have described Sammy as normal, but she was being weird even for her, and that certainly was saying something. "What is up with you?" Straightening up, Mike stood and tossed the tray in the trash can. "Don't be so defensive, Sammy. I only asked to see if you wanted to sit with Maeve and me."

"Oh." Blushing, Sammy made her eyes focus on the floor. She remembered earlier that day, when Maeve had been sitting alone at a large table near the front of Dickinson Hall, trying to sell cupcakes, cookies, muffins and other assorted baked goods to raise funds for the psychology club. Sammy had practically run past the table, without so much as a greeting, let alone any monetary contribution. Maeve had likely been furious, and Sammy couldn't apologize for her behavior when she didn't do anything wrong, really, but Maeve would be expecting one, and it was an awful game of friendly politics Sammy wanted no part of. She'd have to decline Mike's invitation. "Sorry. I mean, thanks for the invite, but I better not."

"Why can't you sit with us?"

Sighing, Sammy moved to tuck her hair behind her ears. Mike, gasping, reached out to stop her. "What?" she asked, alarmed by Mike's sudden concern.

"You're going to get ketchup and shit all in your hair."

"Gross."

Mike snorted laughter. "Here," he said, handing her a pile of napkins he now had no use for.

"Thanks." With a pinched look of disgust and discomfort, Sammy began to wipe the condiments from her assorted limbs.

"No problem. Don't miss the mustard on your left elbow." His grin never left his face, so it was evident that Mike was clearly enjoying Sammy's misfortune. Anger threatened to consume her, like ravenous, wild dogs going after a prime cut of beef. It was only kept at bay by the very same element that fueled it – Mike's simple but genuine amusement. It had been long, too long, since Sammy had laughed at herself. Lately, she had adopted the nasty habit of taking herself too seriously. Smiling despite her nasty habits and best efforts not to, Sammy finished cleaning up and tossed the napkins in the trash can. "So, are you going to come eat with us or what?" Mike asked again.

"I don't know. The last time I saw you guys it was pretty awkward."

Mike shrugged indifferently. "So?"

"It'll be awkward again."

"Only if you let it be that way." Mike slapped her playfully on the arm. "Just come on."

She chewed on her lower lip in thought. "Okay, but if gets weird then ... Eliot?"

"What?"

Sammy shifted her eyes to Mike. "I'm sorry, but Eliot just walked in, and he'll want us to eat together." She waved and Mike turned to see the tool in the plaid shirt clumsily make his way through the crowded dining hall. Sammy had often employed adjectives such as "graceful" and "effortless" when she spoke of Eliot. Mike didn't see it, and honestly, he never had. He thought Eliot was just another guy trying too hard to not try at all. He turned back to Sammy.

"Are you being serious?"

Sammy was confused. "What, Mike?"

"Sammy!" Eliot immediately slipped an arm around her waist and kissed her not-so-chastely on the mouth. Rolling his eyes, Mike found the ceiling very interesting all of a sudden.

"Hey," she smiled. "Eliot, you remember Mike."

Mike extended his hand and forced his lips to curl into an expression halfway between a grin and a grimace. "Hello."

"Hello. It's nice to see you again." Though he shook Mike's hand amicably enough, Eliot's tone of voice was odd. There was a disconnect somewhere, and his words rang false. Eliot turned to Sammy and asked, "Where are we sitting?"

"Actually," Mike began before Sammy had a chance to respond, "I just invited Sammy to come and eat with Maeve and me. You're more than welcome to tag along."

Mike's words seemed to physically irritate Eliot, like some appalling parasite crawling beneath the skin and making it itch. Eliot did not turn to Mike, but remained focused on Sammy. "It's up to you, Sammy. Where would you like to sit?"

The nausea came in waves. She was strongly reminded of the importance of seats when it came to Eliot, how he could sit anywhere and be fabulous, but she was another story. Sammy felt the most obvious choice was to sit with Eliot removed from Maeve and Mike, even though it would not make things better, and Mike would definitely be pissed. Frowning, Sammy knew such a decision would only serve to infuriate Maeve further. Sitting and dining with the other couple would repair relationships, maybe, but Sammy wondered at what cost to her relationship with Eliot. "Um, I think that, well, it might be best, maybe, if Eliot and I ate lunch by ourselves, you know."

"Why?" Mike's tone was sharp. He had no intention of letting things go.

Sammy rubbed her sweating palms together. "It's just that I feel like maybe everyone will be more comfortable that way."

"No," Mike argued, shaking his head. "You're doing what's easiest instead of what's right, and that's fucked up."

"Hey," Eliot interjected. "You don't have to talk to her like that."

"I've known Sammy for a while, alright chief? If I'm offending her, she can tell me."

"Is there a problem? I don't understand where all of the hostility is coming from." Eliot crossed his arms over his chest. Sammy could feel the tension mounting, climbing at an alarming rate to dangerous levels. Gripping Eliot's shoulders in her hands as she moved to stand behind him, Sammy began to push him past Mike to the secluded corner of the cafeteria where her claimed table waited.

"Can we get lunch another time, Mike?" she asked.

"You tell me."

Sammy sighed. "Let me show Eliot where we're sitting, and then I'll come back and swipe your lunch, alright?"

"Fine."

Sammy led Eliot to the table. "I think it's better if you stay here."

"But I haven't gotten my food yet!" Eliot complained, sliding his bag from his shoulder to an empty chair.

"I'll use my meal plan and swipe you some food like I'm doing for Mike," Sammy offered, gently rubbing her aching forehead. "What do you want?"

"This is ridiculous," Eliot grumbled. He walked past Sammy and past where Mike remained standing. Entering the line, he shot Sammy a meaningful look before disappearing amidst the hungry students. This was wrong, all wrong. Maeve, Mike, Sammy and Eliot were all supposed to be best friends and hang out together all the time. Eliot's charm should have impressed the couple, and his intriguing character could make for hours of interesting and entertaining conversation. Completely annoyed, clenching and unclenching her fists, Sammy marched up to Mike.

"Let's go, and make this quick."

"Why are you so upset?"

She threw her hair into a sloppy bun, letting loose strands fall where they may. "You didn't have to be so rude."

Mike scoffed. "Did you give this same speech to your Romeo?"

"No. Why would I when he only defended me?"

"Yeah, I'm surprised he didn't just lift his leg and piss."

Rolling her eyes, Sammy started walking toward the line. "You are the most vulgar human being I have ever met."

Grinning, Mike followed. "Are you honestly telling me you didn't think the way he marched over and stuck his tongue down your throat was weird?"

"No," Sammy said. She bit the inside of her cheek to keep from beaming. She knew she wouldn't be able to withstand the onslaught of taunts from Mike. "I thought it was sweet." She pushed through the turnstile, and Mike followed suit.

"He treated me like a threat. Didn't you notice?"

"That's absurd," Sammy said. She reached in the nearest freezer for a bottle of soda. "You're Maeve's boyfriend. Eliot knows that. We all had dinner together, remember?"

"Yeah, and he was bizarre that night too. He drank blood, essentially, and gave me the death stare."

"No he didn't."

Mike stopped short behind her. "You're blind."

She had to grunt to keep from screaming. "What am I blind to?"

"To everything I just said and the fact that you've totally been ignoring Maeve to hang out with Eliot. You have other friends, too."

Her jaw dropped. "Maeve's been telling you bad stuff about Eliot this whole time, hasn't she? She's gotten to you!"

Mike shut his eyes and rubbed the bridge of his nose. "Don't talk like there's some conspiracy against you and Eliot. There isn't one."

"Really? Because you could have fooled me!" Sammy began digging in her pockets. "I thought the two of you would want me to be happy."

"Stop that bullshit right now." Mike was ready to launch into a whopper of a lecture and demand that Sammy stop the melodramatics, but paused as he became interested in Sammy's obsession with the contents of her pockets, or the lack thereof. "Sammy, what the hell are you doing? Are you looking for something?"

With a quiet kind of dignity, Sammy produced a crumpled ten dollar bill from a back pocket and chucked it at Mike. He caught it deftly, but was shocked and dismayed. With wide eyes, he watched Sammy turn and storm out. "Enjoy your lunch, asshole."

"Sammy! Come back!"

She didn't come back.

Eliot was sitting at the table, looking like he was dying to raise hell, until he saw the ugly grimace on Sammy's face. He stood to greet her. "What's wrong?"

"Nothing; let's just eat."

"She did what?" Maeve asked, scandalized.

"She threw money at me. It wasn't like it hurt or anything, babe." Mike was sitting on the couch of Maeve's apartment with a beer in one hand and the remote in the other, watching the football game. The two windows to Mike's left were open slightly, as the heat was blasting and could not be lowered or turned off. Needless to say, Mike had not caught Maeve in the best of moods and Maeve had been coming back into the living room from her bedroom, where she had been sending a nasty e-mail to her landlord after he had failed to answer his phone. The latest revelation of Sammy's undesired and worrying behavior had caused Maeve to stop dead in her tracks.

"She's unbelievable, Michael," Maeve complained. "Doesn't she miss me? Am I really that replaceable? What's so great about Eliot?"

Mike turned off the television and slowly got to his feet. "It has nothing to do with you being replaceable, or a bad friend, or anything like that. Sammy's just never had anything like this before and she's allowing it to take precedence over everything else."

Pouting, Maeve hugged Mike. "I miss my best friend."

Smiling sadly, Mike rubbed Maeve's back. "I know, babe. Want me to talk to her?"

"Do you think it will do any good?" Maeve asked. She was looking up into Mike's concerned face.

He shrugged in response. "It can't hurt to try though, right? I can't stand seeing you like this." Softly, he kissed her lips and she buried her head in his chest.

Days passed with Sammy seeing Eliot only once or twice for a meal. That was highly irregular. When Sammy complained, Eliot explained that he was busy with work. Sammy, on the other hand, was painfully available – not at all busy. It left her frustrated, and she didn't sleep much either. She awoke late one Monday morning, which dawned gray and miserable. The weather suited Sammy just fine; it matched her internal forecast. Cranky and sore from physical exhaustion, she got onto campus just in time to see her French professor closing and locking the classroom door behind her. Cursing loudly, Sammy essentially assaulted the woman, begging for another chance to take the midterm, pleading to reschedule. The professor wrenched her arm free of Sammy's, lest she get the stink of desperation all over her fancy coat, and explained that it pained her to grant exceptions to her well thought-out and necessary classroom rules. However, she had to admit that Sammy always did her work correctly and promptly. Turning her snooty, French nose up, she told Sammy she would e-mail her a final decision and took small, quick, and stylish steps down the hall. Somewhat calmer, Sammy figured she'd get an early lunch and maybe see if Eliot would like to join her. En route to the dining hall, Mike blocked any further progress. "Hello Sammy."

Sure to completely express her extreme frustration, Sammy groaned loudly and rolled her eyes dramatically. "Hello Mike. Let me give you fair warning: I am so unbelievably not in the mood today."

Mike smiled. "I don't give a shit about what kind of mood you're in. We need to talk."

"Look, if this is about me and Eliot, I already –"

"Wrong," Mike interrupted, grabbing Sammy by the arm. He steered her toward the quad in the middle of campus, just outside the Student Center. "This isn't about Eliot. You just think everything is, and that's where the problem is." He sat her down on a stone bench, but he remained standing. "Maeve misses you, like any good, caring friend would. She would feel this way no matter who you were dating. I don't care about Eliot. You could go out with all the creepers on this campus, and I wouldn't judge. It's when it starts to make you and Maeve miserable that I get involved."

"Did she ask you to talk to me?"

"Yeah; so what if she did? It's not like we aren't friends or that I think Maeve is always right all the time. All I'm asking is that you not ignore Maeve because it makes her grouchy and that sucks for me. You don't look so pleasant or composed yourself either, if I'm being honest."

"Thanks?" Sammy got to her feet. "I'm not apologizing for anything."

Mike raised his hands in front of him, showing he meant no harm. "Hey, I never said you had to. But how about you just give her a call later, so she knows your new boyfriend hasn't thrown you in his basement for safe keeping."

In spite of herself, Sammy grinned. "Ha; that's very funny."

Proud of himself, Mike also grinned. "Okay, now you can walk me to class."

"What?"

"You heard me. Think of it as the perfect opportunity to convince me I'm wrong about your weird boyfriend."

"I never said he wasn't a little weird. And besides, you already seem to have your mind made up," Sammy said, increasing the length of her strides to catch up with Mike, who was already making his way to the humanities building.

"Well, you have been changing ever since you started hanging out with him. As much as you talked about getting a boyfriend, you never forgot who you were. Now that it's happened, it's like you're willing to be whatever for this guy, and that's no good." Mike chose his words carefully. If he pissed her off, she wouldn't call Maeve, and then Maeve would be pissed and yell at Mike when he got back to the apartment.

"You can't have it both ways."

"What?" Mike asked, confused.

"How do you know I'm changing who I am for Eliot if you never see me?"

"Right there- we used to see you all the time. Do you really not miss Maeve? I know you miss me terribly." Mike smiled to show it was all in good humor. Sammy returned the smile, pulling her hair back.

"I do miss her. I want us all to be able to hang out, but it seems impossible with all this tension." Sammy forgot her desire for an early lunch with Eliot as she slipped into easy conversation. If nothing else, Mike was always good for a laugh and for a distraction.

"Then just call her, like I said. If you show her you're going to still be a friend, everything else will be easier. Okay?"

Sammy nodded. The pair parted ways at the sliding glass doors that served as the entrance to the humanities building, set on the hill behind the Student Center. Sammy waved goodbye to Mike before doubling back to the cafeteria and pulling out her cell phone from her always present and always cluttered bag. She dialed Eliot's number and patiently waited for him to answer. As the phone rang, Sammy observed the day, made note of the curled leaves scuttling about her feet in the sharp wind. The colors were beautiful, even in the unflattering gray light that made everything and everyone look somehow shrunken and unreal. Eliot's voicemail reminded Sammy that she had more on her mind than just foliage.

"Hey, Eliot, this is Sammy. I just wanted to see if you wanted to get an early lunch. I'll be in the dining hall for a little bit, so hopefully I'll see you soon. Bye." Hanging up, she eyed her cell phone with real skepticism and with a sense of uncertainty that bordered on contempt. Why wasn't Eliot answering? Did he have class? Was she really about to eat by herself? Sammy supposed she was, seeing no alternative, and entered the dining hall with a real sense of defeat.

Lunch was chicken again. Sammy believed if she ate just one more piece of chicken, she'd start clucking. Finding her meal less and less appetizing, Sammy threw the unfinished piece back on the tray and slid it away from her. She figured she could wait a while longer for Eliot. Not wanting to stare into empty space like the loner she used to be not too long ago, Sammy dove into her bag for her writer's notebook. She only came up for air when she heard Eliot call her name. Like a deer hearing snapping twigs announce the arrival of the hunter, she sat up rigidly and instantly. Eliot was damn near sprinting towards her with a wide smile. His hair was all askew and some of the smaller pieces stuck to his brow, dampened by sweat. Panting and filthy, his shirt was ripped above his chest on the left side, just under the collar bone. Like his face and shirt, his jeans were covered in dark-colored dirt. Eliot's earthy musk reached Sammy's nostrils and she crinkled her nose in disgust. Standing as he approached, Sammy called, "Eliot? What the hell happened?"

"Get your stuff and come with me."

"Excuse me?"

"Come on," Eliot urged. He had reached the table and was gathering Sammy's things. "Let's go."

"Go where?" Sammy asked, although the question was completely superfluous. As she asked it, she was already pulling her jacket on.

"I'm taking you to my apartment." Eliot slipped a strong arm around Sammy's waist and began pulling her out of the large cafeteria.

"Wait, Eliot, I've got to throw out my tray."

"They've got people for that." Eliot had successfully dragged Sammy outside.

"What the hell has gotten into you?" Sammy demanded, but Eliot did not answer.

Mike watched Sammy through the full-length windows of the building. She retrieved her cell phone and Mike silently prayed that she would keep her promise and call Maeve. Reality nastily whispered in his ear that it would be Eliot on the other end, but whatever – it was fine. He had a test to study for. Later that night he'd be having dinner with Maeve and regardless of Sammy or the douche bag she was seeing, it would be awesome. Smiling as he pressed the down button to call the elevator, Mike remembered the first time he ever met Maeve. It had been in the dining hall. He had been impatiently waiting for the moron in front of him to decide on which sandwich would be the best for lunch and move on. It was taking forever and Mike was about to sigh loudly and begin tapping his foot when he heard the young woman in front of him say, "Can I have a Lombardi, please?"

That was Mike's favorite sandwich. It was destiny. He leaned forward to commend the young co-ed on her decision, and it was the exact moment when she began to turn around, when her soft, wavy red hair slid across her back like silk, when her bright, blue eyes that had the mysterious and most eloquent tint of grey to them looked him over, when she stretched her lips to smile at him; it was the exact moment when Mike knew she was what tuition money was really for – opportunities like this.

Maeve was beautiful, really fucking clever, hilarious, and honest. She had never lied to Mike, and it was wholly inconceivable for him to believe she ever would – deception wasn't something Maeve was capable of. The way she'd catch him staring and still be embarrassed even after months of dating, and the way she'd reach for his hand without thought in a crowded room, made his debt to Sallie Mae worthwhile. Maeve was the best part about Mike as a person, let alone his college experience.

A soft ding of a bell and the elevator doors slid open. Mike strolled in without any conscience thought – his mind was very much preoccupied with his lady love, so when someone hurried in after him, hood pulled up and dressed all in black, Mike took no notice. Had he been paying attention, he would have found it odd that the person beside him was dressed in such shady attire and did not select a floor. Even when Mike pressed the button marked with a plain-looking number six, the stranger did not move. It wasn't until the doors slid shut and Mike felt the elevator begin its journey heavenward that he felt discomfort in his side and something warm running down his side. More than a little disturbed, Mike looked down and realized he was bleeding. Light glinting off silver caught his attention and his brown eyes widened when he saw the blade, crimson running in tiny rivers off the edge. He should have moved, should have screamed, but he was shocked. So when the knife came again and again, he succumbed to it. As it turns out, a knife can be very persuasive: quite the motivational tool. After all, it convinced the blood sustaining Mike's life to exit the body post-haste. It was awe-inspiring how fast the floor of the elevator was covered in the sticky, warm stuff. When the doors slid open on the sixth floor, the attacker sprinted from the scene, and Mike lay in a puddle of the very substance he needed, unable to call for help.

After a long day of classes, Sammy's American Literature professor, sometimes known as Professor Windbag but more commonly known as Professor West, liked to unwind with a strong, black cup of coffee and the Arts and Leisure section of the Times. He'd return to his car in the faculty lot behind the Student Center, because his office was uncomfortable and smelled like mildew, and because the library was always crowded and he preferred to avoid students with too many questions and not enough sense to come to his office hours or raise a hand during class. Besides, his building was in Dickinson Hall, and the temperature was never quite right. He wanted to be warm, and his office was nearly a freezer. He'd have his engine idling, more concerned with the biting cold than the fumes, toss his briefcase thoughtlessly – almost recklessly – on to the already cluttered backseat, and lose himself in the culture that seemed to completely disinterest the majority of his students. He'd only stay for ten minutes or so, but it was enough to regroup and relax before returning to an empty apartment.

Professor West had just moved north after an exceedingly painful breakup with his fiancée. For many years, Professor West had been operating under the false notion that all women wanted to start a family, have children, and grow old on some wooden, wrap around porch, with grandchildren circled at their feet and the sun setting in the distance behind rolling green hills. His fiancée had no such dreams, and when Professor West finally realized he was alone, he needed to be alone. He packed up all that was his, threw it in the car, and drove north. For a while, he stayed with friends, hopping from one couch to the next and was desperate for work. After a month of feeling less and less of an intellectual and more and more like a failure, things started to fall into place. After a stellar interview, he landed the adjunct professor gig at the university and found a place nearby. He was ready to begin again, and had put a lot of energy into furnishing it, though the only result of those efforts was a mattress too big for his bedroom without a box spring, and some plastic folding chairs with a plastic table that was too low to the ground to be taken seriously. With all that in mind, Professor West definitely preferred his car. With a contented sigh, the professor would recline the driver's seat back and give the paper a healthy rattle.

More often than not, the professor could very easily block out the raucous of campus life outside his impromptu, snobbish sanctuary. It was no trouble at all ignoring the disappointingly immature squabbles and the overly dramatic scenes created for attention's sake … usually. However, the well-meaning professor seemed to be having a great deal of difficulty focusing on the book reviews. Frustrated, the professor let the paper fall almost soundlessly to his lap and reveal students and faculty milling about in all different directions, some traveling with companions, some moving in solitary style. Nothing out of the ordinary was there to entertain, inspire, or consume him. The professor was ready to give it up and just drive on home. He was just about to put the car in gear when two students moving quickly through the crowd caught his eye.

Miss Thogode, hardly working on her extra assignment, was being dragged along at an alarming pace by the young man Professor West considered to be an interloper. He had not been registered for that class and had weaseled his way onto the attendance sheet. Professor West firmly believed that there was a flaw to the logic behind "better late than never." As a result, he had seriously doubted the authenticity of the young man's interest in American literature, and that doubt was currently being reinforced by the way he was dragging Miss Thogode across the parking lot. Clearly, that was where his real interest laid. Rolling his eyes, Professor West was debating whether or not to dismiss the juvenile drama unfolding before him and head home, or wait until its conclusion, of which he wouldn't dare hope to be thrilling. He decided to stay and observe how things played out when he gave more thought to the fact that Miss Thogode was being dragged, a strong indication she did not want to go where she was being led. She kept looking all around her, and Professor West was wondering if she was looking for a sympathetic bystander, looking for a way out. His hand moved to the handle of the car door, and he was ready to jump out and call to her, to make up some lame reason for needing a moment to discuss something that couldn't wait. His hand retreated to his side when Miss Thogode willingly got into the young man's vehicle.

Professor West was perplexed to say the least. Miss Thogode seemed confused, unsure and yet, she was acting with certainty. He thought the young co-ed showed literary potential – her papers were insightful and well-constructed – and was excited to see what she would make of her extra assignment. He found this display disheartening; maybe she really did have her priorities all askew and maybe he really was giving her too much credit. Professor West was not an idiot; he knew Miss Thogode loathed the sight of him and was only mildly troubled by it. He wondered if her opinion would have changed had he called out to her just before. Well, he supposed it was neither here nor there; she got into the young man's car, and now they were gone. It was about time he himself was gone.

Professor West did his best not to worry about Miss Thogode between his frozen dinner, the grading of papers, and a foreign art film he couldn't make heads or tails of. But just as he was falling to sleep, her face resurfaced on his eyelids, and he was again struck by her complexity. How unsure her face appeared, and yet her body did not hesitate in its movements. Maybe he was thinking too much, as he often did. Besides, Miss Thogode undoubtedly had people she could confide in and people she could seek advice from, and Professor West knew with certainty he did not top that list, nor even make it.

Eliot, with Sammy at his side, pulled into the parking lot of Eliot's building, and together they walked inside his building. Eliot was going to take a shower, so Sammy took a seat upon the couch, prepared to wait patiently. "Sammy? Could you come into the bedroom?" Eliot's deep voice called to her from down the hall.

She rose and went to Eliot without thinking. She passed through the doorway, brow knit in confusion because, though she had definitely heard Eliot, he was nowhere to be found. The bedroom door slammed shut, and Sammy screamed, jumping toward the sound. Eliot revealed himself. Why had he been hiding behind the door? And why wasn't he dressed yet? Grinning, Sammy opened her mouth to ask those very questions when Eliot rushed at her, tossing her on the bed with a violent need. Her teeth clamped on a strange combination of her tongue and her lips, and her mouth was filled with the coppery taste of blood. She quickly pressed her hand to her mouth, eyes shut tight against the pain and the urge to vomit, but her hand was ripped from her mouth. Gasping, Sammy swallowed the blood filling her mouth and started choking. As she was trying to clear her airway and inhale the necessary, vital oxygen, Eliot was pinning Sammy's wrists above her head and against the pillows. His rough, dry lips raked across her cheeks and lips, and his bare legs were sliding against her jeans. "Eliot, stop, I'm bleeding."

"What?" Eliot sat up, breathing heavily. He released Sammy's wrists to free his own hands, freed them to gently take her face in his hands. Sammy used her liberated hands to sit up as well. Though she was bleeding, she couldn't help but notice that Eliot's skin was still damp and slick from the shower and glistened in the lamp light of his bedroom. How could she possibly have managed to bite her tongue at a time like this?

"I bit my tongue."

Eliot laughed softly, shaking his head from side to side. "Let's take a look. Open your mouth," he said. Sammy did as she was told and she trembled at his touch, his fingers trailing gently along her lips to inspect the damage she had inflicted upon herself. Eliot nodded. "Yeah, you definitely did, and it's definitely bleeding. Do you want some ice?" Caringly, Eliot pushed Sammy's hair away from her forehead.

"Do you think it'll help?"

Eliot laughed again, shrugging. "Damned if I know." He moved to sit beside her on the bed, still clad in just a towel, a fact Sammy was all too aware of. Eliot let his hands fall to his lap. "Is this weird?"

"What?"

Eliot blushed. "Me, taking you here to … I mean, how do you feel? Do you feel weird?"

"You need to know something."

"What's that?" Eliot turned to fully face Sammy, but she twisted her face to the side, afraid to tell Eliot what he probably already knew.

"I'm a … I've never … Eliot, you need to know that I'm a virgin." Her face was burning red.

Eliot smiled in response. "I know. I just thought that maybe we were ready." He moved his hands to pick at his towel and Sammy relaxed. Eliot already knew. That was okay, but he was asking to begin a serious conversation, one that Sammy couldn't have with Eliot just in a towel. It made her imagine seeing him naked, feeling his hot breath panting against her neck and face, his hands undressing her and roaming all over her body – she couldn't think of anything else, and she didn't want the first time to be like that. She had had lustful thoughts and nighttime fantasies, sure, but nothing so sudden, nothing so ordinary. Sammy continued to watch Eliot's hands near the towel's edge and gasped. "Eliot, is that blood?" Sammy asked. Following Sammy's gaze, Eliot looked at the shallow cut across his stomach. Cursing under his breath, Eliot pressed his hand tight against his wound, but it was too late; Sammy had seen it. She moved to sit up straighter, swinging her legs over the edge of the bed so they rested on the floor. "Why are you bleeding? And why were you filthy?"

"It's my landscaping job. I got your message and figured we could get lunch together, because my break is early, too. Then I saw you, sitting there, and I don't know …." His deep, husky voice trailed off and he ran his hands down his face, suddenly weary. "I just wanted you."

Sammy leaned over, bending nearly in half, to better study Eliot's stomach. Gingerly, she removed his hand. It wasn't deep, but it was nasty. She looked up at Eliot through heavy-lidded eyes. "I think we should get this cleaned up and checked out."

Eliot gently cupped Sammy's face in his hands. "I'm fine." He tenderly ran his thumb along Sammy's lips.

Sammy nodded and kissed Eliot's cheek. "I'm sorry if I freaked out, but I bit my tongue and it hurts, and -"

"Don't apologize. Your first time should be special and important, and I shouldn't let my lust get in the way."

"Oh, Eliot, I ...." Sammy's cell phone rang loudly from the living room. "I need to get that."

Smiling sadly, Eliot watched Sammy run to her phone. He sighed heavily and lay back against the pillows.

Sammy was alarmed to see Maeve calling. She answered and before she had a chance to say hello, Maeve said, "Ask me where I am right now."

"Uh ... where are you?"

"I'm in the god damned hospital waiting for my boyfriend to get out of emergency surgery."

Sammy swallowed back the rising bile in her throat. "I just saw him earlier today, though, and he was fine. I walked him to class. What happened?"

"He was stabbed, like, fifteen times."

"Do they know who did it?"

"No one saw anything. I find that hard to believe considering it was in the middle of the day on a college campus." Maeve released a sob she had been trying to control.

"I'll be right there," Sammy promised. She ran back to Eliot, tears pouring down her face, and begged for a ride to the hospital. Eliot didn't pause to ask the inane questions, but simply got dressed and held Sammy as tightly as he could on their way to the hospital. Sammy needed to get there, talk to Maeve, and see Mike: all that was priority number one. Thirty minutes later, Sammy was out of the car, out of breath, and rushing to the front desk. Everything was quiet, white, and so sterile it was startling, suffocating. Sammy's fingers lingered at her own throat as the pastel-scrubbed nurse behind the desk impatiently waited for Sammy to speak, but she could only stutter. Thankfully, Maeve came walking around the corner. Her eyes were swollen from crying and nearly as red as her hair. The two friends rushed to each other and embraced, holding each other to better express what they couldn't bring themselves to say. Both were shaken, sorry, and in need of a friend. Inquiring in hushed tones about Mike's condition, Sammy followed Maeve into the dimly lit hospital room. Mike was not awake. His breathing was heavy and labored; it was the only sound in the room other than the beeps and clicks of running machinery. It made Sammy uncomfortable – quickly, she sat beside Mike's bed but left the chair nearest the patient open for Maeve.

"The doctors haven't said much of anything – the damage was minimal though, thank God. He was up earlier, but I don't know when he'll be up again. Can you stay long?" Maeve spoke in a soft whisper and basically collapsed into the chair next to Sammy and nearest to Mike. She seemed tired, weary – and that was understandable. Sammy offered her friend a broken smile; it was the best she could do.

"I'll stay as long as you need me to." Gently, she patted Maeve's thigh. Lowering her gaze in a sign of humbled gratitude, Maeve noticed dried blood on Sammy's knuckles and fingertips. Instinctively, Maeve reached out and seized Sammy's hand.

"What happened?"

Sammy shook her head dismissively. "Eliot cut himself doing landscaping, and I tried to help him clean the cut and whatever."

Maeve flicked her eyes to Sammy's face. She noticed dried blood at the corners of her lips. "What happened there, then?"

Sammy shrugged. "I bit my tongue like an idiot."

Maeve opened her mouth to reply, maybe ask another question, when Mike groaned loudly. Sammy was instantly forgotten as Maeve turned to her boyfriend, taking his hand in hers. Slowly, Mike's eyes opened and he smiled at Maeve. Her whole face lit up, and Sammy released a deep breath, relieved. "I'm going to let you two catch up and get coffee. Maeve, do you want anything?"

Maeve shook her head impatiently. With great effort, Mike turned to Sammy. He was still smiling brightly. "Hey. I'm glad you're here."

Pausing in the doorway, Sammy nodded. "I'm glad you're here too, buddy. Do you need anything?"

Mike shook his head. Leaving the pair to the company of each other, Sammy headed down the hall. Her sneakers padded softly against the tile. Now that the initial fear and anxiety had passed and she had seen Mike, she decided she liked the quiet, wanted to be fully absorbed in the vast whiteness all about her. To not exist, to not worry, to be able to go back to being alone and living in dreams and on the printed page; it was all easier, so much easier. She was at the vending machine before she realized it. The crappy cup of coffee was warm at least; not hot, but warm. She dutifully carried it back to the room where Maeve and Mike were deep in conversation.

"So, we're going to get dinner tomorrow night?"

"Definitely; I'll call you."

"Alright, then I'll talk to you later."

"Goodnight," Sammy called to Maeve in the cold, wet air of an evening in late November. She and Maeve were scheduled to grab an early dinner on campus the next evening. Afterward, they would order ice cream and bring some to Mike during a visit. Sammy promised Maeve she'd go and visit every day. There was plenty of time in between classes and that way Mike would never wake up alone. Sammy pulled her keys from her pocket. The clanging metal made an awfully lonely sound in the vacuous silence of the near deserted parking lot. Getting nearer to the white Buick Skylark that was lacking all hubcaps and shamelessly displaying a bright red sticker, which indicated the vehicle had most certainly failed inspection, Sammy noticed a slip of paper tucked carefully beneath a windshield wiper. If it turned out to be a ticket Sammy would go nuts, although, it would be the most appropriate ending to her abysmal day. Careful not to rip the paper, Sammy gingerly removed it to read its contents. It was not a ticket.

It was a note. A strong feeling of déjà vu came over her. There was no signature beneath the message, and the message itself was incredibly brief. Only two words were written on the slip of paper.

"I'm sorry."

She eyed the writing and gulped when it was immediately familiar to her. The same hand that had written this note was the same hand that had written the one she found the day Rob was buried. But she couldn't be sure, or at least she didn't want to be. The content was too generic, too universal of a sentiment to be unique or connected to the other note. Lots of people could be sorry for a number of different things. Maybe the author had left the note on the wrong car. That made sense because Sammy could think of no one who had wronged her. Sammy decided she had more important things to worry about than random, indecipherable notes left by strangers, so she crumpled the note in her fist. She didn't give it another thought on the drive home.

MANDI BEAN

Chapter Eight
Wading into the River of Blood

"That boy is a monster." ~ Lady Gaga

3:00 AM arrived quickly. Sammy lay on her back, staring at the ceiling above her. Sleep came in brief, tantalizing waves. Sighing, she rolled over onto her side. This lack of sleep thing was not romantic, did not make her feel like a heroine. It just made her agitated and exhausted all the fucking time. Throwing the covers off in a quiet kind of rage, Sammy decided she could stay in bed no longer. A trip to the kitchen for a glass of water would be enough to change the scenery and break up the monotony. Hopping out of bed, a knock against the window sent her right back under the covers. With a racing heart, she peered out from behind the shaking sheet to see if the culprit was only a branch, like she hoped, or a threatening stranger.

It was Eliot.

Seriously?

Surprised, Sammy threw the covers to the end of the mattress and lifted the window open. Eliot looked to her with calm and patient eyes, and Sammy released a deep breath. Because of the hour, she thought he might be in some kind of trouble. Relief washing over her, Sammy whispered, "You scared me. Aren't you tired? Do you have any idea what time it is? Aren't you freezing?" She paused for a breath and had every intention of inviting Eliot into her bedroom, but Eliot was already crawling inside. He wasn't saying a word but fell quickly to the bed. Eliot lay down and gently took Sammy's hand in his own. He coaxed her closer and from this distance, it became evident that he was worried about her. Sammy's relief waned and she stepped against the edge of the bed. Eliot slid over, closer to the wall and Sammy understood that Eliot wanted her beside him. Shifting her weight from foot to foot, Sammy hesitated. "Eliot, I'm not going to –"

Eliot shook his head. "I'm not here for that, Sammy. Please don't think about me like that. I just know that you need me right now. Let me be there for you."

Sammy squeezed his hand. "I don't know if I can handle all of this. Maeve and I just started talking again but only because Mike was stabbed, and I don't know. People I love keep getting hurt, Eliot."

"It's not your fault, Sammy. Rob wasn't your fault, either."

"I know. Or, at least I know I'm supposed to know that."

Eliot smiled. "If you need me, you have me." Eliot tugged her hand. "Problems won't seem so insurmountable in the morning. Let's just lay here."

Still, she hesitated. She had thought being needed would be divine and that it would give her a greater, better purpose. She only knew how to be needy, taking and taking. But the man in her bed was still there all the same, asking for her to be needy. Eliot most certainly had what Sammy required, but maybe, just maybe, Sammy had what Eliot required – maybe it didn't have to be clear. Sammy climbed into bed beside Eliot, facing him. She planned on not saying anything, planned on maybe going back to sleep, but Eliot thwarted her plans, as he usually did, by wrapping his arms around her. He pulled her close so he could bury his face in her hair gathered at the crook of her neck. Sammy held on tightly, and soon her body shook with sobs. Eliot could only hold her close, and he did that as best he could.

Sighing contentedly, Sammy let her eyes flutter open. She was warm and cozy...

And staring at Eliot.

She sat up abruptly and shook her sleeping partner vigorously. "Eliot! Wake up! If my parents come in, we're dead!"

"They're not here," he mumbled.

"What? How could you possibly know that?"

"I got up to pee, and there was a note on the kitchen table for you."

Sammy nudged his side half-heartedly. "What did it say?"

Eliot sighed dramatically and rolled over to better see Sammy. Lying on his back, he said with a yawn, "There's an assembly at the elementary school, and they went to watch your little brother do something, or something like that."

"Oh. Okay then." She smiled down at him. "Want some breakfast?"

"Can I get it with some coffee?"

"Absolutely you can." Sammy quickly kissed Eliot's forehead and hopped from the bed.

Warmly smiling, Eliot watched Sammy leave the room. He sauntered out into the kitchen about twenty minutes later when the delicious scent of sizzling bacon was strong enough to lure him from the bed. He lingered in the doorway, observing silently as Sammy slid a loaded plate onto the kitchen table.

"Smells great," Eliot said as he stepped into the room, a means of announcing his arrival.

"I promise that it tastes great, too," Sammy said over her shoulder. She was finishing up her own plate in a red college shirt and flannel boxers. Her long, dark, wavy hair was piled high atop her head. Eliot felt the word "beautiful" rush to his lips, but he bit it back. Instead, he asked if the coffee was done. Sammy answered, "Oh, yeah, can you pour two cups?" Turning, Sammy held her breakfast platter in one hand, and a plate of bagels in the other. Voila – the domestic goddess. Eliot was most certainly impressed, but he'd be damned if Sammy knew it. He sent her image screaming from his mind as he filled two mugs of a deep shade of green with coffee. The two sat simultaneously across from one another, and Eliot dug in immediately. Sammy was just as hungry as Eliot but had bigger, looming questions to ask, which lessened her appetite. "Is everything okay, Eliot?"

"Huh? Of course, and this really is all delicious." Eliot spoke through a mouth full of food.

"Thanks, but I mean, are you okay?"

Eliot set his silverware meticulously beside his plate and took great care in cleaning his mouth with a napkin. "I've never been better Sammy, I promise. You make me nervous when you keep asking, though."

"I'm sorry. I guess I just need constant reassurance." Sammy's voice cracked.

"If there is something wrong, then we'll talk about it. Trust me, okay?"

Sammy's jaw twitched, as she slid her ailing tongue against the roof of her mouth. "I'll try."

He sighed and reached for her hand across the table. "You've got me, Sammy. I'm not going anywhere." Eliot kept his eyes locked on Sammy's and watched them squint and widen with what Eliot prayed was comprehension.

"It can be rainbows and butterflies and bunnies all the time?" Sarcastic though she was, she squeezed Eliot's hand. "I know I'm a lot to handle, but if you can handle my rollercoaster emotions, then there's no reason for me to not handle your … well, there's bound to be something wrong with you." Sammy laughed, but Eliot did not join in.

"Are you happy with me? Be honest."

Sammy inhaled deeply. Retreating within herself, she closely regarded the human being staring back at her. She thought that the best analysis would be conducted if she detached herself from the subject; all scientific and whatnot. Or would a simple list of pros and cons suffice? He was hot. He was passionate. Sammy realized she could go on and on like that for hours and make a list of thousands. The fact of the matter was that Eliot was a beautiful composition of everything she wanted, and Sammy did like him for it, and she thought she could love him if he could do the same. Sammy grinned. "I am extremely happy with you, Eliot. Are you happy with me?"

Eliot suddenly looked as if he was about to cry. "I am extremely happy with you, Sammy."

Sammy took Eliot at his word.

Breakfast ended and Eliot showered while Sammy cleaned up the kitchen. Reappearing in the doorway, he leaned against the doorjamb with a pleasant, genuine smile. Cue the sweeping music and slow-motion running. Beaming, Sammy walked over to Eliot. He wound his index finger in a loose strand of hair that had liberated itself from her ponytail. "How about we do something tonight?"

Sammy clicked her tongue. "I would love to, but I promised Maeve we'd get dinner and then visit Mike at the hospital. Maybe you and I could visit him some time? I think he'd appreciate it."

"Oh. Yeah, maybe we could do that." Eliot spoke slowly and shifted his weight to stand tall. His arms hung limply at his sides.

"Can I call you after?"

"Sure, but I don't know if I'll answer, because I'll most likely be sleeping. Calling it an early night."

"Is everything okay?" Sammy asked, scrutinizing Eliot with raised eyebrows.

"Yeah, of course. I'll see you later." Eliot quickly, roughly kissed her forehead and practically ran for the door. Dismayed, Sammy followed him.

"Eliot, are you sure everything's okay? You seem upset."

"Bye, Sammy." Eliot shut the door behind him and that was that. She pulled her bangs back in frustration.

Sitting on the outrageously uncomfortable plastic couch in the lobby of a small, local diner near campus, Sammy shifted her weight. She didn't think she could sit for much longer. The seat was not only hard as a rock, but an offensive shade of orange. Rising to stand upright, Sammy was just about to step outside when Maeve walked in, causing the bells above the door to jingle. "It's about time you showed up, you tool. You're the one who said seven o'clock."

Maeve smiled. "Mike woke up just as I was leaving. Remember him, my boyfriend that got stabbed? Feel like an asshole yet?" In response, Sammy playfully swatted the back of her friend's head. The girls giggled as the young hostess showed them to a booth near the bar. Each ordered a beer and debated appetizers.

"Have the police found the guy that hurt Mike yet?"

"Oh, I've been meaning to tell you!" Maeve let her menu close. "They think the same weapon used to kill Rob was used to stab Mike. They think the crimes are related."

Sammy blinked slowly. "Oh. Wow. So, wait, what … does that mean?"

Maeve shrugged. "The police are looking into it. I guess we just have to wait and see what they come up with."

Sammy nodded, letting her eyes go out of focus. Maeve discussed which dinners looked the most appetizing and about what Mike usually orders while they're out, and Sammy nodded and laughed in all the right places. But she didn't really come back to the table until the meals arrived. She had been in a dimly lit bar, staring at a bleeding Rob.

Dinner was delicious and enjoyable, as Maeve was able to keep Sammy distracted from the reemergence of Rob's death. Though Maeve spoke a lot, and quite often about Mike, Sammy kept mum about Eliot. She was content to just enjoy Maeve's company without it being awkward – a return to normalcy. It was less tense that way, and besides, if no one else could see the light radiating from within Eliot, then she'd be more than happy to keep his beacon all to herself – it was enough to illuminate her world. It was more than enough, really.

A few hours later, and a few drinks later as well, Maeve and Sammy walked out into the parking lot. Though it was crowded with vehicles, the two young women were the only people in sight. The soles of their shoes echoed against the smooth pavement in the thin night air. They had decided not to visit Mike in their tipsy state tonight but would go see him early the next morning. Reaching Sammy's car first, Maeve was about to bid adieu when she noticed a folded sheet of paper tucked deliberately beneath one blade of the windshield wipers. Had Sammy noticed, she would have been overcome with a near fatal dose of déjà vu. Maeve was the one to notice first, however, and as Sammy unlocked her door, Maeve retrieved the note, read it quickly and handed it to Sammy. "What the hell is this?"

The message was the same, as was the handwriting. "I'm sorry." Sammy placed her hand on her forehead, eyes widening. "This is really bizarre. This is the third time I've gotten a note like this, exactly like this."

"When did you get the other ones?"

"The first was at Rob's funeral. The next one was when I saw Mike and you at the hospital yesterday."

Maeve inhaled sharply. "The day Mike got stabbed? What if this is from the guy who did it? Do you still have the other notes?"

Sliding her hand down her face, Sammy sighed heavily. "Let's calm down, okay? We've just got to think about this rationally. Do you think there's any reason to believe the guy who stabbed Mike and killed Rob left this note?"

"Well, it's a very strong coincidence, isn't it?" Maeve asked, popping her hip and resting her hand upon it. "You were the last person Rob was trying to talk to and the last person to see Mike before his attacker, so maybe the bastard saw you with these guys and has sudden pangs of remorse. Plus, the same weapon was used both times!"

Clenching the note in her frightened, white-knuckled fist, Sammy shut her eyes against the looming questions opening up before her. There were a million ways to handle the situation, but which was best? "Maeve, maybe I should take this to the cops tomorrow. It's not like I can just let this go."

"Wait a second, Sammy. You don't have the other notes, and the cops don't have a handwriting sample to compare it to, because there are no leads. There are no suspects." Maeve was frowning and pacing back and forth before Sammy's car. "They'll start inventing suspects, and you know who they'll come after?"

Sammy shook her head.

"Us! We'll be suspects! What else do Rob and Mike have in common? Do you want to be hauled down to the station and interrogated? They can make us admit to stuff we never even did!"

"Whoa, stop. You sound crazy right now. Do you realize that? Why are you so paranoid?"

Maeve spun to face Sammy, angry. "I'm not paranoid! I've done nothing wrong!"

"Right, so there's nothing to worry about. We should go to the cops —"

"Maybe I don't want to know who did it!"

"What?" Sammy was shocked.

Maeve crumpled against the hood of Sammy's car. "What if it was someone I know? What if I'm the reason Rob's dead and Mike's in the hospital?" She began to sob heavily, and Sammy wasn't sure how much of it was the booze, the discovery of the third note, or if it was both of those things, so she just kept talking.

"I don't want to upset you, Maeve, but there's a killer out there. He's targeting people we know. What if we're next? That's why we have to do something."

"This is your entire fault," Maeve breathed.

"What?"

"Rob wanted to be with you. Now he's dead. Mike and I wanted you to spend more time with us, and now he's laid up in the hospital, and I could be next." She sat up, pushing her hair from her face. Maeve was taking deep breaths, trying to calm down. "All of this started happening when you met Eliot."

Furious, Sammy rounded on Maeve. "What the fuck is that supposed to mean?"

"Open your eyes, Sammy. Take these notes to the cops, and the first person they're going to look at is Eliot. He's the outsider." She crossed her arms over her chest. "What will that do to Eliot, to be handcuffed and thrown into the back of the cop car as his girlfriend just looks on, with all his family and friends in Maine? Do you think he'll ever talk to you again?"

"Maeve," Sammy screamed, "what the hell are you trying to do? What in God's name are you talking about?"

"If you go to the cops, Sammy, things could get worse. Let them figure this entire mess out, okay?" Maeve spoke calmly, almost soothingly. She rubbed her friend's arm affectionately, and Sammy's head was spinning. She had never been so confused. Maeve's reaction to the note and the proposed plan of police involvement had been odd, to say the least. Maybe it was the booze, or the stress of having Mike in the hospital, or the notion that the person who had done those horrible things was someone she knew. Either way, Sammy was tired and broken and needed to leave.

"Yeah, well, goodnight. I'll see you tomorrow morning." Sammy opened her car door and then slammed it shut, not giving her friend a chance to reply. This was lunacy. Peeling out of the parking lot, Sammy was attempting to breathe in and breathe out deeply, calming herself. The notes unnerved her enough. The four of them should all be going on double dates and hanging out – not making hospital visits, not fighting amongst each other, and not trembling beside a handsome man in bed at three o'clock in the morning. The whole thing was ridiculous.

Deep in thought, Sammy didn't realize she passed the turn for her home. Subconsciously, she knew she was going to Eliot's apartment, but the surface refused to acknowledge this growing need or dependency. Killing the engine some twenty minutes later, Sammy turned off the lights and unbuckled her seat belt. Focusing on the mindless, menial task of parking the car kept her from getting angrier and prevented seeds of doubt from taking root in her soul and growing into a monstrous redwood tree, with twigs and branches painfully poking her skull as constant reminders that Rob was dead; a walking, breathing bad idea that it could have been all her fault. The gravel crunched under her soft soles as she marched up the path to Eliot's humble-looking, beige front door. She pushed the doorbell twice, slightly impatient, shifting her weight from foot to foot. No one came, and, after five minutes, it didn't sound like anyone was going to come. Puffing her bangs up and away from her eyes, she began to knock on the door. It was a decent release of the mounting frustration, but did not bring Eliot or anyone else forth. Nothing stirred inside. Turning away from the stubborn locked door, Sammy dug in the pocket of Eliot's sweatshirt she had claimed as her own and removed her cell phone. She was calling him, cursing him for being so unavailable. Sammy called Eliot once more, after leaving a voicemail the first time, but still there was no answer. Discouraged, Sammy slowly trudged to her car, tired and careless. The day had been going so well, progressing so positively, but it had crashed and burned terrifically. It had transformed into a bright ball of fire, burning out of control and simultaneously consuming and destroying all she loved. Mike was in the hospital, Maeve was a wreck, Rob was still dead, and she had no way of getting in touch with Eliot. Terrible sensations of both alienation and isolation slinked with a seductive kind of danger around her naked throat, tightening it, and making it hard to breathe.

A sense of eerie calm had settled over Maeve. She wasn't crying or shaking, but was steady and sure. Maeve knew that if she just kept her head on straight, thinking both logically and rationally, she'd be all right. Smiling serenely, Maeve unlocked the door to her apartment building and climbed the stairs, running through the itinerary in her head again and again. Not a soul was in sight and all things considered, that was most likely for the best. She reached her floor and readied her keys in her hand. She was all set to unlock her apartment door when she noticed someone else had already done so. Not only was the door unlocked, but it was slightly ajar. The breath traveling from Maeve's lungs caught in her throat and burned there, seared the sensitive lining of her throat. Maeve realized she had two options. She could enter her apartment and meet whatever it was that waited for her, or she could flee the premises and escape to the nearest precinct. Maeve allowed her intuition to take over completely and something told her to go inside. Curiosity may have killed the cat, but she had to know who was in there. The door creaked loudly as she slowly opened it wider. There was no movement coming from within so hesitantly, carefully, Maeve took a few steps inside. Still, no movement came and she debated calling out when someone very familiar rose from his seat on the couch. Maeve smiled ruefully. "You scared the hell out of me, but I should have known."

Driving home was uneventful. The blaring music drowned out all attempt at thought. The pounding drums and growling guitars created a peaceful kind of sanctuary. Sammy was able to continue the trend in her darkened bedroom with a locked door that was essential. Curling into the tiniest ball she could, Sammy held herself together quite literally, linking her pale arms around her shins with her knees neatly tucked beneath her chin. She closed her eyes and listened to the music playing softly. Her breathing deepened and somewhere along the line, she fell asleep.

Her eyelids slowly opened when the gentle but constant, and therefore annoying, tapping made it impossible to remain sleeping. Rolling over onto her other side, Sammy lazily searched for the source of the sound. She found it easily enough as Eliot was once again outside her window. The hard part was moving. Though Sammy knew she had to let him in (it would be cruel to just leave him sitting out there in the dark and the cold), she was exhausted. All of this was emotionally draining. She loved the drama, embraced it and propagated it without being malicious, but maybe a life worthy of the silver screen wasn't really all it was cracked up to be. Maybe, just maybe, when the credits rolled or the cover closed it was out of necessity because real people weren't as resilient as fictional characters. Did ink and paper make for stronger stuff than flesh, blood, and bone? Sammy didn't have the energy to form an answer. Sighing, she climbed to her knees upon the mattress, and Sammy slid the window open and moved back, allowing Eliot to climb inside. He did so, and shut and locked the window behind him. Leaning back against the wall with his head against the windowsill, Eliot sat upon the mattress and watched with patiently focused eyes as Sammy fell lazily back into the bed. "Where were you tonight?" Sammy mumbled with her face in the pillow.

As he grinned and crossed his strong arms over his firm chest, Eliot asked, "Can I not see you for one night?" He watched Sammy's body tense. "Calm down. It was just a joke. I thought you were having dinner with Maeve and then visiting Mike?"

"I was, but dinner went late and ended badly, so we didn't visit Mike."

"Badly? Why? What happened?" Eliot moved to lie beside Sammy, carelessly running his fingers through her hair. It was an instinctive, soothing gesture, and Sammy released a deep breath.

"We got into an argument about these notes I've been finding on my car. I wanted to take them to the police but she said I shouldn't because then you would be a suspect." She awkwardly craned her neck to catch a glimpse of Eliot.

"Wait. What notes? Why would I be a suspect? What would I be suspected of doing?"

Sammy frowned. "The night of Rob's funeral, I found a note on the windshield of my car, and all it said was 'I'm sorry.' I found identical notes the night I left the hospital after visiting Mike and then again tonight. Maeve thinks the notes have something to do with Rob's murder and the attack on Mike, and I do too, but she doesn't want to go to the police, and I don't understand it. She thinks you'll be implicated, and I guess that's because things started happening when I started seeing you. I don't think you did it, clearly, but Maeve thinks if they brought us down to the station the cops will bully us into saying something that isn't true, and we'll all get each other into trouble."

"It's okay. I don't think that's something any of us have to worry about. I think Maeve's been watching too much Court TV," Eliot whispered, his lips close to her ear, grazing it. His hot breath assaulted her neck, and she trembled. "She's only targeting me because she doesn't like me, and you do, and that's affecting your friendship. She's angry about what's been happening, and since I'm the new guy, I'm getting the aggression." Eliot was speaking very matter-of-factly, like he was removed from the situation. It worried Sammy; shouldn't he care that he was being called a murderer and being blamed for senseless acts of violence? Shouldn't he be worried Sammy might be infected with these thoughts, and that everything would end?

"Yeah, but how does that make you feel?" Sammy rolled over onto her back to better see Eliot. He softly kissed along her jaw and neck.

"If she doesn't like me, then she doesn't like me." His lips got caught up with Sammy's for a moment or two. "Does how Maeve feels about me change how you feel about me?"

Rolling over onto her side to completely face Eliot, Sammy sighed. "No, but it does make things harder. I don't want my best friend to hate my boyfriend and accuse him of atrocities."

Wonder of wonders, Eliot grinned. Sammy assumed the revelation would be more than disheartening, but here he was, smiling and pressing his body closer against hers. Inhaling sharply, Sammy closed her eyes as he whispered, "That's the first time you've ever called me that."

Eyes still shut, Sammy laughed softly. Her warm breath mingled with Eliot's and she was complete; she didn't need absolutely anything else. There was nothing left to understand – it was all right here. "I hope that's okay."

Kissing Sammy's soft eyelids, Eliot breathed against her skin, and she had an inexplicable desire to propose an idea – that she and Eliot stay in bed beside each other until their bones turned to dust, until all the clocks stopped ticking, waves rose above buildings to crush them with their might, and flames engulfed the spinning globe she called home. Armageddon could wreak tragic havoc, and Sammy would be perfectly content to welcome the end of time with Eliot beside her. She wouldn't fear the darkness or the uncertainty of whether there was life after death and what that meant precisely. Sammy knew this was what she had always wanted and needed. Eliot confirmed all this when he said, "I just want you. You're all I care about."

Sammy truly decimated Eliot's mouth with her own ravenous lips. There was a rushed but absolutely necessary clash of teeth, lips and tongue. Her hands assaulted his body, fingers following its contours. The craziness was worth it. To love and be loved - that was the meaning of life – reason enough to take another breath. The muscle in her chest was free to keep contracting so long as she wasn't the only one who noticed, or believed it necessary that her heart keep beating. Eliot climbed on top of Sammy, sucking and biting her neck as his hands gripped her hips, pulling them up closer against his own. Then Eliot froze, suddenly breaking the kissing and impassioned embraces to seriously look at Sammy. "Is this okay?"

Words seemed wildly unnecessary. Lips mashed together, Sammy began unbuttoning Eliot's shirt, eager with desire and fumbling. She slid it off of his firm, smooth shoulders. Discarded, it fell to the floor beside the bed. Her fingernails, bearing chipped polish, scratched down his back and then circled to the front of his jeans. Still too eager and therefore clumsy, her fingers slipped as she unbuttoned and tried to unzip his jeans. Eliot stilled her hands.

"Sammy, are you ready for all of this? I don't want you to regret anything with me."

Smiling, Sammy gently pushed Eliot's hair from his slightly dampened brow. "I'm ready. I want it to be with you, Eliot, please." Resuming the hungry kisses, Eliot's clothes were soon crumpled on the bedroom floor. Sammy's joined his shortly. The delightful, delicious pressure... The moonlight slanting in through the blinds... The rise and fall of their bodies and heaving of their chests... it was perfect.

The moonbeams gave way to sunbeams, and Sammy lay on her side, head propped up by her bent elbow and hand. She watched the steady rise and fall of Eliot's chest. His angel's face was turned away from her to the side. Dark, careless hair curled down his neck. Briefly, Sammy wondered if he was as passionate about her as she was about him, but only briefly. Coming to a conclusion could be catastrophically painful. Hesitantly, Sammy tugged at his dark hair with shaking fingers. The gesture was meant to be tender and loving, but it was really more selfish than anything else. She needed the comfort found in the physical contact, needed him like an alcoholic needs a parting drink at last call; a shot to remember. Because that's what Eliot was - some kind of addiction. Sammy thought about him constantly and would plan her entire day around their encounters. He was all that mattered, and unhealthy as that was, it was inconsequential because it was true. And it had all happened so fast, as sudden and as quick as lightning, and as quick as Eliot's hand moved to close around Sammy's, nestled in his hair. In startling contrast, Eliot turned his face to hers slowly. Despite Sammy's increased heart rate, Eliot smiled and brought Sammy's trembling hand to his lips. He kissed it lightly. Still, Sammy trembled. The sun was coming in strong slants through the blinds. Sammy watched the rays lick her lover's face and arms like some irritating, overexcited puppy. Groaning, his eyes squinted against the luminescent intruder, and then Eliot asked Sammy what time it was. She reached out for her cell phone. It was 8:54 AM. Wow. Sammy placed the phone back on the windowsill and noticed a comfortable pressure against her middle. Eliot's arm was wrapped securely around her. Smiling in spite of herself, she looked down to see Eliot's face, feigning sleep. It was precious and perfect, and Sammy couldn't help herself – she kissed his eyelids. Grinning almost instantly, Eliot kept his eyes closed as he said, "I was hoping you'd do something like that."

She laughed softly. "Are you going to stay for breakfast?"

"Absolutely, but let it be my treat this time. We'll go out."

Infinitely happy, Sammy bit her bottom lip to keep from beaming like a juvenile fool. "Okay, great. I've just got to take a shower."

Deeply kissing Sammy as he held her hair back and away from her face, Eliot grinned wider. "Me too." The young couple occupied themselves in a far-from-cleanly manner until they were showered and ready to go.

Chapter Nine
A Bad Trip

*"The truth is that I only really wanted
to be wanted by you."* ~ Damien Rice

They sat in a booth near the front of the restaurant. Eliot had left to use the bathroom, and Sammy was patiently waiting for his return. She couldn't believe what had happened last night. Smiling so wide that her cheeks were sore, she'd laugh for no particular reason every now and again. Though it was cold outside, the sun shone brightly and she was warm and cozy in Eliot's sweatshirt. Sammy was bursting with joy and, in her exceptionally radiant mood, she reached for her cell phone to scroll through her inbox, a means of keeping busy until Eliot returned from the bathroom. She couldn't just sit and stare off into space or watch the diners around her; both would be creepy. She'd been through the menu, already knew what it was she wanted to order, so the cell phone was definitely the best way to pass the time. A small frown began as messages flew past without a single one from Rob. Someone had deleted his messages.

Eliot returned from the bathroom. "This is the second time I've seen you sitting alone at a table, going through your phone and looking like you're about to cry." Smiling, Eliot shook his head slowly. "What's wrong?"

"The messages from Rob are gone."

"Weren't they from a while ago? Maybe your phone deleted them automatically to make room for incoming messages."

"No," Sammy said, her voice rising. "I specifically saved these. They would have to be manually deleted. Someone went through my phone and got rid of them."

Eliot's brows furrowed. "Why were you saving them?"

"I really need to explain that?" Sammy asked rhetorically, paling. "He was my first boyfriend, and he was murdered sending me a message. Of course I saved them, to remember. Those messages were the only physical proof I had of Rob, and now they're gone."

Eliot leaned forward. "I'm sorry. I understand why you would want to save them, at first, but time has passed and you're with me now. I don't understand why those messages are still so important."

Realization hit Sammy like a strong, horrible odor and her stomach flipped over. "Eliot, did you delete those messages?"

"Like a month ago, and that only proves that they weren't that important to you anymore, Sammy. If you had been reading them every day, I wouldn't have gotten rid of them." Eliot squirmed uncomfortably in his seat and had stopped making eye contact with the young woman opposite him.

"Are you shitting me?" Sammy was shouting. "How dare you! It is never up to you to decide what's important to me!"

"Sammy, please calm down –"

"No, no, I will not calm down!" Sammy clumsily got to her feet. "I need to leave."

Eliot sighed heavily. "Don't be childish. Sit down."

"Fuck you." Sammy pulled Eliot's sweatshirt up over her head and threw it at him. "I loved Rob. You had no right to erase those messages."

"You had no right to keep the messages. Do you even care how you hanging on to Rob like that made me feel?"

"You're crazy!" Sammy screamed. "He's dead, Eliot! You had no competition from him! I literally gave you everything last night. What more do I have to do to prove to you I'm all yours? I've already lost my friends! Want me to give up my family too?"

Eliot reached for her hand. "Sammy, just stop yelling and please sit down."

"Don't touch me," she spit back. Sammy marched past the startled waitress and past the handful of intrigued onlookers. She threw open the doors and marched right out into the cold with no jacket and no ride home. It didn't matter – she would call her dad. He'd be at the store with Mom and her little brother (that's what the note on the fridge said, and, frankly, Sammy was fucking sick and tired of getting notes), but he would come and pick her up and bring her home, and then she would call Maeve. Together, they could get brunch and visit Mike. If Eliot called, she wouldn't answer, not until she had a handle on her emotions and knew exactly what she was going to say. Eliot had no right removing Rob from her tangible memories. It wasn't fair.

Sammy called Maeve three times while she waited for her dad to come and pick and her up. She called Maeve another three times once she got home and watched her phone anxiously as she cleaned her bedding. She was a storm cloud, hovering about from place to place and raining her misery down upon anyone and everyone she talked to. Her mom tried to ask what was wrong, but Sammy had shot her down harshly. Burned by her daughter, all Sammy's mom did was tell Sammy that the rest of the family were going to visit Aunt Ellen in Pennsylvania that weekend and that numbers were on the fridge. Shortly thereafter, everyone departed, and Sammy had the house to herself. All things considered, that was probably for the best.

Waiting for Maeve to call back, Sammy plopped herself on the couch for some mindless television. She snacked occasionally, always keeping an eye on her phone. No one called. No one sent her a text message. Hours passed. Around eight o'clock that evening, there was a frantic banging on her front door. Sammy had a sinking feeling it would be Maeve, bleeding and begging for shelter. All day, after leaving Eliot at the local IHOP, Sammy had entertained the very real possibility that Rob and Mike's attacker had found Maeve. That in mind, Sammy hurried to her front door and threw it open wide.

Eliot collapsed into the threshold, covered in blood.

"Oh my God, Eliot!" Sammy immediately knelt beside him and gingerly tried to assess the damages. "Eliot, what happened?"

He was gasping for breath and scrambling further inside the doorway. "The guy … who got Rob and Mike … is after me." He kicked the front door shut behind him and lay on his back, trying to compose himself. Sammy was struck with terror.

"What do you mean?"

"Some big son of a bitch ambushed me at my apartment. I only got away because a neighbor came home." Eliot looked Sammy in the eyes for the first time since dragging his bleeding body across her doorstep. "We need to get out of here."

Sobbing, Sammy asked, "Shouldn't we get you to a hospital?"

Eliot shook his head. "I'll be fine. He just beat me up a little. If he comes after you, though, there's not much I can do. We've got to leave."

"What about the cops? I think it's about time we called them!"

"There's no time. He could be on his way here." Eliot struggled to his knees, assisted by a frantic Sammy. "I grabbed my bags already, so come on. We'll go to Maine, stay with my parents and call the police from there."

"But what about classes? And my parents?"

"You can call them once we're on the road and fuck classes. He's coming after us!" Eliot got to his feet, obviously in a great deal of pain. Sammy wanted desperately to help him, but he wasn't really in need of help. He just needed her to listen and do as he said. "Sammy, please let me keep you safe. Please pack a bag and come with me. I'll answer all questions once we're on our way."

Sammy nodded, though she was crying. Turning, she sprinted up the stairs and grabbed what she could; some toiletries, a couple of outfits and pajamas, her cell phone charger, and her purse. Hurrying back down the stairs, Eliot was already waiting with the door open. She followed him out instinctively, pausing only to lock the door behind her. Sammy observed Eliot wince with pain with nearly every step. "Eliot, should I drive?"

"That'd probably be best, yeah." He threw her the keys.

They stopped to fill the tank and get some coffee for Sammy, and before they were on the road for half an hour, Eliot was asleep. Sammy tried to get Maeve on the phone about five more times. There was still no answer, so Sammy resigned herself to playing her iPod loudly and sipping the now tepid cup of coffee to stay awake. The roads were nearly empty, but still Sammy kept checking the rearview mirror for the ominous looking car that had to be following them, plotting their respective demises. Eliot had escaped once, but could he do it again? Would he get hurt saving her? What had happened to the neighbor? Sammy stole a glance at the sleeping man beside her and, for the first time ever, doubted him. Why would he rush to her aid so quickly, especially when he was injured and they had fought so bitterly that morning? Why didn't he want to go to the cops? Why did he already have a bag packed? All those questions had to be answered, but Sammy supposed they could wait until morning and that she should be grateful Eliot had come for her at all.

Morning broke over the interstate with an understated beauty. Sammy greeted it with an exaggerated yawn, and Eliot stirred beside her. "Good morning," he groaned. "Where are we?"

"Somewhere in New England, I think. I've been too exhausted to be more precise."

Eliot laughed quietly. "Do you want to pull over and get some breakfast? I'll take over after that."

Sammy didn't smile. "Will you answer my questions?"

"Of course," Eliot said as his own smile faded. He sat up straighter in the passenger seat. He eyed Sammy warily as she took the next exit and searched for a restaurant. She was still angry, confused, and scared. Her emotional instability would make everything much harder, harder than it had to be. He rubbed the back of his neck roughly, frustrated. Sammy didn't notice her boyfriend's rising agitation as she pulled into the parking lot of some local diner. Even when Eliot slammed his door after climbing out of the car, even as he remained silent walking in, and even though he headed straight for the rest rooms instead of waiting with her, Sammy didn't notice how visibly aggravated Eliot was. This lack of interest in her significant other should have startled Sammy, as it possibly marked the beginning of a severe disconnect. Sammy was too frustrated to care; an ironic commonality between her and Eliot. She sat and stared through the menu, allowing herself to become (Lost? Trapped? Did it matter?) absorbed in her thoughts.

Eliot announced his arrival by clearing his throat. "I figured I should clean up first. Otherwise, people might stare and ask questions."

"What's so wrong with having questions? I have a few, myself." Sammy calmly closed the menu and placed it directly in front of her. Calm, cool, and collected; it was crucial she remain that way, so Eliot wouldn't be able to dismiss her concerns as theatrics.

"What?" On the other hand, Eliot was having some trouble retaining his composure. He just wanted her to understand, to figure it all out so this wouldn't be necessary.

"Why can't we call the cops now? We've put quite a bit of distance between ourselves and your apartment."

"If you want to call the cops, go ahead. What is it you're going to tell them?"

Sammy crinkled her brow. "That my boyfriend was attacked by the same person who killed Rob Hall and hospitalized Mike Bower."

"Sammy," Eliot spoke slowly, "what evidence is there?"

"The same weapon was used on Rob and Mike."

Eliot shook his head. "I wasn't stabbed."

Faltering, Sammy was beginning to get upset. "What about the notes left on my car?"

"What about them? You didn't save any of them."

She slammed her palms down on the table. "Eliot, you said that the guy was after us –"

He took her hands in his. "I know what I said, but the police need evidence. We don't have any. Calling in based on a suspicion that can't be verified is only going to make us look suspicious."

Sammy frowned. "How come you already had a bag packed?"

Eliot averted his gaze. "Well, I was already on planning on going to Maine. After our fight, I had no reason to stay in New Jersey."

"You weren't going to call me and try to work things out?" Sammy was fighting back tears, but she wasn't exactly sure why.

"I was but from Maine. I was going to come back, but I thought we both needed time to calm down."

"Why did you delete those messages?" Sammy asked, lowering her voice to a whisper.

Eliot leaned in closer and said, "I thought I was helping. I didn't want you to hang on to him. You weren't sleeping. I guess it made me mad to think I wasn't enough for you."

Sammy took her hands from Eliot's and leaned back in the booth as the waitress came to take their orders. Not a word was spoken between the two as they ate their meals. Sammy tried calling Maeve several times but still there was no answer. She was becoming incredibly worried and thought, if nothing else, the two should call the cops to have them check on Maeve. Sammy had half a mind to tell Eliot but knew he'd only argue with her. When

Eliot grabbed the check to pay, Sammy didn't complain or offer to pay half. She simply walked back to the car, climbed into the passenger's seat and did her best to fall asleep as soon as possible. She didn't even want to look at him.

Sammy awoke when the car slowly rolled to a stop some hours later. The sun was coming in strong through the windshield and Sammy could feel her shirt stuck between her back and the seat. She sat up slowly, feeling a dull, aching pain in her neck. She must have slept on it funny and as she tried to stretch, she had a strong desire to get out of the damn car and walk around. A sharp intake of breath from beside her made Sammy turn, and when she did, she found that Eliot was sweaty, pale and grimacing in pain. Concerned, she gently grabbed his shoulder. "Eliot?" she called hesitantly.

"I just need a break. The pain's intense." His breath was shallow. He killed the engine, removed the key from the ignition, and fell back in his seat like he'd just run a thousand miles. Slowly, delicately, he turned his head to Sammy. Sorrowful, tired eyes met hers. "Five minutes is all I need. The gas light was on, too."

Sammy looked out of her window and realized they had stopped at a gas station. Turning back to Eliot, she wondered what was going on- was there internal bleeding or something? Was he tensing and cramping from driving? She had to do something. "I'll be right back," Sammy said. She hurried from the car into the convenience station beside the gas pumps. She purchased some chips, strong ibuprofen, and water – lots of water. Running back to the car, Eliot appeared to be sleeping but when Sammy softly called his name through the open window his eyes opened. He smiled sweetly. Sammy opened the car door and knelt beside the vehicle. "Here, take two of these." Sammy handed Eliot two pills and she handed him a bottle of water. His eyes remained focused on her the entire time it took to pop the two ibuprofen pills into his dry, shaking mouth, unscrew the cap on the bottle, take a large swig of water, and then replace it. Sammy tried to keep eye contact but couldn't. She began talking to the pavement. "Okay, so let's get you in the other seat." She unbuckled Eliot's seat belt and, slipping his arm around her neck, Sammy managed to get Eliot to his feet. Together, they shuffled to the passenger side.

Eliot was staring at Sammy.

Sammy pretended not to notice.

She was about to buckle him in when Eliot placed a hand upon her shoulder. "Could you please get me another shirt from the back? This one is sweaty and kind of bloody." Sammy nodded silently and did what had been asked of her. Coming back, Sammy saw that Eliot was attempting to remove his soiled shirt, but he was failing – the pain was winning. She rushed to his side.

"Eliot, let me help," she said, grabbing a sleeve. Carefully, she pulled until his arm was free, doing the same on the opposite side with just as much care. It was when she grabbed the bottom of the shirt to pull it up and over Eliot's head that her heart broke. Dark, deep bruises of all sizes covered his entire torso. The asshole must have taken a bat to Eliot. The skin was swollen – the ache must have been terrible, and his first thought had been of Sammy and her safety. Eliot hadn't even been to a doctor. Tears spilling over, Sammy dropped to her knees beside her seated boyfriend and allowed the discarded tee shirt to slip from her hand to the pavement. "Eliot, what did he do to you?"

Sadly, Eliot smiled. "It looks worse than it is, I promise." He searched Sammy with those burning eyes. "Did you get another shirt?"

Wiping her eyes, Sammy nodded and lovingly dressed Eliot. She buckled him in, shut his door, and as she passed behind the car to the driver's side, she allowed herself a few broken sobs. Everyone she cared about was getting hurt (or going missing) and all she could do was cry about it like some stupid, silly, little girl. That was all Sammy was – a dramatic, self-indulgent, lonely, bitter girl. She wasn't a heroine. She wasn't romantically tragic. She wasn't anything but scared. Drying her eyes, Sammy took one last steadying breath before climbing in behind the wheel. She was just about to start the engine and get back on the highway when Eliot called her name, softly.

"Please don't hate me. I couldn't live if I thought you hated me."

"Eliot, I don't hate you. I don't think I ever could." She tried to control her breathing, to stop the hysterics. "Just sleep."

Night was coming on slowly as Sammy drove through the violet hour, catching glimpses of the wintry New England countryside. Churches that had been standing since the revolution had snow gathered on their roofs. The bare trees glinted silver with hanging icicles. It truly was a beautiful drive, and Sammy would have enjoyed it had she been able to get Maeve on the phone. The irritating rodent that was worry chewed consistently on her brain and made her irritable and emotional. She had watched Eliot, sleeping peacefully beside her, with varying amounts of envy, love, and anger. She had shut his window once he had fallen asleep but not before she noted the way the breeze had been blowing his dampened hair about his magnificent face. If nothing else, he was beautiful. His expression seemed to be peaceful, but Sammy wondered about his pain. Her stomach rumbled loudly, and her thoughts turned. It was well past dinner time and Sammy was hungry. She thought it'd be a good idea for Eliot to eat something other than pills and potato chips. Reaching out, she shook his shoulder. "Eliot? Eliot?"

Groggily, Eliot asked, "What is it?"

"Are you hungry? I'm thinking we should stop for dinner."

"Sounds great," Eliot agreed, opening one eye to look at Sammy. "How long was I asleep for?"

"You were out for a couple of hours, at least." Sammy stole a glance from the corner of her eyes. "How are you feeling?"

"Much better," Eliot said. He sat up straighter and grinned. "Thank you very much."

Sammy stayed quiet.

"Let's just hit up a drive through. We'll switch and eat but keep making time." Sammy agreed, and in no time at all she was no longer driving but enjoying a greasy burger and fries and listening to the radio. From time to time, she'd have to lift Eliot's drink or his burger to his lips or hand him some fries, but it wasn't a big deal. She was comfortable – comfortable enough to ask Eliot about Maeve. "Have you tried her parents' house?" he asked.

Sammy shook her head. "I don't have that number."

Eliot raised an eyebrow. "Really? That's weird. You guys have been best friends for a while now, right?"

Sammy nodded. "Well, it's been about a year. So maybe it hasn't been all that long."

"Where'd you meet? In class?"

"Yeah … kind of like us. Maeve and I took the same gen-ed math class. It was awful," Sammy laughed. "I got a C. She did better than that, though." Sammy paused solemnly. "I just want her to be okay, Eliot."

He took her hand in his and held it tightly. "Call the school. If she hasn't been to class, then we'll call the cops." Eliot kissed Sammy's hand. "I'm sure all this worrying is unnecessary. Maeve can't have her cell phone with her when she visits Mike, which is all the time, and she can't answer in the middle of class." Eliot eyed her warily. "Didn't you two have a fight the last time you talked?"

Sammy rubbed her eyes with her free hand. "Yeah, but I've called like a million times."

"She might not have gotten all of them. Once you cross state lines, service gets pretty shoddy."

Shrugging, Sammy began to absent-mindedly chew on her thumbnail. "Maybe, but we can't call the school until Monday. What if –"

"If she's not at Mike's bed side, I'm sure he'll get nervous and call the police and check up on her."

Falling silent, Sammy turned her head to watch the world pass by outside the window. Eliot had the heat going in the car. The Garden State had been teetering on the precipice of winter and it only grew colder the farther north they travelled. The low rattle of the heater was the only sound, and it filled the car completely. Sammy felt like she was obligated to break the silence, to say something. But what would she say to Eliot? Should she apologize for her theatrics at breakfast? Should she demand an apology from Eliot for deleting the messages? Or should she just turn the radio on and forget the whole thing? Leaning forward to press the required buttons for the radio, Eliot stopped her when he said, "Sammy, I'm sorry."

She turned to look at him fast. "What?"

"I'm sorry about deleting the messages. I had no right to do it at all, let alone behind your back. You're not the only one with insecurities, and I know that's no excuse, but it's a reason," Eliot spoke as he released a deep breath. "Can you forgive me?"

Sammy looked at Eliot for a good minute before answering. She thought about how he deleted the messages and how angry that had made her. She thought about the sunrise they had watched together, the nights they spent together, and she knew what her answer was, what it had to be. "Yes; of course."

Eliot beamed like a little kid, and took his eyes off the road long enough to kiss her lips. "This can be a good trip. I'm excited for you to meet my parents."

A whole new kind of horror grabbed hold of Sammy's insides and wouldn't let go. With a queasy smile, she turned to stare out the windshield, wishing she were one of the bugs meeting its demise against the transparent surface.

They stopped at a motel that night and slept in separate beds. It had been Sammy's decision. Though she was beginning to forgive Eliot for erasing Rob's last messages, she still felt like something was amiss and thereby felt it'd be most responsible if they didn't sleep together. Eliot swore up and down that he wouldn't try anything and promised it'd be enough just to have her beside him. The sentiment was touching, but Sammy was stoic, sturdy, and unwavering.

She fell asleep staring at Eliot's back.

Chapter Ten

The Lunatics Run the Asylum

"I may be romantic, and I may risk my life for it,
but I ain't gonna die for you. You know I ain't no Juliet."
~ Amanda Palmer

They left the motel at the crack of dawn and arrived at Safe Haven Asylum of Ellsworth, Maine in the early afternoon. The tires rolled slowly up the long, gravel drive, crunching against the tiny rocks with each revolution. Each side of the winding lane was lined with trees, their bare limbs stretching upward to the gray, frigid sky. The air was bitter cold and it viciously seeped in Eliot's car through tiny cracks near the doors and windows. The heat was blasting, but still Sammy had to suppress chills that assaulted her whole body. Eliot noticed the tremors. "Are you still cold?"

Sammy smiled at Eliot. "I don't know if it's the weather or my nerves."

"Why would it be your nerves?"

"I'm meeting your parents, Eliot. I'm meeting them at the mental institution they operate. It's a little nerve-wracking."

Shaking his head, Eliot chuckled dismissively. "We're staying at the house, not the asylum, and they're going to love you. My dad's a little cold, but he's like that to his own family. It's the weather. We're supposed to get one hell of a snow storm this weekend."

"Think we'll be snowed in?"

Eliot shook his head as the car slowly rolled to a stop before an enormous white mansion, reminiscent of the Southern style plantation homes. Rolling down the car window, Sammy didn't even notice the biting cold as the image of architectural beauty before her consumed her. Four picture windows, complimented by long, black shutters were on the left and right side of the front of the house, as the center featured a balcony and regal front door with several wide, stone steps leading up to it. Potted plants and fancy, curling railings lined the steps, and Sammy half-expected to see roaring, stone lions and Greek statues lining the expansive yard before it. There were none, however. The lawn was plain, but massive. "Eliot, your house is –"

"Thanks," Eliot mumbled. His tone made Sammy turn. He seemed uncomfortable. "I'll grab the bags if you want to head up the steps and knock."

"Not without you," Sammy said, shaking her head. Eliot laughed and opened his car door. Sammy followed suit, and the couple climbed from the car. Eliot retrieved the bags from the trunk, and Sammy waited, bouncing from foot to foot to stay warm. A very audible click in the icy quiet caught her attention, and she turned to see a severe looking woman in a smart-looking pantsuit standing in the doorway. Her light blonde hair was pulled back neatly into a long ponytail. She waved from the warmth of the house and Eliot waved back.

"That's my mother. She's very excited to meet you."

"Great," Sammy said with as much enthusiasm as she could muster which, admittedly, wasn't much. She took Eliot's hand, and together they ascended the stone steps.

"Eliot, welcome home. It's been too long." Mrs. Andrews was beaming as she held her arms open wide. Eliot let go of Sammy's hand to share in his mother's embrace, which was touching to observe. As Sammy observed, so she was observed. Mrs. Andrew's steel gray eyes took in the young woman awkwardly standing in the threshold, too nervous to even come inside and out of the cold and shut the door. Mrs. Andrew's smile remained, as timidity was a quality to be admired in a young woman; something feminine, albeit antiquated, lost in the modern age. Sammy, feeling Eliot's mother's gaze upon her, froze – which wasn't particularly hard to do considering half of her was still outside. She didn't dare breathe until Mrs. Andrews gave some kind of sign. Would she accept Sammy, or would Sammy be rejected? Sensing the building tension, Eliot turned out of his mother's embrace to look at Sammy. His face showed he was anxious as well. After one last, brief moment, Mrs. Andrews spoke. "You must be Sammy. Come in out of the cold, sweetheart."

Breathing easy now, Sammy stepped forward into Eliot's home and shut the door behind her. The heavy door closed with a loud boom that echoed throughout the vast mansion. Sammy was then hugged tightly by Mrs. Andrews. Hesitantly, Sammy returned the embrace. She was surprised, to say the least. Her dark eyes found Eliot's, and he shot her an encouraging smile. Sammy relaxed a little more. "It's a pleasure to meet you, Mrs. Andrews."

Stepping back and still grinning brightly, Mrs. Andrews said, "I'm sure you must be exhausted after the drive, but I'm hoping you'll join me for hot chocolate in the dining room."

Hot chocolate sounded like a wonderful idea. "I'd love to," Sammy agreed. "Just tell me where to drop off my bags and –"

"Oh, right there is fine," Mrs. Andrews interrupted. "The help will bring them to your room."

"Oh." Sammy felt dumb, and her cheeks burned an almost alarming shade of red.

"Eliot, your father is expecting you in his study. You may join us afterwards."

Eliot's beautiful face paled noticeably, and there was a hint of dread in his voice when he spoke. "Mother, please. Haven't you –"

"Go," Mrs. Andrews said. It was a stern command that Eliot did not argue with. He kissed Sammy's forehead with an aching kind of tenderness before heading up the spectacle of a staircase. Sammy watched her lover leave with an anxious curiosity until Mrs. Andrews grabbed her hand. "Come along; this way, Sammy." Eliot's mother led the young woman to the right and to the rear area of the house, along parquet floors adorned with Oriental rugs, past mahogany bookshelves, priceless pieces of art, and hallway after hallway. When they finally reached the dining room (through the expensive looking kitchen, with its slate tile flooring, rich, wooden cabinetry and seemingly endless supply of appliances), Mrs. Andrews seated herself at the head of a long, oak table; the centerpiece of the room. Sammy sat to the right of the matriarch, observing the intricate chandelier hanging low from the center of the ceiling in awe.

She had never felt so poor or so out of place in her entire life.

"Truth be told, I'm glad we're spending these few moments alone." Mrs. Andrews smiled warmly at Sammy. "You're the first young woman Eliot has ever brought home."

"Really?" Sammy blushed again. "I've never been brought home before, so this is a first for me, too." She laughed loudly, even though neither of them had said anything particularly funny. Sammy swallowed hard.

"Eliot speaks very highly of you," Mrs. Andrews said. A maid arrived to deliver the hot chocolate. Sammy didn't mean to gawk, but she had only ever seen maids in movies and was disappointed when the wizened woman departed quickly. Mrs. Andrews sipped gingerly from her steaming mug before patiently eyeing Sammy. Stomach sinking, Sammy realized Mrs. Andrews was waiting for her to speak.

"Oh, well … Eliot's really good to me – too good, actually. I'm still trying to figure out how I deserve him, and why he's attracted to me." Sammy laughed softly, but then quickly cleared her throat. She knew she should say more about Eliot. "Your son is beautiful, intelligent, patient, passionate, kind … and he makes me feel singular and unique in a world of six billion people. Eliot is one of the greatest things to have ever happened to me, and I know I am blessed to have him in my life." Sammy averted her gaze to her own steaming mug. "Eliot kind of saved my life. He sort of saves my life every day." Sammy hadn't intended to be so honest or so intense. She made it sound like her life revolved around Eliot and that he alone gave it meaning. Sammy didn't want that to be true, but did that wanting change anything? Was it true all the same?

"Do you love my son?"

Sammy looked up quickly, ripped from her self-reflection. "I'm sorry, what?"

"I asked you if you loved my son."

Fuck.

Shit.

Balls.

How the hell was she supposed to answer that question? Sammy's hands were shaking badly – she couldn't even pick up her mug. "Um, it's only been a few months …." Sammy began answering one way and thought it sounded weak and lame, so she rapidly changed direction. "But I've given Eliot all of myself, and he's accepted me and all of my juvenile craziness again and again. I've accepted him, too, and have depended on him and he has never let me down. He …" she paused, faltering again, "… he is the love of my life. I love him very much."

Sammy looked to study Mrs. Andrews's face, to gauge her reaction to Sammy's response. Tears had filled the older woman's eyes and were now spilling over, rolling silently down her smooth cheeks. "If you'll excuse me, Sammy." Without another word, Mrs. Andrews slowly and gracefully pushed her chair back from the table, rose, and left the dining room. Sammy didn't see which way she went, as she stared at the tabletop and fought off waves of nausea. Clearly, she had said something terribly wrong. The horrible possibility that this may be the last weekend she would ever spend with Eliot settled over her like some fatal, highly communicable disease. She simply sat in the chair, staring blankly ahead until her hot chocolate turned cold.

Sometime later, the sound of advancing footsteps startled Sammy and snapped her out of her maddening trance. Jumping and turning to the sound, Sammy saw Eliot approaching. She leapt to her feet, fighting the urge to wrap herself around his ankles to keep him from sending her away. "Sorry that took so long. My father had a lot to say." Eliot came to a halt mere inches from Sammy. His eyes were red and swollen. Had he been crying? Why would he be crying? "Where's my mother? Did you scare her off?" Eliot asked good-naturedly. It was a corny attempt at humor, Sammy felt, to mask the fact that he was upset. Had his mother already talked to him and convinced him to get rid of the trash downstairs?

"I think I actually did. She ran off crying after she asked me if I loved you."

Eliot grew pale for the second time that day. An unnerved Eliot unnerved Sammy – he was strong and stoic; he didn't rattle. She was the one that was supposed to go to pieces, but here Eliot was, disturbed because his mother had fled from his girlfriend in tears. Could you blame the guy? Eliot idly rubbed the back of his neck and asked, "What did you say?"

Sammy pulled her hair back. "I said a lot of things, some really intense things, actually – things I've never even told you."

"Yeah, but what was your answer?"

Mumbling, Sammy said, "I said I love you very much."

Laughing, Eliot threw his arms around Sammy and crushed her mouth with his. Mouths and limbs entangled, Eliot lifted her off the ground and spun her around, laughing against her precious mouth. After a few spins, Eliot set Sammy down and cupped her face in his hands. "I love you too, so much."

Sammy gripped Eliot's shoulders. "This is spectacular news – really fantastic – but why was your mother crying when I told her?"

Becoming very still, Eliot began to look at Sammy in a whole new way, almost like he was seeing her for the first time … or for the last time. It was her turn to hold his head in her hands, but Eliot wasn't going to break in front of her. "I, um, wouldn't worry about it. She's always been emotional. You're the first girl I've ever introduced to her, remember, and my father has been trying her patience a lot lately. She has a lot on her plate." He kissed her lips. "Let's go unpack before dinner."

Sammy was staying in a large bedroom across the hall from Eliot's. It was decorated in calming, varying shades of lilac and lavender, and Sammy liked it very much. The big picture window at the opposite end of the room let in slants of burning orange as the sun set. It was beautiful to see, and Sammy stopped what she was doing to watch the scene unfold. The power of the light was nearly overwhelming, and she had to squint her eyes against it. It reminded her of not too long ago when Eliot had suddenly appeared at her bedroom window and taken her to watch the most important sunrise of her entire life. Eliot, Eliot, Eliot – so much had happened so fast, and Sammy had no idea as to what it all meant. She couldn't make heads or tails of any of it, of the odd behavior, extreme circumstances, or her own feelings. Rob was dead, Mike was in the hospital, and for all intents and purposes Maeve was missing. Sammy wouldn't allow herself to lose sight of those facts, but at the same time, she was about to have dinner with Eliot and his parents in their completely awesome mansion. The mundane parts of the situation appealed to her, so was it really a sin to enjoy the little moments? Was it really so selfish to not be consumed by the past or be terrified of the future for just one god damn night? The present, the here and now with Eliot … didn't that matter? Gentle tapping at the door saved Sammy from herself.

It was Eliot, as it always was. Eliot the savior, the white knight. "Are you ready to head downstairs?"

"Yeah."

Eliot held out his hand, and Sammy took it. He kissed her cheek lightly before making the return trip to the dining room. As they walked, hand in hand, Eliot whispered a constant string of tips and tricks to surviving an Andrews Family dinner. Eliot placed a great deal of emphasis on the fact that Sammy shouldn't expect much from his father. He went as far as to reveal that Mr. Andrews didn't believe Eliot should be seeing anyone, and that Sammy in particular was distracting him from prior obligations and preventing him from making good on previous promises.

"What prior obligations?" Sammy asked. Unfortunately, she asked just as they arrived at the long, oak table. Sammy sat beside Mrs. Andrews, and Eliot sat opposite Sammy, beside his father. Mr. Andrews was devastatingly handsome, much like his son, but also incredibly intimidating. There was no merriment twinkling about his dark eyes, and his strong chin and thick brows framed his face in the most severe of manners. He was an authoritarian – a scary man. When he spoke, Sammy was strongly reminded of Jeremy Irons as Scar in *The Lion King*. She knew it wasn't the best analogy, but she was too nervous to think of a better one.

"Good evening, Sammy." His voice boomed like a slamming door. "Please excuse my absence this afternoon. Work has been particularly important as of late." Mr. Andrews paused to shoot Eliot a meaningful glance signifying something Sammy didn't understand. "I apologize, also, for keeping Eliot from you."

"Oh, that's okay. I'd just spent plenty of time with him." Sammy paused to smile sweetly at Eliot. "And besides, it gave me the opportunity to meet Mrs. Andrews."

Mrs. Andrews did not smile. She only nodded her head in Sammy's direction. The first course, some kind of fancy soup, was served, and Mr. Andrews continued the idle conversation. "Eliot tells me you want to be a writer, Sammy."

"I do."

"Has any of your work been published?"

"No, not yet."

"That's a pity."

"Father," Eliot interjected coldly, "Sammy's only twenty-one years old. She has nothing but time and talent ahead of her."

"You seem very protective of her, Eliot. Why is that?"

Eliot gritted his teeth. "I am protective of her, because you are attacking her."

The atmosphere of the dining room was uncomfortable and reaching outrageous levels of it. Sammy wanted to bring it back to normal. "Eliot, it's okay. I don't feel attacked." Gently, Sammy tapped Eliot's shin with her foot. She turned her eyes towards his father and took a deep breath. "I'm trying to get published, sir. I've sent a short story to five different magazines recently. Now it's a waiting game until I hear back."

Mr. Andrews appraised her coldly. "Which magazines?"

Sammy's throat was dry. "Some specialty magazines dealing in science fiction, fantasy, and horror."

He sipped from his crystal water glass. "You consider that literature, do you?"

"Father." Eliot was still angry.

"Some of the best literature, yes. Stephen King is a personal hero of mine." Nervously, Sammy tucked her hair behind her ears. "What's your genre of choice, Mr. Andrews?"

"I prefer non-fiction, works that deal in abnormal psychology and groundbreaking treatments for various related disorders. Immersion in work leads to success."

Sammy nodded with a queasy smile. "I couldn't agree more, sir."

"My career is incredibly important to me. I would sacrifice anything for my work, as it benefits the greater public and is my passion." He nodded to indicate his son. "I have instilled the same values in my son."

"That is an impressive work ethic, sir."

Eliot tapped Sammy's shin with his foot. "You'd have to agree that there's more to life than work, though. There's love and happiness and art and pain and destruction and the good and the bad."

"Eliot, may I speak with you in the kitchen?" Mr. Andrews sounded furious.

"No. We are eating dinner. It can wait."

"Now!" Mr. Andrews did not ask Eliot again. He demanded his presence. Eliot threw his expensive linen napkin against the pricey china, climbed out of his chair violently and stormed out of the dining room. Mr. Andrews's movements were more controlled, seemingly more deliberate. When they had both left, Sammy released a breath she had been well aware of holding in, and laid her weary head to rest upon her arms, folded on the table.

"Get out."

It was the first thing Mrs. Andrews had said since the awful meal had begun. Sammy raised her head slowly to stare incredulously at the older woman.

"What?"

"There's no time to explain. They'll be back any minute." Mrs. Andrews did not make eye contact with the petrified younger woman beside her, but spoke quietly and quickly. "If you want to live, you need to leave this house now."

"Mrs. Andrews, what are you talking about?"

"They'll kill you if you let them. They've done it before."

"Who will kill me?"

"You stupid woman, I can't make it any plainer!"

"Is everything okay, Elizabeth?" Mr. Andrews had returned.

"I feel ill. I think it's best if I retire for the evening." She rose to her feet.

"I agree. I'll escort you upstairs." Mr. Andrews took his wife's hand and led her up the stairs.

It was the last time Sammy ever saw Mrs. Andrews.

Eliot came back in the room a few moments after, absolutely livid. Sammy rose to meet him. "Eliot, what –"

He didn't engage Sammy in conversation, but only grabbed her hand and hurried up the stairs. Sammy could barely keep up and was fearful of falling. She had to run to keep up. He took her back to her bedroom and slammed the door shut behind him. "Fuck!" He picked up some decorative trinket from the dresser and threw it against the wall, smashing it into tiny, porcelain shards.

"Eliot, calm down!" Sammy screamed.

"He expects too much of me! It's not fair!" Another trinket smashed.

"Who are you talking about, your father? What does he need you to do?"

Suddenly, Eliot turned and punched the wall. "I hate him! He has me trapped! He damn well knows I can't turn back now!" He left a thick trail of blood smeared against the lavender. Sammy gasped and backed away.

"Stop it! You're scaring me!"

Eliot turned to Sammy and rushed to her, arms open wide. "I'm sorry, Sammy. I am so, so sorry." He wrapped her tightly in his arms and buried his face in her hair. "You have to believe me that I never meant for you to be involved in all of this."

Sammy's voice broke as she gently rubbed Eliot's back, trying to soothe him from his manic, frantic state. "Involved me in all what, Eliot? It's really frustrating not knowing what you're talking about."

Eliot began sobbing and fell limply into Sammy's arms. Unsure of what to do exactly, Sammy sat the both of them on the bed and held Eliot, running her fingers through his hair, kissing his cheek soothingly. He was breaking, falling to pieces in front of her, and Sammy's fear of not being good or strong enough for Eliot loomed in front of her. He needed her, but Sammy wasn't sure if she could handle all of this. "Can I stay with you tonight?"

Sammy wondered if she should say no. Would it be callous to tell Eliot that she needed time to think things over, especially since his mother's warning that had scared the shit out of her? Should she be packing her bags? However, when Sammy looked at Eliot really and truly suffering in her arms, she knew the answer. There was no way she could leave him. The dependence ... it worked both ways. "Of course," was all she said, and Eliot kissed her deeply.

Sammy woke up beside Eliot, encircled in his strong arms. It was a feeling she loved and lusted after, but didn't think she could ever become accustomed to. Discreetly, Sammy inched closer to Eliot and released her breath, settling in to go back to sleep. Lips softly kissing the back of her neck caused her lips to curl into a smile and for her eyes to open again. "Good morning beautiful," was Eliot's whispered greeting.

Rolling over to face her beloved, Sammy said, "Good morning handsome." She smiled.

"How about some breakfast in bed?"

"That sounds ... amazing."

Eliot kissed her deeply. "Don't move a muscle. I'll be back." Eliot climbed out of the huge, impossibly comfortable bed, and Sammy listened to his bare feet pad gently against the carpeted bedroom floor and against the wooden floors of the hallway, until she couldn't hear anything except her own breathing. Sammy was happy. She wasn't thinking about Rob, or worrying about Mike and Maeve. Instead, she was enjoying the moment like she promised herself she would. Sammy lost herself among her happy thoughts, among fluffy pillows and warm blankets.

Sammy traveled back to herself when the bedroom door burst open to reveal Mr. Andrews, a long, hypodermic needle with a syringe clenched tightly in his right fist. His thumb was on the trigger, so to speak. "Damn it, Eliot, this should have been done while she was still sleeping!" He took a few predatory paces towards Sammy. Confused and terrified, all she could think to do was scramble back against the headboard, clutching the blanket all around her.

Eliot appeared in the doorway next, breathless. "I wanted to reason with you! There's still time to find someone else!"

"Your relationship with her will compromise any future endeavors and you know it!" Mr. Andrews turned from his son to the young woman on the bed. "Hold her down, Eliot."

Grunting with aggravation, Eliot grudgingly climbed on top of Sammy. The realization that something was terribly wrong and that bad things were about to happen to her finally began to dawn upon Sammy. Screaming for help, she struggled against Eliot, punching and kicking with all the strength she had. Her hesitation had been too long, however, and Eliot had the upper hand from the beginning. Before long, his limbs pinned hers and Mr. Andrews administered a rather heavy sedative.

Sammy was out cold.

Sammy's eyes popped open. The movement was so fast it seemed involuntary, much like the frantic and frequent contracting of the muscle in her chest, the muscle that seemed to be more trouble than it was worth. All she saw was a snowy white ceiling. Something was terribly, terribly wrong, and it was that suffocating and frightening knowledge that woke her up of its own accord. But what was it exactly that was wrong? The eight pounds of crap in her skull was doing nothing to help; why couldn't it work overtime like her heart? Berating her organs, Sammy abruptly realized she was thirsty, very thirsty. She made to turn her head, and to roll over and out of the bed she was in, but multiple leather straps trapped her against a gurney and made any movement impossible. Sammy's face went pale. Her throat tightened and her stomach turned unpleasantly. Her heart, already working double, began to beat so fast she could feel it in her ears. Sammy, faced with a lack of other options, found herself darting her wide, panicked eyes from side to side. Why was she in restraints? Where was she? Gasping for breath and grasping for any kind of memory that could offer answers, Sammy barely heard a door somewhere to the left click open, but the sound that followed was unmistakable.

"Sammy?" Eliot called. He shut the door and this time, Sammy couldn't help but hear it click. His face appeared before her. "Oh, good – you're up."

"Eliot, what the fuck is going on? Let me go!" Sammy screamed and thrashed against the straps.

"I can't let you go. It's too late now. We're already halfway through the experiment. It would be foolish not to finish at this point." Eliot suddenly looked like he was about to cry. "You never should have told me you were a writer."

"Experiment? What the fuck are you talking about?" Her voice was breaking and cracking at random intervals. Her sanity was following suit.

Eliot sighed and spoke slower, as if he were dealing with an especially dense toddler. "My father and I are observing and reporting upon the psychological and physical effects torture has on creative types. We've compiled enough data to report on psychological torture on a female writer, aged twenty-one … you." He regarded Sammy, imprisoned before him, with great interest. "Today, we begin the more physical phase of the experiment. After each method of torture, you'll be asked to write creatively for forty-five minutes to an hour, so I can see if the torture inhibits your ability to create."

Sammy didn't understand everything Eliot said, but the phrase "physical torture" set off bells and whistles and loud alarms. "Eliot," she sobbed and pleaded, "you don't have to do this! You can't do this! You said you loved me! Please, please don't do this!"

Kindly, Eliot smiled and kissed Sammy's forehead. "I do love you, Sammy. That's why I'm allowing you to be a part of this groundbreaking study. Your sacrifice will help countless others. My father explained it all, helped me to see reason." Eliot's logic was flawed to say the least, and he knew it. He was lying to himself and the woman he loved. His face clouded over. "Besides, you don't love me anymore, and I'm a big subscriber to 'if I can't have you, then no one can'."

"I love you, Eliot, I swear! You haven't hurt me yet. No harm, no foul!"

Slowly, Eliot shook his head. "You won't be able to love me once you understand what I've done to psychologically cripple you."

"I won't care!" Sammy's throat burned. Her voice was hoarse. "I promise! Everything can be like it was!"

"Sammy, I killed Rob."

She stopped screaming. She stopped breathing. "What?"

"I killed Rob, put Mike in the hospital, and essentially made Maeve go missing to ensure I was the central figure in your life. I needed your trust, and for you to be completely dependent on me. My efforts were successful. How else were you going to come to Maine?"

"Fuck you, you mother fucking bastard!" Sammy's voice was back with a vengeance and she struggled against her restraints hard enough to rock the gurney.

"No, Sammy, listen – I tried to stop it several times. The clock was against us. I endured blow after blow from my father for you, but the experiment must come first. I realize that now."

"Dear God, someone help me! Help!"

Eliot punched her hard and fast in the mouth. Blood poured freely and already, she could feel her bottom lip split and swell. He punched her across the face a total of ten times, working over each side evenly. Next, he assaulted her sides and ribs. Sammy was positive she heard them crack and that blood was pouring freely inside as well. Lastly, Eliot focused on her thighs.

Then he used a wooden bat.

Her screams brought no salvation.

Eliot left after the beating, and a nurse came in to feed Sammy and clean her up. The nurse didn't heal the wounds, nor offer

Sammy any kind of painkiller, and Sammy cursed the woman and her family. She didn't eat, and when Eliot asked her to write, she couldn't. She only sobbed.

The beatings continued for three more days, at least. Bruises barely had a chance to begin to fade to a pale yellow before ominous patches of black, blue, and violet took their places. Sammy began to eat, but refused to write.

After the beatings came the boiling.

Over a period of what Sammy believed was two days (but it was hard to tell since she all she saw was the snowy white ceiling and the shadows that played across it), Eliot dipped both of her feet and her left hand into a large, silver pot of boiling water. He held each appendage in the pot, under the water, completely immersed, for thirty seconds with minimal time to rest in between. The pain was excruciating and impossible to accurately describe. Though Sammy had always considered herself verbose and articulate, she wasn't surprised to find herself at a loss for words, considering the circumstances. Her right hand had been spared because Eliot asked her to write, and she needed that hand to do so. Surprisingly, after the beatings and the boiling, Sammy was able to compose a short poem:

Roses are red, violets are blue
You're a monster, and I fucking hate you

Eliot stormed out of the room, slamming the door shut behind him. All Sammy could see was the ceiling, but she heard the hurt and anger in the strength Eliot had displayed and had felt the whole room shake with his effort. It made her smile, despite her cracking, bleeding lips.

Eliot would choke her until she nearly passed out. Eliot cut straight, deep lines along her arms, legs and stomach. He sliced the palms of her hands and the soles of her feet. Sheets stained red, Sammy was only moved so the gurney could be hosed down and cleaned. She stood as they did so, which was no easy task considering her feet were burned and sliced. Two burly men in white scrubs held her up and she did her best to remain silent. Eliot walked in.

"How are you feeling?"

In response, she spit in his face.

Outraged, Eliot punched her in the stomach and left the room, presumably to wash his face. Sammy's hospital gown matched the soiled sheets as wounds reopened and oozed. Still, Sammy grinned.

Days, maybe even weeks, passed. Eliot removed the nails from Sammy's left hand. Slowly, he pried them from the skin with thin splinters of wood. He broke every single finger on her left hand. He attacked every pressure point. He dunked her in icy water at random intervals for varying lengths of time. Then he would return and repeat the activity but with scalding water.

Crying, Sammy was forced to squat, blindfolded for what felt like hours.

Speakers blared a cacophony of sound so loud that Sammy's head would pound and her body would shake. It would happen without warning, and Sammy's heart raced as it lived in constant fear.

Sammy never left the room where her misery started, though she had left the gurney now and again. The room had one giant picture window, which led Sammy to believe she was still in the house. Other than that, the room was really unremarkable - just the fucking awful gurney and a desk. A large, bright lamp hung overhead and the wooden floor was old, scratched, and bare. Eliot must have his materials, his torture devices, brought up to the room, as there was nowhere to store them. When the two burly men would strap her back onto the gurney, she wouldn't struggle, wouldn't fight back at all. It would be futile; Sammy knew she didn't stand a chance. She was conserving her energy for the opportunity she was positive would arise for her escape and survival. Sammy knew hope and the will to live were the only things keeping her alive. Sure, life was filled with horrors and cruelty and disappointment, which Eliot embodied, but she had loved and had been loved. She had the felt the sun stoop and spread its warm rays to lovingly caress her face and had felt the eyes of another observe the beauty in that exact moment. She had inhaled sweet, crisp breezes mixed with the breath of another and inhaled life. To know, even for a few months, which is nothing next to a lifetime, that someone found her worthy of special, unique attention was worth taking another breath. Sammy would fight tooth and nail for that breath.

Except Eliot had pried Sammy's nails from her fingers on her left hand, and he had also begun to rip out the teeth in the back of her mouth. She had screamed and cried, struggled against her restraints, and thrashed to survive. Remaining teeth and right fist clenched, Sammy howled for a savior. When it became apparent that she was really and truly alone, she implored death to be swift and sure. Death had yet to make an appearance, however, and Sammy teetered between hope and despair. Eliot's supposed remorse didn't help to tip the scales towards one emotion or the other. Eliot had been enigmatic before, but this confusion was supremely dangerous, and Sammy knew she would die at his hands – or at least that it was a startlingly real possibility. Sammy feared Eliot and what he was capable of, but more so, she was afraid the irreparable psychological damage would take its toll and she would lose the will to live.

Blood was leaking from the corners of her bruised, broken mouth. Both of her eyes were nearly swollen shut from the painful sobs that wracked her entire body, and both of her eyes were blackened from the brutal, consistent beatings. Blood was dried and flaking around her nose and ears, and the whole room reeked of the coppery smell of death and suffering. Sammy didn't know the hour or the day. She assumed it could be December, but being unable to determine the length of her blackouts, she admitted it could be January. Covered in bruises and ravaged by a dull, aching pain, Sammy wasn't ready to die. The old girl still had some fight left in her, but she was sore and tired. Every time the door clicked open and Eliot walked in, Sammy's breath would catch in her throat. He kept warning her that he was going to have to kill her once he had collected all of the data necessary to complete the study, but wouldn't be any more specific about the deadline (pun intended - ha, ha!). She smiled at her own morbid wit, but didn't laugh. To give in and make noise, to succumb to the hysteria, would be to admit defeat. Allowing her mind to crack and break into dangerous, pointy shards would rob her of any chance at survival.

One day, the door opened slowly, and Eliot walked in by himself. As he leaned over Sammy, she noticed he wasn't wearing his white coat or plastic gloves. That was odd, as was Eliot releasing her from the gurney. The leather straps were undone and dangling from either side. Though Sammy was liberated from her bonds, she was too afraid to move. The lack of immobility was too obvious of an opportunity. Something was up. This was it then – her time to die. Metal scraped against the floor, causing Sammy to grimace. Eliot was pulling a chair closer to the gurney. He sat, and Sammy twisted to face him. Strangely, Eliot didn't look so hot himself. Dark circles claimed the space beneath his eyes; he was sweating freely and was paler than she remembered. Something else had changed too. It was hard to describe, but he had walked in with something like a limp, shoulders slumped. His grace and beauty were gone, along with his confidence. Sammy wondered if any of it had ever really been there or if she had imagined it. Her imagination had proved to be dangerous – it had concealed a manic killer in the form of a lover and a savior. She had been so desperate and lonely that she had allowed herself to be manipulated and tortured because of her juvenile desires.

She hoped that whatever Eliot had planned next would be quick.

Eliot cleared his throat. "I'm sorry I killed Rob."

Rob – hearing the name took her back to the day she and Eliot had left for Maine on this bizarre trip into hell, the day all remaining evidence of Rob and his affections for her had been dismissed and permanently removed, and she had permanently affixed Eliot in her life, so to speak. Sammy felt like fucking puking, staring at Eliot, wide-eyed and open-mouthed, like a zombie or comatose patient. She may have still been lying on the gurney, but she was gone.

Sammy was back at the bar. Maeve and Mike were somewhere on the other side, most likely chugging beers and swapping spit. Rob was sitting beside her. He was smiling kindly, but his eyes were somber, sad, and clouded over. Shaking slightly, his hand reached out to tuck Sammy's long, sweeping bangs behind her ear. He wanted to see her better. Rob's fingers lingered near her ear before moving to trail down her cheek and neck. He cleared his throat, and leaned close to whisper to her, making sure he would be heard above the music and raised voices. "We could have had some good times."

Looking down at Rob's knees, her lips twitched for just a moment to display a half-hearted smile.

"Just be careful, alright? Something doesn't feel right and you know it. Keep your guard up, okay?"

Tears were falling. She nodded.

Rob laughed softly, almost imperceptibly. "You know, I had big plans for you the night I was going to surprise you. If I had been able to, that would have been a night to tell our grandkids about."

Smiling only made her cry harder. Rob wiped the tops of her cheeks dry, that sensitive area just under the dark rings of her eyes. "It'll be okay, Sammy. It will all be okay."

"I never meant to hurt you like this," Eliot said. Sammy snapped back to reality and released a shaky breath, but said nothing to Eliot. He had killed Rob – she knew that and needed to pull herself together.

"I'm sorry I put Mike in the hospital."

Silence.

"I'm sorry Maeve's missing and that I lied to you for so long, Sammy."

Silence.

"I love you."

"I don't believe you." That last line had been so unbelievable, Sammy felt forced to respond. Her voice was hoarse and cracking, and the tears still streamed freely. "Fuck you. You're a liar."

Eliot reached out to caress her cheek. Sammy jerked her face away as sharply as she could, but she was sore and tired and the contact was made possible. "I need you to believe me," Eliot pleaded. "It killed me to hurt you."

"I don't give a fuck what you need. I gave you everything I had, you horrible piece of shit."

Eliot pulled his hand away. "You said you loved me."

"So did you."

"I meant it."

Sammy laughed. "You're unbelievable. Love isn't like this. Kill me now, or leave me alone."

Eliot cleared his throat. "I'm sorry to say our time together has come to an end, but I'd like to take this opportunity to also thank you. The information you've provided will be most beneficial to future analysis."

Sammy responded with the old standard of silence.

"Can you move?" he asked.

Curious, Sammy moved her liberated limbs in wonder. Turns out she could move, but not without pain. Confused as she often was in Eliot's presence, Sammy turned to face her beloved monster. "Can you stand, Sammy?"

Eliot extended his hand, to perhaps help Sammy, but she didn't take his hand, didn't use his strength to find her own. Such practices were exceedingly unhealthy. After all, look at where they had gotten her: bruised, broken and bleeding next door to a mental institution. She may not have been a patient in the strictest of senses, but she was there all the same. Sammy had envisioned many things for her future, like publications and marriage and family. Being an experiment hadn't made the list. With real effort and pain, Sammy swung her legs over the edge of the gurney nearest Eliot. Carefully and delicately, she slid forward until her bare soles brushed against the linoleum floor. It was cold, uncomfortably so, but it was wonderful to feel the ground beneath her feet once more. When she attempted to put her full weight upon the floor, to stand of her own accord, her knees buckled. Eliot moved to catch her and helped her stand upright with a gentle tenderness not unfamiliar to her. It was amazing how the monster was revealed but did not replace the prince within. Did she still love him? If he were to apologize sincerely and ask her to stay there with him forever, what would she say? Unsure and nauseous, Sammy looked into Eliot's face. "Sammy, I need you to know that I did love you. I've been honest about that every step of the way."

Her heart broke and splintered into shards, floating about inside her and able to poke her painfully at random intervals for the rest of her life. "You're a liar, Eliot. You've done nothing but lie to me."

"Not about this."

"Fuck you. I'm not having this conversation again."

Eliot released Sammy. She did not fall, and Eliot's eyes widened in surprise. "You're stronger than I thought."

"You don't know me at all." Sammy summoned all her strength and brought both of her fists crashing against Eliot's face. The blow was feeble, but the shock of it was great, and that was what Sammy had been after. Eliot staggered backwards and Sammy began to run.

Eliot had not shut the door behind him.

Chapter Eleven
The Beautiful Monster

"Bang, bang; he shot me down. Bang, bang; I hit the ground.
Bang, bang; that awful sound. Bang, bang;
my baby shot me down." ~ Nancy Sinatra

Sammy had never run so fast in her entire life. She knew that she would never run as fast again and was okay with it, because never again would she be in an even remotely similar situation. Her blistered and bruised feet were now bleeding, leaving a trail for Eliot to easily follow her progress. For a moment, it seemed despair would force her muscles to seize up and stop working, and that she would just fall into a heap on the carpeted landing just before the staircase and cry. What was the point in trying? Eliot was in way better physical condition than she was, so he could run faster and longer. He would catch her and kill her, and that'd be that. Sammy reached the start of the stairs and surprised herself by beginning her descent.

Despite the negative thoughts parading about her head, Sammy's legs kept pumping. The rapid changes of emotion were something Sammy understood; she wasn't what someone would call stable. However, unless she focused on survival and hope, she'd be done for. Eliot had preyed on her instability, had used it against Sammy every step of the way. She needed to somehow channel that odd energy into something positive. Sammy had to grow up before Eliot cut her down. Those thoughts, and her legs, had carried her into the kitchen. She was right; they had been in the house. Looking around her, Sammy knew it was a straight shot down the long hallway off to the right to the front door. Getting there was the key to getting out, but she paused to rummage through the drawers for a weapon. Eliot would not come unprepared.

"Don't make this harder for me, please." Eliot suddenly appeared at the opposite end of the kitchen, leaning against the doorway. Spinning around to face Eliot at an alarming speed, Sammy sent the kitchen drawer and its contents that she had been looking through crashing to the floor. A silver scalpel in Eliot's hand caught the light and glittered. "There's no need to draw this out."

Sammy began backing away instinctively, slowly, and she tried to control her breathing. She found the latter increasingly difficult to do as Eliot stalked forward, inch by inch, biding his time before he attacked. "Eliot," she began, her voice straining to be audible, "I'm not going to let you kill me."

"I understand that you want to live," Eliot began, "but I do not believe you're willing or able to do what is necessary to live."

Sammy raised an eyebrow. "What are you talking about?"

"To live, you're going to have to kill me." Eliot frowned. "Can you do that?"

Continuing her halting, backward steps, Sammy tried to stifle a sob. "Eliot, I don't want to kill you."

"You do if you want to live."

Frantically, she shook her head. "You can let me go. I'll walk out the front door, and it'll be like none of this ever happened."

He laughed. "Don't be simple, Sammy. It doesn't suit you. Your choice is to kill or be killed. My choice is to live without you or disappoint my father and ruin all of his hard work. If I let you live, I'd be destroying everything he built over decades for a few moments of lust." He shook his head slowly, sadly. "Our decisions have been made for us."

Sammy backed against the far wall of the kitchen, right beside the doorway opposite the one where Eliot had entered the kitchen. Staring Eliot down, she said, "You're out of your mind."

Suddenly screaming, Eliot charged at Sammy. Having to maneuver around the island in the middle of the kitchen slowed him down only slightly, but it was enough for Sammy to find her stride after she spun to her left and ran to the front door. Eliot's footsteps were fast and furious behind her. In a few moments, Sammy stretched her arm what seemed impossibly far and circled her trembling fingers around the crystal doorknob. It took all that she had to wrench the heavy door open, but she did it.

The car was in sight, nearly buried beneath the blinding snow. She could get to it, maybe, but –

The door slammed shut under her and Eliot's weight. He had collided into the back of her. She tried to open the door again, but Eliot was stronger, healthier, and she was too scared to do anything really helpful to her cause. Grabbing Sammy by her shoulders, Eliot spun her around and then slammed her back against the door. Sammy's skull also knocked against the heavy door and for a few moments, she saw stars.

"Do you know what our last session together consists of?" Eliot was smiling, but tears were pouring down his cheeks. It was pathetic. Sammy shook her head, terrified and trying to think of what to do next. This was no time for a conversation. "I'm going to give you a Glasgow smile. Do you know what that is?" Again, Sammy shook her head and squirmed fearfully in Eliot's arms. "I slit your mouth from ear to ear, and the scars that remain resemble a big smile, like the Joker from *Batman*. You saw that movie." Sammy needed to run, needed to get free; but how? Eliot was still rambling. "That in and of itself isn't deadly, but if I were to then punch you in the stomach or make you scream in pain, you'd bleed out because the wounds would be constantly kept open. It's a beautiful piece of irony, isn't it?" Grinning, Eliot took his shining scalpel and tried to slip it between Sammy's lips. The metal in her mouth helped her to concentrate and she brought her knee up as hard as she could against Eliot's groin.

Immediately, he doubled over in pain and that was awesome – exactly what Sammy wanted – but in doubling over, Eliot managed to slice Sammy about half the distance he was aiming for. Sammy screamed, but the pain only grew worse. She shut up, focused again, and turned. She was out the door in a matter of seconds.

It was incredibly cold. No shoes and a flimsy hospital gown were not going to cut it for very long. Sammy debated going to the car, but assumed it was locked and that Eliot had the key since it was his car, after all. She needed a plan B and quick. Scanning her surroundings, her eyes spotted what looked like a tool shed behind the house and to the right. Sammy took off running again, knowing her bloody footprints in the snow would lead Eliot right to her. It seemed like she constantly lost before she won, but she wouldn't follow that runaway train of thought down an unfinished track. Her imagination had gotten her into this mess – now she needed her imagination to get her out of it.

Sammy reached the shed and threw the doors open. The fact that it wasn't locked Sammy took as a sign from God Himself that she was finally getting things right. However, a quick visual scan of the wooden shelves and pegs robbed her of her divine inspiration. The shed was unlocked because it wasn't used anymore – there were no tools, no sharp or blunt objects which could be used as a defensive weapon. About to leave and seek sanctuary elsewhere, Sammy noticed an object near the door, on the cold, hard ground. It was a metal pipe, rusted and abandoned. She imagined that some careless worker had dropped the pipe while clearing out the shed and had left it. Carefully, Sammy bent and picked up the pipe. She felt the cold, fatal weight. It would be enough to kill Eliot, and that was what she had to do, regardless of whether or not she was emotionally prepared for the undertaking. She shivered and looked about the shed one last time. There was nothing else that would be useful, and her breath expelled in white puffs of vapor. If she wanted any kind of chance at survival, she'd have to get somewhere warmer than where she was now. The house was no longer an option, so Sammy cautiously stuck her head out from the shed and looked left. Set further back on the sprawling property was what could only be the asylum. Squinting against the dazzling brilliance of a winter sun, Sammy was just able to make out the remnants of truly beautiful topiary. In the warmer months, the scene was most likely emblazoned with emerald green slopes of lawn, that were covered in flowers of the most vibrant shades of color. It would be beautiful to behold. Now, excusing Sammy's somewhat jaded and cynical presence of mind, it was barren, frigid, and wasted. It was not inviting by any stretch of any imagination, but Sammy was fairly confident the building would be shelter enough from the snow and the cold, and momentarily, from Eliot. Sammy knew he would be gaining and was anxiously waiting to hear his shoes crunching against the snow.

It was now or never.

Sammy stepped out of the shed and looked right one last time, convinced Eliot would be standing there, lips twitched and twisted in an insane smile. The scalpel clutched in his angry and confused fist would catch the sunlight and twinkle innocently. Thankfully, Sammy knew better than to give into the illusion her mind was trying to present before her. She would not panic, would not slow, and definitely would not stay where she was a moment longer. She took off for the asylum, running as fast as her wearied legs could carry her.

Eliot, upon receiving the surprisingly strong blow to the groin, had doubled over in pain and fallen to the carpet before the front door. He wanted to regain his composure before he resumed trying to kill the girl he loved. He'd be embarrassed for her to see him like this, so weak and confused and desperate. Eliot knew Sammy admired his strength and confidence, and ending her life was bad enough; he didn't want to disappoint her. His face lost its purple pallor, and he climbed to his knees. His dark brown eyes bored through the front door, and it was almost as if he could see what lie beyond it. Sammy was hobbling somewhere, somewhere she'd be safe. But Sammy, poor Sammy, she was wrong. She was not safe anywhere. Sammy would not be safe until she was dead, because Eliot would not be safe until she was dead. His father could be exceedingly convincing, particularly when he employed certain tools. Eliot had hoped Sammy would notice the bruises he wore that matched her own, that she would notice his missing fingernails and pulled teeth. Consumed by her own misery, as his beloved so often was, Sammy had not realized Eliot was torturing her on the point of torture. His father was cruel, calculating, and cold. Eliot had worked so hard to become the antithesis of his father, had been so proud to discover his soul, and for what? Here he was, about to kill the only girl who had ever caused his face to blush, who had ever caused his heart to pump double time, sending blood everywhere and helping him to appreciate the miracle of life. Slowly, Eliot clamored to his feet and began to walk to the front door. If he didn't kill Sammy, his father would kill him. Eliot was not sure if he could kill Sammy, despite what he had wanted her to believe, but he was sure he'd rather die at her hands than at those of his father.

Throwing the front door open, an icy wind greeted Eliot. It rustled his un-tucked shirt about his waist and caused the hair near his brow to bend closer to his forehead. Sammy's bloody footprints were easily visible; they went to the abandoned shed and then to the equally abandoned asylum. Eliot frowned sadly. Sammy would not be prepared to comprehend or process what she would see, smell, and feel. It would cripple her, and Eliot would have an unfair advantage. Wasn't that always the way, though?

Sammy had a nasty habit of choosing and loving exactly what was worst for her. Smiling sadly now, Eliot increased his pace, jogging alongside Sammy's bloody path.

Sammy skidded to a halt once she was inside the asylum. The door echoed shut behind her, and already she was bewildered. Where were the employees, the administrators, the custodians? Where were the patients? Hell, where was the furniture? She assumed she was in the front lobby, but there was no welcome desk, and the chairs along the wall beneath the vast windows were torn and tossed, stuffing exposed. The lights were off, and, looking up, she could see the carcasses of smashed bulbs. Someone must have climbed a ladder to be able to reach so high up and she was surprised someone had cared that much about smashing a fucking light bulb. The whole thing was nonsensical and the only fact glaring obviously before her exhausted mind was that the place was abandoned and had clearly been abandoned for a while. Eliot had lied about everything, absolutely everything. Why was she surprised? She shook her head slowly, still searching about her. She needed to focus and start making decisions; Eliot was likely just a step behind. Any moment the door would open and he'd be there, crazed and homicidal. Steeling her resolve, breathing deeply, Sammy took off running again, following her instinct leading her to the right.

The hallway was narrow and long. She flew past what were once offices. Stealing glances inside revealed toppled filing cabinets, overturned onto tile floors. Papers which were probably important were strewn about everywhere like trash. Desks were smashed, drawers were removed, and chairs were not where they should be. What had happened? Sammy was not sure, but was more frightened than she had been outside in the cold. She debated whether or not she would be better off battling the climate than getting herself lost in the ruin of an asylum once she reached the end of the hall, but her decision was made for her. There was a loud boom that echoed in the stillness and bounced down the walls to her. Then, there was his voice. "Sammy? Sammy, I know you're in here! Please come to me! Don't put yourself through this. It's unnecessary!" Eliot was shouting, calling to her. Not bothering with a response, Sammy decided to climb the stairs to her left, in a stairwell guarded by heavy, metal doors.

A departure at the second floor would be obvious, but Sammy did not possess the strength to keep climbing. Becoming completely exhausted was not an option, and energy conservation was crucial to continuing on. Sammy exited onto the second floor and decided she should hide somewhere, surprising Eliot with her fury and the metal pipe. She needed some kind of advantage, and the element of surprise was the only advantage readily available. Quickly, she dashed into the nearest room; the first door on her right. It opened easily despite its weight and ominous appearance. A small, glass window was in the center. Sammy wondered if she was hiding in a padded room, and she wondered if that was a good idea as she slipped inside.

The smell of death was overpowering. When it was coupled with the stingingly sweet smell of sweat and the coppery smell of blood, it was damn near fatal itself. Hiding in the room was not a good idea. Upon the floor was the corpse of a young man. His arms were stretched out, towards the door, and his left leg was bent inward at the knee. He had been crawling toward the door, desperate for salvation. Blood emanated around him, had dried to resemble some sick kind of shadow, like the tracing of a body by a childish, clumsy hand. Sammy's own hand covered her mouth, trying to stifle the scream and keep the bile in her throat. Blinking back tears, she tore her eyes away from the dead man to the walls, which were not padded but were instead covered in artwork that was haunting. Each painting only featured three colors; red, black and gray. One was a distorted, screaming and scarred face – just a human face. The gender was not discernible, but the horror and pain were evident. Others were just blending of colors and shapes that instantly made Sammy uncomfortable. Still others were words. Some read, "Fuck you." Some read, "Let me die." Some read, "Kill me." The room had not been a haven for the dead man. What use would it be to Sammy? She wrenched open the door and fled, further down the hall. There were many other doors to try. She picked one on the left side of the hall.

She did not rush inside this time. She stepped in slowly, almost hesitantly, and let the door close softly behind her. The smell of death was unmistakable and there before her was the corpse of a young woman. Wavy, dark hair hung heavy in her face and obscured her features; Sammy was unable to discern her features and could not see her properly. Small pools of blood had gathered around the four legs of the metal chair the corpse was propped in, and the chair had been placed in the center of the room. The lights overhead reflected oddly against the dried crimson pools, and Sammy wanted to focus her eyes and mind elsewhere. However, it was impossible to look away and the best she could do was to follow the dried rivers of blood on the front legs of the chair. The woman's wrists had been slit, and her arms had been tied to the arms of the chair, palms facing upward. The dirty hospital gown she wore had been soaked through with the same liquid; her throat had been slit. Sammy's shocked and ever-widening eyes looked to the woman's face. As much as the woman's hair created a veil of sorts, it could not conceal one staring, empty eye.

Sammy immediately turned to the left and vomited, doubling over and pressing her palms into her knees as her body heaved and shook to purge it of bile. With the acid came the horror, the regret, and the overwhelming sadness, all in a pink colored puddle on the floor. With a trembling hand, Sammy shakily wiped her mouth clean and could clearly her hear lungs expanding and deflating greedily. Her breathing was loud enough to fill the room, enough to fill her universe, but there was something else; something soft and almost soothing. It was melodic. It was music. It was terribly out of place, and Sammy straightened up. Her head twitched left and right, up and down, searching for the source of the music. In the back corner of the room, plugged in neatly, was a small, cheap-looking stereo and CD player. Small, digital numbers glowed at Sammy in a muted shade of red. A guitar was being strummed gently and a female voice was singing in a crisp, clear voice. Blinking back tears, Sammy knew with absolute certainty that the CD playing had been recorded by the dead woman in the room. The sense of tragic horror enveloping Sammy was practically palpable. The dead woman before her had composed a melody, created lyrics, had given birth to art, and now she was dead because of it. The artist and this musician were Eliot's victims; her brethren. How many others were hidden behind innocent-looking doors? How many corpses were tucked away on the other floors? Sammy didn't want to know; couldn't discover the answer if she wanted to survive and be normal at some point down the line.

Sammy left the room and had every intention of going back the way she had come, of taking the stairs to the ground floor and getting the hell out of this slaughterhouse, this death trap. She was only a few steps from the stairwell when she heard approaching footsteps and the muffled, but still distinct, sound of Eliot's voice calling out her name. She thought she might get sick again and scurried backwards, scrambled back down the hallway. There had to be another stairwell somewhere; Sammy's confidence was solely based on federal fire safety requirements or something like that. Finally, at the opposite end, before another set of double doors, was the stairwell. She forced her legs to pump faster than they had for some time. Looking through other doors for shelter would be redundant. She couldn't, was physically unable to hide in a room with a dead body. Her mind was fragile enough as it was and, quite frankly, had already endured its fair share of abuse. No other psychological warfare was necessary. Galloping down the steps to the ground floor, Sammy pushed open the heavy door and ran right into Eliot.

Slamming hard into Eliot, Sammy rebounded back against the door she had just worked to open. Eliot looked just as surprised as

Sammy and was unsteady on his feet for a moment. He was pale and seemed to be covered in a thin, ever present film of sweat. He licked his dry, cracking lips and said, "Sammy." Just that one word; like it summed up everything, as if it was all he could say. Sammy wanted to sob, to rush to him, hold him, and beg him to take it all back and plead with him to make everything go back to normal. But that was silly, and Sammy understood that now. Tearing her eyes away, and forcing the rest of her to follow, Sammy began to hobble down the stairs.

She could hear Eliot approaching slowly, following. "Is that a metal pipe? Is that for me?" he asked. Sammy did not respond, aside from moving faster. Eliot quickened his own pace and added, "You're not going to use that to kill me. That's much too intimate of a murder weapon. You don't have the stomach for it, Sammy. Could you really watch my chest rise and fall for the last time? Could you really watch the light leave my eyes?"

Sammy couldn't listen to that. She shut her eyes for a moment, and shook her head to clear it. Her battered soles found the ground floor, but Eliot's thudding footsteps were not far behind, were – as a matter of fact – definitely closer than they had been just a moment ago. Damn near running, Sammy struggled to open the metal door separating the stairwell from the lobby, and had thrown her weight against it, only to have the door creak open. Precious time was being lost and Eliot would surely have her now. Sammy was bracing for the rushing whoosh of air that would precede the slash of the scalpel that would end her time on earth. She pushed harder and harder against the door, eyes clenched tight from the strain and finally, she was making progress. Indeed, the metal door flew open. When Sammy opened her eyes to rush through, Eliot was significantly closer; standing beside her, actually. He had opened the door and was still holding it open. She looked to him wide-eyed. "I do love you, Sammy. I swear to God that I never lied about that. You deserve a fighting chance." She couldn't move, couldn't breathe, and couldn't think. What was he doing? Was this some final kind of psychological torture he was sadistic enough to inflict? Big, glistening tears had begun to fall from the far corners of his dark eyes. Sammy was still, and Eliot grew incensed suddenly. "Take the fighting chance, you stupid bitch!" Wildly, he struck out with the scalpel and made a decent slice along Sammy's arm. The pain woke her up, and as she screamed, she projected herself forward across the vast expanse of the lobby to the great, wide doors that marked the main entrance. Bloodied footprints marred the already defaced tile. Her breath was becoming increasingly difficult to catch and she knew she had to make her move soon; she physically could not keep running. He would win in the end that way. She had to turn and make her final confrontation, but some part of Sammy she could not identify decided she'd do it in the sunlight, rather than an abandoned asylum.

Back in the brilliant sunlight, Sammy ran a few more paces before turning to face the end and whatever that meant.

Eliot was leaving the building to join her, two paces behind at the most, and he was crying again, hollering broken phrases, hurling words at her like they were dishes from an open cabinet. Like those dishes, they crashed to her feet, useless and broken. She took a few steps forward and just as Eliot tensed his muscles to swipe at Sammy with the scalpel a second time, she took her swing, gripping the pipe tightly with both hands and praying her aim was true.

She caught the side of Eliot's face. He spun and hit the ground, blood spraying against the blanket of snow. Shock was slowly descending upon Sammy. The metal pipe was vibrating in her hands, ripe with tremors. Confused, she looked down at her shaking hands, and Sammy realized they were covered in blood. She unclenched her left fist, and brought it up before her unbelieving eyes. She could not discern the color of her flesh; everything was a sick kind of crimson, just like, she realized upon closer inspection, the rest of her body was. It couldn't have all come from Eliot; she had only hit him once, and had witnessed blood fly out against the sheet of white beneath their feet. The stress must have been causing old wounds to open, and the blood flowed forth freely. Sammy brought her free left hand near her face and let it hover over her latest wound; the gash on her face was fresh and was surely contributing to the mess. A mess she was indeed, as blood ran down her alarmingly pale arms and dripped from the fingertips of the hand that had left her face to hang limply at her side for just a moment, as she stood there, stunned and unmoving. It had just dawned on Sammy that she hadn't allowed herself time to heal, but she couldn't be too hard on herself as there hadn't been any time to waste; nor was there any time to waste now. Despite the precious, crimson liquid that was slowly draining from her body, the metal pipe was still clutched tightly in her right fist. Eliot was crawling away at a snail's pace, coughing up some precious liquid of his own. Her stomach twisted as she observed Eliot turn his head to the side and spit, expelling blood and shards of teeth. She had shattered the smile that she had lived to see. What was she doing? She loved this young man; how could she end his life? Well, he had tried to end hers, and all is fair in love and war and all that. Sammy smacked her face once or twice to stifle a sob and get control of her raging, conflicting thoughts and emotions. A twinkling amidst the frozen snow helped bring Sammy back; the sun had reflected against the scalpel, which had flown from Eliot's hand when he had been struck. He was crawling towards it now, slowly but surely, stretching his crooked fingers out, grasping and reaching. Screaming, more out of anger at his tenacity to be a murderer than anything else, Sammy brought the pipe down across the back of Eliot's knees.

He howled in pain and sprawled out against the blanket of snow, flat on his stomach and straight as a board. Loud cracks echoed in the eerie winter silence, and Sammy was glad, hoping she had broken something. Eliot turned onto his back to stare incredulously at Sammy. Eliot wasn't a beautiful boy anymore, not at all. Sammy's bare, bleeding heels crunched numbly against the icy snow as the sun shone down in crisp, vibrant rays. Vaguely, Sammy was aware that she had transformed into a barbarian of sorts, into a monster no better than Eliot's, and that was fine because it had all been Eliot's doing; every monster needed a creator. "Sammy," he said, barely able to get the words out, "look at you now. What have I done?"

"What? Was this not part of the plan? Oh, I'm sorry," Sammy retorted.

Eliot rolled back onto his stomach. He continued talking with Sammy, yelling back to her as best he could over his shoulder. "This isn't you, Sammy. I don't know who this is, but I know I have to destroy her." Eliot began crawling again, this time with urgency. He was making notable progress. Sammy was having none of it.

She swung the pipe twice as hard as she could against Eliot's back. She caught him twice more, once in each side, before Eliot collapsed onto his stomach. The air exhaled from his battered lungs in a great rush. The blood was now trickling from the corners of his mouth and from his ears. Delicately, with genuine pain and effort straining the once glorious lines of his face, he rolled onto his back, smiling weakly. His eyes, no longer burning – perhaps dimmed by current events – only flickered as they connected with Sammy's. Turning his head to the side, he coughed. Crimson splattered against white again and Eliot eyed it nervously, but soon turned his attention back to Sammy. "I never thought it would end this way."

Sammy lowered the metal pipe in her hands. "How did you think this was going to end, Eliot?"

"Honestly?" In between coughing fits, Eliot sputtered, "I thought we'd go side by side, decades from now, in adjacent hospital beds … 'til death do us part type of deal."

Sammy couldn't be allowed to believe Eliot, even for a second. "You made me do this."

"I did," Eliot admitted. "Remember that I taught you more about yourself than Rob ever could have. He never would have endured this for you."

Sammy raised the metal pipe in her hands and brought it crashing down against Eliot's abdomen. He screeched in pain. It was a terrible sound and, though she cringed from it, Sammy said, "You didn't know Rob. Don't you dare fucking talk to me about Rob."

"Sammy," Eliot wheezed, "I love you."

The metal pipe crashed across his shoulders. "Shut up!"

"In my own crazy, fucked up way, I love you, and you know it."

Sammy screamed and smashed Eliot's knees a second time with the pipe, which was now sticky with blood. In her fury, she meant to attack again, but the pipe paused above her head. Her hands began to tremble, as did her lower lip. Eliot's countenance was heartbreaking. Through all the blood, his eyes were kind and patiently focused on Sammy, and something like a tired smile hung about his lips. How could Sammy kill Eliot? He had lied to her and had shed her blood. Eliot had tried to *kill* her and now here he was, defenseless before her, looking all kinds of pitiful and tragic. He was whispering that he loved her, even though she was working him over with a metal pipe. Didn't that make her the monster now? Resolve weakening, Sammy dropped to her knees beside Eliot. She lowered the pipe and let it nearly fall beside her, gripping it only loosely. "Eliot …"

"Go on, Sammy; don't let me manipulate you again. Be free of me. Be strong." Turning to look at the clear, blue sky above, he added, "Maybe this was part of the plan all along."

Eliot was smiling peacefully, albeit sadly. Sammy was doing her best to be numb. She launched a second attack against his middle. She thought she heard ribs crack and grimaced. Now gasping for air, Eliot's remaining white teeth were stained a repulsive red shade. The end wasn't near for Eliot Andrews; it was here. Before he joined the dearly departed, Sammy had one last thing to say to her beloved monster. "I don't need your permission to kill you, you fuck. This is for me and Rob and the life you stole from us." Eliot leapt up at the mention of Rob's name and Sammy swung like a New York Yankee. Eliot's skull cracked against the pipe. His chest that Sammy had once so lovingly kissed ceased to rise and fall.

Blood was splattered against her face, her neck and her hands, though very little of it belonged to her. She had the sudden urge to lick her lips and satiate her dry mouth, but she was afraid she'd taste Eliot's blood. His scent - black coffee, burning wood and sleepless nights - was now tainted with the faint smell of copper, of fear and of death. Stomach flipping end over end, Sammy turned to the side and vomited. Everything came rushing out; the romance, the memories, the blood, the bile, the anguish, the tears, and the horror. All of it left her in one fell swoop and nothing remained; nothing but a blackness that beckoned her forward. She tumbled into it freely, not caring about finding an exit or escaping. She had slain the beast. What more could anyone possibly expect from her?

Maeve was in a fury, driving at an almost indeterminable, but definitely illegal speed. Eliot had not called as planned. When she had tried calling the Andrews home, she had received no answer, and she had begun to panic. Eliot knew how hard it had been, initially, to allow Sammy to get closer to Eliot. Eliot had been there to hold trembling Maeve in his arms when she finally conceded to help facilitate Mike's injuries. She had given Eliot everything he had asked, because she believed in the work he was doing; helping the greater good, and she was proud to be a part of it, as should Rob, Mike and Sammy. The study Eliot and his father were conducting would have invaluable and lasting contributions. If creative people could still create, and still essentially exhibit higher-level thinking skills while under extreme torture, then creative people would best be suited for entirely different careers; careers within the government, maybe – sent to dangerous places in exotic locations to protect other citizens, like citizens lacking the proclivity for fancy and imagination. Eliot had explained it all to Maeve the summer she had been interning at his father's psychiatric hospital, the summer after her senior year of high school.

She had applied for the internship because she knew, even as a naïve young woman, that psychology was going to be her field of interest, particularly abnormal psychology. The internship, which admittedly had seemed unorthodox and almost too good to be true, had been a blessing. Maeve had been able to learn so much, observing the patients and the respective treatments. She would dutifully take notes, filling notebook after notebook, before and after the more clerical duties that were required of her. She could easily recall sitting behind the tall, white desk that was the centerpiece of the hospital lobby, straight ahead once one walked through the wide, ornate double doors. She had been mindlessly making sure each paper file had an electronic replica, a task that had taken two weeks to complete without any end in sight, when the vision of beauty that was Eliot had strolled through the door. He was smiling broadly, as if daring someone to ask him why he was doing so, and walking tall. His skin was deliciously bronzed from the New England sun and his hair had sun streaks throughout.

"Hey," he breathed, and the scent was something akin to optimism and eternal youth, despite the hint of tobacco laced throughout. It was like a noxious gas that placed Maeve under some antiquated spell; her lips curled into a smile and her dreamy eyes took in all of Eliot as he asked where his father was. Maeve gave him appropriate directions and watched the young man until he was out of sight, unabashedly craning her neck and leaning up and over the desk. He returned some hours later and asked her to join him for dinner that evening. They had slept together, and while cuddling in Eliot's enormous bed, among fluffy pillows and endless, elegant blankets, he told her of a groundbreaking study he was beginning with his father and how he would love for Maeve to help. Naturally, Maeve thanked him and graciously accepted the opportunity, finally feeling like she was right where she should be; that her life was finally beginning.

When the murders started, she was disturbed and had thought about going to the police. Mr. Andrews had been instrumental in helping her to see reason (the jury was still out on whether it was the beatings or the extortion), but Maeve began to understand that it was all for the greater good, though that term was never exactly defined by anyone involved in the study. She stopped sleeping with Eliot after sitting in on a session between him and a subject. Eliot's smile had unnerved her when he sliced the subject from ear to ear, and, needless to say, the attraction had quickly dissipated. Maeve began dating while attending class and the special sessions at the hospital, and whenever she met someone with artistic ability, she readily informed Eliot.

They were making real progress, really starting to create a definitive conclusion, when the hospital lost its funding. The number of patients had drastically waned as attentions were pulled elsewhere, and, before anyone had realized it, the building was in disrepair and boarded up. Maeve had been devastated to see the beautiful place so forlorn and neglected, but again, it was all for the greater good. The experiments could be easily conducted elsewhere and, after all, the work needed to be completed.

To think Sammy had almost been the undoing of everything.

Life was rolling along smoothly, which never happens. Maeve had met Mike and thank God he did not have one creative impulse in his sculpted body. He was safe and beautiful, and she really liked him. Then Maeve met Sammy, and she found a genuine friend. She had hid Sammy from Eliot, kept her a secret as to keep her protected. How was Maeve supposed to know Eliot was trolling the creative writing classes? How could she convince Sammy to avoid taking the class she was most passionate about without giving up the whole operation? Maeve had to let things take their natural course.

Then Eliot began to behave strangely, to talk of quitting his line of work and of Sammy. It was always Sammy this and Sammy that and how he thought she was his salvation. Maeve had to choke back the vomit; Eliot was forgetting that Sammy was one of many girls he had bedded, and that she was a writer – the subject to conclude the study. When the work was published, they would all be rich and famous and more than that, society would then be privy to knowledge which would drastically change... everything, for lack of an appropriate, more specific term. Maeve's pleas fell on deaf ears, and even Mr. Andrews was having trouble in convincing his son to stay the course. Maeve had a sinking feeling all would end badly as a result of Eliot and Sammy, and here she was, leaving the side of her beloved beaten boyfriend to bail Eliot out of his mess.

Mike had been an unfortunate sacrifice, but he would wake up and be blissfully unaware of who Maeve really was and what she had done in the name of science. She would kiss his dampened brow and gently explain how Eliot had snapped and killed Sammy – that she and Mike had been right all along about Eliot's instability. Her bottom lip would quiver with emotion when she described how Eliot realized tragically too late what he had done, and then took his own life. Mike would want to help Maeve heal, and he would take her into his arms and all would be well.

Maeve eyed the 9mm on the seat beside her. It caught the winter sun and glittered. She increased her speed and tightened her grip on the steering wheel. If everything was going to end, it was going to be her decision. Eliot had been so willing to sacrifice others for his vision. Why should his life be any different? Sammy was obviously expendable, knowing too much to remain alive. Maeve would be the victor.

Sammy came to later, though she couldn't say for sure how long she had been out. The sun was still shining, so she prayed it had only been minutes. She needed to get to a hospital and as soon as possible. Sitting up slowly, mindful of her aching joints and throbbing muscles, she inhaled quickly as she remembered where she was. Eliot lay beside her, cold as stone, dead. His eyes were open and vacant. The light that had burned so brightly, had promised shelter and warmth from the adolescent storm Sammy had created for herself, had been snuffed out by hers truly. A small, pitiful sob escaped her lips as she climbed to her knees. He had beaten her, lied to her, tortured her … yes, but he had been everything. Sammy felt nauseous again and inhaled deeply, counting backwards from ten until the moment passed. Her numeric sanctuary was disturbed by a tiny, metallic click near her ear. Confused, she turned toward the sound.

There was an icy, silver gun pointed in the center of her face. Maeve was at the other end. The breath caught trying to escape in Sammy's throat was finally released. Sobs of the more joyful variety appeared. "Oh, Maeve, thank God. I thought something terrible had happened to you."

Maeve's voice was breaking. "What happened?"

"I'm okay, but I should get to a hospital. Maeve, it was awful. I just want to go and get away from here."

The gun had not lowered, but Sammy didn't seem to notice. Or if she did, she didn't care. Maeve asked another question. "Is that Eliot?"

Sammy turned to the body beside her. Technically, she supposed, it was the boy that called himself Eliot. But Sammy realized she had never really known him at all. Tears threatened once more, but she exhaled deeply and let it pass. "Yes. He tried to kill me, Maeve. He…he…oh my God…"

"Shut up." Maeve's voice was stern, almost cruel. Sammy turned back to her best friend in surprise.

"What's wrong?"

"You killed him." Maeve seemed panicked, almost grief-stricken. And in truth, she was; Sammy wasn't supposed to end Eliot's life. That had been Maeve's responsibility, Maeve's privilege for everything she had given up for Eliot. It wasn't fair.

Sammy's head hurt. She couldn't understand Maeve's reaction. It was illogical, nonsensical. "I had to, Maeve. Did you hear me? He was going to kill me."

"It wasn't supposed to be like this."

Sammy snorted. "You're telling me." Wiping her ever-weeping eyes, Sammy tried to get to her feet when she was struck by the metallic gun in Maeve's hand.

"Sit down!"

Sammy collapsed into a heap, fresh blood trickling warmly and slowly down her face. She was missing something. Something was askew. Maeve hadn't meant to hurt her, surely. What would be the reason? Maeve must not understand. Sammy had better start explaining, or she might get whacked again. "Maeve, Eliot was a liar. He wanted me dead. He killed Rob, and he tried to kill Mike. Don't you get it?"

"We worked so hard and for so long. I told him bringing you into this would ruin everything. And then! And then he started to love you. Mr. Andrews and I tried to reason with him, but it was too late." Maeve shook her head slowly. "I told him to leave you alone. Now look at what you've done!"

Sammy squinted her eyes. It hurt to breathe, let alone think. "You knew about this?"

"I've been working with Eliot since my senior year of high school. I interned here last summer and got in on the ground floor of a study that would change everything. Eliot and I would travel to different places, find different artists, and bring them back here. We were so close to the end that I could be with Mike and start to settle down, and he was supposed to find a female writer, but he found you. He got his priorities all confused." Maeve was crying. "It was brilliant, and you ruined everything. You don't deserve to live."

The gun became steady in Maeve's hands. Exhaling deeply, Sammy closed her eyes. Death had come for her after all, in the most unexpected form. She didn't want to spend her last moments dwelling on Maeve's betrayal, so she focused on seeing Rob again. Those laughing, light blue eyes and innocence would be reward enough for all she had suffered.

When the gun went off, she didn't feel a thing.

She hadn't expected the end to be so painless. She didn't even fall backwards. Sammy opened her eyes and looked down. There was no fresh blood, no bolts of pain coming from a visual realization. There was nothing. Had Maeve missed?

Sammy's eyes looked to her former friend. Maeve's mouth had formed a round circle of horror. She dropped to her knees, hands cradled against her chest. Blood seeped through the tiny spaces between her fingers and one last breath passed through Maeve before she fell face first in the snow. Sammy's field of vision opened up to the landscape Maeve had hid from her. Police cruisers and policemen in two solid lines were approaching, as was Mike, on crutches. She heard her mother scream her name from somewhere nearby, but she slipped back into unconsciousness.

EPILOGUE

"I heard Maeve talking to someone on the phone while she thought I was asleep. She was talking about you, and how you had to be killed. You'd been missing for a week, maybe two, so as soon as she left the room, I called the police. Detective Taylor followed her, but she ditched him at an exit on the Maine turnpike. He called in reinforcements and was able to track her down again, in the nick of time." Mike took a deep gulp from a glass of water. His hand shook slightly.

Sammy had been in the hospital for a week now. She was incredibly weak but was on the road to recovery. In between mouthfuls of air, she said, "I'm so sorry Mike."

He shook his head quickly. "Knock that shit off." He looked at the tubes and wires, listened to the beeping machinery. "How are you?"

Sammy smiled. "I'm okay. I'll be crazier than ever, but I'll be breathing." She paused for a moment to catch her breath. "What happened to Eliot's parents?"

Mike frowned. "Their last name wasn't even Andrews. I don't remember what it was, but the mother was found hanging in her bedroom closet, and the father put a bullet through his head as the police entered the house." He took another large swallow of water. "There was no mental asylum, by the way. I mean, there was, but the building was all run down. There were no patients or anything like that. It hadn't been functioning in years."

Sammy didn't bother to tell Mike she knew about the last part. She grimaced and asked, "Do Rob's parents know it was Eliot?"

Mike nodded. Sammy let a few tears roll down her cheeks. There was a knock at the door. Sammy's professor from American Literature walked in. "Miss Thogode? Are you awake?"

Sammy gave a cautious, little wave. She was very surprised to see him and did her best to keep her emotions hidden from her tone when she said, "Hello, Professor."

Mike cumbersomely climbed to his feet. "I'll head out. I'll stop by later in the week. Hang tough, kid." He smiled kindly before exiting the room on his crutches. The professor took his seat.

"I hope I didn't scare away your company, Miss Thogode."

Sammy laughed softly. "I'm sure you did." She paused to breathe deeply, to readily greet the awkward silence that was sure to descend. Then she remembered she had wanted to ask him something. "Did you get my extra assignment?"

The professor looked very serious. He pulled his briefcase onto his lap and began to search through it. "I did. I asked for thirty pages, Miss Thogode. Do you remember?"

Sammy nodded.

"You turned in two hundred and forty five pages."

Sammy shrugged. "I guess I had a lot to say."

The professor pulled the manuscript from the briefcase and then placed the briefcase neatly on the floor beside him. "Also," he said, flipping through the pages, "your characterization of me was particularly harsh." He looked at Sammy, not the hint of a smile in his face. She was worried.

Frowning, she tried to articulate an apology. "Sir, I only –"

He broke into a radiant smile. "It's brilliant. You wrote what you knew." As he continued, his smile began to fade. "Unfortunately, what you knew was pain and suffering on an unprecedented level. You knew evil in its most attractive and damaging forms. The fact that you completed my assignment at all, let alone wrote about what you've been through, astonishes me." Gently, he patted her hand. "You get an A, obviously."

"Even though it was late?"

The professor laughed heartily. "Better late than never, right?"

Sammy smiled.

ABOUT THE AUTHOR

Mandi Bean is a New Jersey native and a high school English teacher. She graduated from Montclair State University. This is her first novel.

Made in the USA
Middletown, DE
14 December 2021

55854811R00146